IF YOU'RE READING THIS

This is a work of fiction. All the characters, organizations, and events that are portrayed in this novel are either products of the author's imagination or are used fictitiously.

If You're Reading This © Rae Lloyd, Esther Lloyd
All Rights Reserved
Except as permitted under the US Copyright Act of 1976, no part of this publication may be reproduced, distributed, or transmitted in any form by any means or stored in a database or retrieval system without the prior written permission of the author.

Cover Design: K.B. Barrett
Editing: Courtney DeLollis
Proofreading: Michele Ficht

www.raelloyd.com

For my sister, Chanie. You are the bravest person I know. You walked through hell and still learned how to stop and smell the flowers. Thank you for fighting.

Playlist

If you enjoy listening while reading, please use the QR code above to access the playlist.

TRIGGERS:

This story explores dark and emotional themes, including mental health struggles and trauma. Some chapters contain:
• Suicidal thoughts and behavior
• Childhood sexual abuse (non-graphic, mainly off page)
• Physical and emotional abuse in foster care (non-graphic, mainly off page)
• Depression, PTSD, and self-destructive behavior
• Mentions of death, near-death experiences, and brief gun violence
• Flashback nightmares, and medical settings (non-graphic hospital/morgue scenes)
• Strong language, dark humor
• Some sexual content

"Sometimes even to live is an act of courage."
Seneca

If you're reading this, it's done. I'm gone. Finally...
You'll probably say I gave up, but I would argue to say that
I gave in. I didn't give up. I just stopped waiting for change,
for the light at the end of the tunnel. I tried to find it. It
doesn't exist. I stopped lying to myself and calling it hope.

It wasn't one particular thing. No dramatic moment. It
didn't happen all at once. This has been a long time
coming. I'd be shocked if any of you are surprised because I
wasn't exactly quiet about how I felt about life, or at least I
didn't think I was. Not with what I've been doing for the
last eighteen months. But maybe I wasn't obvious enough
since so few of you really understood what was going on.

The fact is, since I was born, it's just been a slow kind
of leaving. Like just watching myself slowly dissolve.

And there was no one to tell. No one who cared. No
one to try to stop me. And maybe that was the worst part.
Then again, maybe it wouldn't have made this easy.
Because if people cared, they would have tried to make me
feel guilty for being this broken. But luckily, I don't have
anyone to do that. Not even the millions of people who
watched me walk into lightning, touch high-voltage electricity, and sit through a hurricane. You all hit like and
share. You commented. You gave me millions of views. But
none of you ever really asked, if who I was after the
cameras turned off, was okay. You just loved the chaos and
the danger. But you didn't love me. No one ever loved me.

There is something wrong with this world. How you
watch people destroy themselves and call it entertainment.
The fact is, pain gets more views than kindness because for
over a year, I've been trending and you've been watching a
man scream for help in twenty different ways, and still I
went unheard.

Before you try to figure out where it all went wrong, I'll save you the trouble of digging into everything. I want you to know that he hurt me. The world let him. No one stepped in. Not a teacher, not his wife, not CPS, not the authorities, not a doctor. No one stopped him.

So don't talk about me and wish I had found forgiveness. Or say, what I did was not the answer. Fact is, what he did to me was unforgivable. I never got over it. Some things cannot be fixed. Despite that, I did try to build a life for myself. I built something out of the wreckage. I filmed it. I named it. I uploaded it. I survived it. But it wasn't enough.

I just never learned how to want to stay. Not when staying meant carrying the weight of being alive, alone.

If there is anything after this, I hope it's quiet. I hope it finally feels like enough.

-me

Chapter One
The End

Die Trying ✔

@dietrying

20m Subscribers · 22 Videos

December 2025

They say it only takes a moment for your entire life to change but for me it wasn't just one moment; it was multiple moments that led to the eventual implosion of my life. It wasn't God, it wasn't the universe, it wasn't karma. It was just the usual fuckery of being human. A thousand paper cuts, none deep enough to kill me on their own, but together? Together, they made it so I couldn't feel anything but the ache.

I was close to thirty years old when I finally decided I was done. It wasn't a dramatic decision. It wasn't as though something more had happened to push me over the edge. I just woke up one morning and realized I had grown really tired of it. The waking up part. The dragging through the day part. The going to sleep to do it all over again part. I finally got to a point where I was just too tired to hide from it anymore. It was a very rational decision, or so I thought. I just didn't want to keep going any longer. I had done my time. My happy ever after wasn't coming. So, I was done.

But I didn't want to be the one to end it. Not directly. That would mean I chose it. That I took some kind of control. Something I really hadn't had a lot of in my life. Call me a coward, but I didn't want to be the one to end it; rather, I wondered if the universe would do me the favor. So, I came up with a plan. Twenty opportunities. Twenty stunts. Twenty chances for the world to finish the job.

And if by some miracle it didn't... Then I would.

That was a year and a half ago. And here I was—still fucking alive. Not because I'd clawed my way toward survival. Not because I'd changed my mind. Just because fate had a sick sense of humor.

My hand hovered over the mouse pad, scrolling through footage. The twentieth and final stunt. I had checked off the last death-defying opportunity on my list by playing chicken with another car down an expanse of highway, almost finally getting it done until the other driver had swerved at the last second. The file was labeled "20_FINAL_CHICKEN.MP4," and it blinked in the folder like it was taunting me. Like it knew there was nothing left for me to film. At least not according to my list.

I opened Gmail, clicked compose, and addressed the message to Carter, my editor. The only person I'd spoken to regularly over the last eighteen months. Not that we'd ever met in person. I could walk past him on the street right now and not know it. I only knew his voice from the voice notes and phone calls. He'd taken me on as a random client after my first video went viral. Now he edited all my footage, curated the thumbnails, and monitored the monetization. I had stopped touching the back end. I just did the stunts and emailed them over. He cleaned them up and made them digestible for an audience hungry for destruction.

To: **CARTER**

Cc:

Subject: **Last One**

From: ● Hide My Email

Message Size: 3.7 MB

That's it. Use whatever clips work. No outro on this one

. 20_FINAL_CHIC
KEN.mp4
3.7 MB

I hovered over "Send" for a moment longer than I meant to. Not because I was unsure. Just because once I clicked it, there really was nothing left.

With a sigh of resignation, I hit send. The tab closed out just as I saw the accidental second attachment.

IfYoureReadingThis_FINAL.pdf

For a second, shock had me completely frozen as my mind ran through the facts. The document had been in the same folder as the video footage. I must've clicked both by accident. Or maybe not by accident at all. Maybe some part of me was ready to be seen. I just wasn't aware of it if I was.

The little "Sent" confirmation pop-up blinked at the bottom corner of my screen like a slap to the face. There was no undo button. No other choice to be made here. Carter had it now. The whole damn thing. All of my truth.

I didn't move. Didn't dare to breathe.

The panic didn't come the way I thought it would. It wasn't a flood to my system. It didn't take over my body in one shell-shocked moment. No, it was a slow, creeping warmth along my spine. Like my body couldn't decide whether to care or not. Like I couldn't choose whether I wanted him not to read it—or if I wanted to see what he would do once he did.

Maybe that was the funniest part of it all. After all this time, waiting for fate to show up and intervene... maybe it finally had. With a fucking file attachment.

I sat back in my chair and stared at the ceiling. There was a crack in the plaster above me that looked like a crooked smile. I'd watched it for many nights over the last six months, waiting for it to grow wide enough to split the ceiling in half and bury me in drywall. But like everything else, it held on. Just stable enough to avoid a catastrophe.

Just like me.

My YouTube channel had blown up almost immediately. "DIE TRYING" had reached one million subscribers in two months. People seemed to enjoy the idea of a man tempting fate for reasons he wouldn't explain. They liked the mystery. The aesthetic of danger without the messy backstory. The stunts were so insane, the risk was so real, and I never once revealed my name or why I was doing it, which left my viewers clamoring for information about me that they never got. I thought maybe that's what made it work. People saw something in me they couldn't figure out—some anonymous blend of desperation and calm. Like a man trying to make eye contact with God and daring Him to blink.

The money and views came fast after that. Ads. Sponsors. Affiliate links. I didn't touch most of it. I didn't need much. I lived in a one-room studio apartment above a shut-down bar. I had one chair. One couch. One set of dishes. A few items of clothing that I rotated through when I felt like getting dressed. So now most of the money sat in a savings account under my name, slowly accruing interest for no one in particular.

I had no friends, no family, no legacy to pass it on to. I'd thought about leaving it to Carter, but that felt weird. We weren't really friends. Or were we? He did a job. I did a job. It didn't make us anything more than pixels on a screen. I'd considered giving it to a charity, but that felt too performative. Too much like trying to scrub all the trauma out of my story with a "good deed."

I'd even fantasized about setting it all on fire and recording it as my very last video for my channel. I'd withdraw the money in cash, light it up and throw it off a cliff, letting it scatter, becoming ash in the wind. But that was too cinematic. Too symbolic. And I wasn't trying to make a statement. I was just trying to end something that had gone on for too long.

I glanced back at the second attachment. My letter was ready, and I didn't even really know who I had written it to. My followers, I guess. All the frenzied, obsessed fans that I had accrued over the last year.

I didn't think the letter was too long. It said just enough to explain that this wasn't an accident. That I hadn't been hacked. That there wasn't anyone to call.

If you're reading this, it's done. I'm gone. And finally... You'll probably say I gave up, but I would argue to say that I gave in. I didn't give up. I just stopped waiting for change.

I'd been more honest in my letter than I'd been in years. Although, I didn't cry when I wrote it. I hadn't really felt anything. Probably because I'd been planning this for a while. I didn't know how I'd end it yet, that part I was still figuring out. But being that the stunts hadn't worked, it was now on me.

The world had twenty chances. And it hadn't taken any of them. So now I had to.

I stood up slowly, my knees cracked from being pushed too hard. My body was tired but not broken. That was the irony of it all. After all the things I'd put it through—jumping onto a moving train, getting high in a one-hundred-degree desert, crossing a dangerous bridge and speeding in a car along a treacherous road—I was still intact. I didn't even have a limp. No dramatic scars to point to. All I had left was me, a man, who kept waking up when he didn't want to anymore.

I walked over to the window and opened it. The city was loud as usual. Sirens. Car horns. Laughter. Somewhere, someone was falling in love or getting high or screaming into the void. And here I was, breathing in stale apartment air and wondering how much longer I had to hold on and pretend.

The problem I faced was that I didn't want to make a mess. I didn't want to traumatize anyone. That was the thing about doing it yourself—no matter how quiet you tried to be, someone would find you. Some stranger would have to carry the weight of that image for the rest of their life.

So, I had to plan carefully. I needed to take my exit gracefully. Just like my comments insinuated, dying right could be an art form.

I'd always been good at suffering silently. Might as well go out the same way I'd lived. Quiet and unproblematic.

Chapter Two
Lake Jesup

(Uploaded: June 7, 2024. 3:14 a.m.)

My list had started with alligators.

Not skydiving. Not fire. Not some dramatic plunge off a cliff or a bridge. Just water thick with heat and the potential of death—silent, green, and so still it made your brain wish for sound.

I'd picked the Everglades because it felt like the perfect place to come across nature's beast. They could be brutal, but they were also indifferent. The Everglades was the kind of place that didn't care what you wanted, and it offered a death that didn't wait for your permission. Nature was pure that way. If something grabbed you, it grabbed you. If something bit, it bit. Simple.

Lake Jesup, specifically, was perfect. Locals said it had one of the highest alligator populations in the country. More than thirteen thousand of them. People said you could see their eyes hovering above the water at dusk like ghost lights. Waiting. Watching.

It was hot the day I drove up there in an old rental car. Not just summer hot. It was Florida-hot. Swamp-hot. The kind of heat that seeps into your skin and bones like you're being swallowed whole by it. My shirt was soaked before I even reached the bank, but I left it on. I didn't want to look like I was preparing for something. I didn't want to strip down and make it seem like I cared if I died with a shirt on or not. After all, this wasn't a planned dive or a carefully edited educational TikTok. No, this was a test. A quiet, dangerous dare.

The GoPro was already rigged in a tree, angled just right to catch whatever might come my way. Its red light blinked, patient. Like it knew what I was about to do and had no intention of stopping me. Not that it could. Not that anyone could.

I didn't say anything to the camera. I didn't offer a vlog-style intro. I gave no explanation to my madness. I just walked into the frame, stepped out of my shoes, and stood at the edge of the water like I was about to baptize myself into some dark cult religion.

I wasn't one to lie to myself; I was scared. I didn't want to be. I'd told myself I wouldn't be. But my body had other plans. My chest was tight; my palms were slick with sweat that wasn't just due to the heat. My brain had signed the waiver to my demise, but my nerves hadn't. I hated that about myself—that my body clung to life even when I didn't want it to.

The water was even darker than I had expected. Murky, like old coffee left on the counter too long. It didn't splash when I stepped in, it just accepted me, like I made sense existing there amongst the decay.

I walked in like I knew what I was doing. The water came up to my knees first. Then my thighs. Then I forced myself to keep going until it reached my waist.

The surface was slick with algae and fragments of leaves. Gnats buzzed low around me. Cypress trees rose up through the water like gnarled fingers.

With a deep breath of resolve, I kept going until it came up to my neck and then I let myself float. As the water closed over my ears, the stillness was instant. Like I'd pressed pause on the world.

It's funny—how loud my thoughts got when everything else went quiet. Under the surface, my breath roared in my ears. My skin prickled with awareness. Every part of me felt raw and alert, like I'd peeled off a layer of me that I didn't know I had been wrapped in.

I began to drift. My eyes closed on their own as I waited. Surely it wouldn't take long. I was a hunk of bait. It had to be any second now.

Any. Second.

But nothing came.

I opened my eyes. The sky above me was flat and bright, cloudless. A single bird glided overhead. It felt like it was mocking me.

I thought about the stories I'd read. The guy who bent down to wash his hands at the water's edge and never stood back up. The teenager fishing off a dock who disappeared mid-sentence. The woman who watched her dog get pulled under and jumped in after him—neither came back.

I wanted that. That moment. The sudden flash. The pull. The drag. My heart thudded as a splash came from behind me.

My chest snapped tight.

I turned my head slowly, barely daring to move. The water rippled out in rings just feet away. Something had broken the surface. Something big.

Another splash startled me again. It was closer this time.

And then I saw it.

Two eyes. Low, black and unblinking. A snout floated just beneath the surface, gliding toward me like the slow curve of a question I already knew the answer to.

I froze. I didn't make a sound, didn't swim. I just stayed still, despite my body screaming at me to get away. *Let it come*, I thought.

It got closer. And then even closer.

Ten feet.

Five.

I whispered, "Come on. Do it."

It brushed against my leg. A slick, heavy touch. Despite the stifling heat around me, my skin went cold. The instinct to move, to flail, screamed through my bones—but I held myself still. I stayed. I offered myself up like a sacrifice in board shorts.

But it didn't bite me. It just slid past me like I wasn't even worth the trouble. Several more seconds passed, and then just like that—it was gone.

I moved and began to tread water. My legs trembled beneath the surface, and my heart jackhammered in my chest. More than the adrenaline and disappointment, fear assaulted me until I was drenched in humiliation. I had been touched by death, only to be rejected.

I didn't remember pulling myself out of the water. All I could recall was the feeling of my knees hitting the muddy shore in surrender. My hands digging into the dirt. The scream that built in the back of my throat, but never fully formed. Instead of hollering out my anger, I grabbed a rock and hurled it into the thicket of trees.

"You coward," I muttered. Not sure if I meant the gator. Or myself. Or the Universe.

The GoPro's red light blinked from the tree reminding me that it had seen everything. More than I had wanted it to see.

I crawled over and sat beneath it. Wet. Breathing too hard. Feeling too much. Or maybe nothing at all.

That's when the airboat arrived. Loud, whirring like a broken chainsaw. A uniformed wildlife officer cut the engine and stood, waving at me. "Hey! You okay over there?"

I didn't answer.

"You're not supposed to be in this area. It's restricted. Too many gators."

I stared at him, water dripping down my arms. I must've looked like hell. I only stood when he called me over to get in his boat. He didn't ask for my name. Didn't write me up. Just muttered about tourists and idiots and how someone's always got to be the cautionary tale. He dropped me off at a nearby dock and drove away like I was an errand he hadn't wanted to deal with.

I sat on the dock for a long time. Watching the water. Waiting to feel something. I didn't.

THAT NIGHT, I pulled up the footage from the GoPro.

My fingers hovered over the keyboard longer than necessary before opening it up and pressing play.

There I was—walking into the water like I had a purpose. There was something strange about watching it back. Like it was someone else. Someone braver. Or dumber. Probably both.

The moment the gator passed me—my face barely flinched. I looked... calm. Resigned. There was something hollow in my eyes that I hadn't seen in the mirror yet. It scared me a little.

I sat in the dark, clicking through frames, pausing where the predator had brushed against my leg. You couldn't see it well, but I remembered the weight of its body. The video held proof that death had been right there next to me, touching me... and still hadn't taken me.

And for reasons I still didn't fully understand, I opened YouTube and created a channel. I titled it: Die Trying. Not because I wanted to be known. Not because I cared if anyone actually watched it. But because I needed it out of me. Because if I didn't, the experience would fester inside of me until I went crazier than I already was.

I uploaded the footage. Added a title: Swimming in Gator-Infested Waters, No F's Given. I didn't bother writing a description. Didn't add hashtags. No fancy music. No intro. No explanation. It was just me and the swamp and a gator that ghosted me.

The video went live at 3:14 a.m. I quickly shut the laptop before I could feel any regret and lay down on the floor, arms outstretched, water still drying in my ears.

I hadn't died. Not today. But maybe—just maybe—the world had finally started paying attention.

Chapter Three
The Knock

Die Trying 

@dietrying

20m Subscribers • 22 Videos

🔔 SUBSCRIBE 👍

December 2025

The knock came at 9:42 a.m.

I was mid-dream. Something about floating down a lazy river made of whiskey, surrounded by cheerleaders in an astronaut uniform. I tried not to sleep much because not all my dreams were of whiskey-soaked riverbeds. Most of the time they were nightmares. The sweaty, screaming kind that woke me up and didn't let me fall back to sleep. The knock came sharp and loud, like the real world was smacking me on the head with a hammer.

I ignored it. Obviously. Nobody knocked on my door.

Despite my denial, the second knock came. Louder this time. I grunted, rolled over, and buried my face in the couch pillow that still smelled like burnt rice from the time I tried to warm it up in the microwave to put on my neck after I had held onto a tree branch during a howling hurricane.

I was fully awake when the third knock came. Followed by a pause. Then another. Slightly less urgent and more of a tap-tap.

I blinked at the ceiling. "If this is Jehovah's Witnesses, I swear to God you'll wish I were already dead."

I pulled myself up. My joints protested. My blanket fell to the floor. The laptop on the coffee table had gone dark hours ago, although I knew if I tickled the mouse pad, it would kick back to life, and the screen would still be open to my latest YouTube video.

Another knock.

"Jesus, okay!"

I stumbled toward the door. T-shirt inside out. One sock on. Hair probably looked like I'd fought someone in my sleep, and maybe I had. But I didn't care who saw me. I had no one in my life who mattered. Uber Eats left food and vanished, and besides them, literally no one else came here.

I opened the door to find a man standing in the doorway. Shorter than me, although I was 6'1, so a lot of people were. He was probably in his early thirties, if I had to guess. Curly brown hair that he had clearly tried to tame and failed as it sprung out around his head in model worthy waves. He wore wire-rimmed glasses. I didn't know if they were just for show or if he actually needed them. A bag was slung over his shoulder, and he wasn't smiling. In fact, he looked wrecked, like he hadn't slept.

And I had no fucking clue who he was. I made a noise in the back of my throat as if to say, "Can I help you?"

"Danny?" he said.

I blinked. "Who's asking?"

He let out a breath. "I'm Carter."

I stared.

"My—your editor. Carter. From the channel."

I continued staring.

"We've talked for over a year."

I narrowed my eyes. "Why are you here?"

He blinked. Then exhaled and walked inside without asking. Just brushed past me like we were buddies getting ready to watch the game together.

I shut the door slowly behind him. "Sure. Come on in. Make yourself at home. You want a LaCroix?"

He turned back to me, holding up his phone.

And there it was. On the screen in front of me. The letter.

IfYoureReadingThis_FINAL.pdf

There in all its glory, displayed in blue-light horror.

My stomach dropped. "Oh," I said.

"You sent it to me by accident," he accused.

I nodded. "Yeah. Pretty much. Whoops. My bad."

Silence.

"So..." he said, voice a little shaky, "is it real?"

I shrugged, heart pounding. "Doesn't really matter if it is, don't ya think?"

He lowered the phone.

"I didn't mean to send it," I added. "But I didn't try to unsend it, either. I didn't know if I could do that. But that probably tells you everything you need to know."

He looked around the room as if it held answers. But all he saw was a crumpled blanket, a crumpled receipt from my dinner order the night before, and a crumpled me.

"Danny," he said, voice lower now, "you've been doing these stunts for what—eighteen months?"

"Yup."

"Twenty of them?"

"Mmm hmm."

"The whole time you actually wanted to die?"

I shrugged again. "I wanted the universe to do it for me, but clearly it didn't."

"So what now? You're gonna do it?"

I didn't answer.

He looked like he was holding something down—grief or rage or disbelief. Maybe all three. It unnerved me.

"I can't let you," he finally said, lips set in a determined grimace.

"You can't stop me." I almost laughed. "And you have nothing to do with this."

"You made me a part of it, Danny."

That made me flinch. "I didn't ask you to come here."

"You sent me the letter."

"By accident."

"But it wasn't a draft. You signed it. You wrote it like it was done."

I looked away. The floor was safer than his face.

"You've got millions of people watching your videos. They'll be horrified."

"They don't know me."

"I do."

"No, you don't."

He stepped closer. "Danny, I've edited your footage for almost two years. Every clip. Every scene. I've watched you almost fall off the top of a moving car and scream into a storm and laugh like you'd finally lost your mind. You may not really talk to me, but I know you."

I swallowed. Hard.

"I know you don't want help," he said. "I know you think this is inevitable. But I'm standing here. In your shitty apartment. Because I care."

"Fuck you. My apartment is great." It wasn't.

That word. Care. I wanted to punch it. Rip it apart. Scream. Instead, I laughed. Sharp and ugly. "What's your plan, Carter? Are you gonna inspire me out of it with a Ted Talk? Show me cute cat videos until I change my mind?"

"No," he said, flinching. "I want you to agree to go to therapy."

"Fuck no."

"Danny—"

"No. Absolutely not."

He paused, looking at me like he was recalibrating.

"Okay," he acquiesced, as if he had any say in this at all. "Then let's make a deal."

"Carter. You need to shut the fuck up."

He ignored me.

"You did twenty death-defying stunts. So do twenty therapy sessions. After that I'll leave you alone."

I shook my head. "They are not even close to being the same thing."

"Why not?"

"Because one is dying slowly in a chair while someone asks about your mother and the other is swimming with literal sharks."

He didn't budge; his eyes bulged a little behind his glasses. "Twenty sessions. And if you still want to go through with it after that, I promise I'll back off."

I stared. "You're serious."

He nodded. "Completely."

"I don't do therapy."

"Fine," he said. "Not therapy. Life coach."

I choked. "That's worse."

"I'll find someone who won't ask about your feelings. Someone who won't even try to fix you. Just show up and talk. Or don't. But go twenty times. That's the deal."

"And if I say no?"

He squared his shoulders. "I'll delete your whole channel. You'll disappear. Your whole legacy will be gone."

"You can't do that. I'll change my password."

He scoffed. "Don't insult my hacking abilities."

I squirmed, my bare foot rubbing along the ragged edge of the rug.

"Your channel is your proof," he continued. "Of what you did. What you survived. What you tried. You want to be remembered after this, right?"

I didn't answer. Did I?

"Twenty sessions," he repeated. "Or it's all gone."

The silence between us stretched.

I hated him. For showing up. For caring. For seeing me even if he had no idea who I really was.

I hated that I was considering saying yes.

Finally, I sighed. Painfully. Feeling wounded by his threat but more so by his concern. "Fine."

"Fine?"

"I show up to twenty sessions. Nothing more. And no therapy bullshit. If she says the word 'inner child,' I'm out."

He smiled, exhausted. Relieved. "Deal. I'll find someone, and I'll send you their info when I do. I'll even make your first appointment."

"Carter?"

"Yeah?"

"You're a crazy motherfucker."

He laughed. "No, my guy. That's you."

I didn't say anything. He wasn't wrong.

But for the first time in a long time, I felt something other than empty. I wasn't sure if it was dread. Or relief.

Chapter Four
Jupiter, FL

(Uploaded: July 9, 2024. 1:45 a.m.)

If the alligators in Florida's backwaters didn't want me, maybe the ocean's predators would.

The next thing on my list was sharks. Sharks would want me, wouldn't they?

I'd done my research and picked Jupiter for a reason. The waters were teeming with them that time of year—lemon sharks, bull sharks, blacktips, even the occasional hammerhead if you got lucky, or unlucky, depending on how you looked at it. But I wasn't going in to see the sights. I wouldn't have a cage. No prepared bait. Well, I was the bait. It was just me, some cheap fins, a matte black scuba suit, and the GoPro mounted like a confession on my chest. The black neoprene with borrowed air was strapped to my back. I looked like someone who planned to come back.

If I drowned, or got shredded, hopefully the footage would float. If I didn't, well... the outcome didn't really matter to me as long as I wasn't here anymore to ponder it.

The guy I had hired to man the boat hadn't asked very many questions. Probably thought I was another influencer with more ego than brain matter. I didn't tell him otherwise. Just slipped him a wad of cash and asked for a spot where sharks liked to pass through. "Don't chum the water," I told him. "Just give me twenty minutes and turn the boat off."

He said, "You got a death wish or something?"

I smiled. "Something like that."

He shrugged and pointed out to a patch of sea that looked exactly like every other stretch of ocean I'd ever seen—blue, endless, quietly mysterious. Then he cut the motor.

I listened to his instructions and fell in backwards without overthinking it. I didn't even let myself say goodbye to the world around me. I tried to ignore the twinge of guilt that I felt knowing that he'd be left with the bloody aftermath. He'd have to tell the police what happened. I hoped it didn't give him any issues. I wasn't an asshole; I just didn't want to be here anymore.

The ocean snapped shut over my head like a trapdoor, sealing me in. Cold enveloped me instantly—like sharp, wet hands gripping my chest. For a second, I hovered just beneath the surface, suspended in blue, feeling weightless and enjoying the quiet. The salt burned my exposed skin. The pressure around my ears deepened as I sank further. I didn't fight it. The water welcomed me like an old friend.

Everything was soundless chaos. The bubbles around my ears roared, then vanished. The water was a murky green-blue, and sunlight rippled down around me like ribbons. I kicked, pushing myself lower, deeper than I should've gone, and looked down at the camera strapped to me. The red light blinked, indicating that it was recording.

Later, when I watched the footage back, it started with a flash of bubbles and a muted breath. Then the camera steadied, revealing my silhouette moving through the open water—small, grainy, a human shape in a world where humans didn't belong.

At the two-minute mark, the first shark appeared.

It glided into frame like a ghost. A lemon shark, maybe six feet, sleek and slow-moving. It didn't even glance at me. Just kept swimming.

Then another. And another. Blacktips this time, thinner, faster, more erratic. I floated in their path. Still. Waiting.

At six minutes, one circled me. Just once. Close enough that I could see the texture of its skin in the footage—gray and smooth, with that sandpaper shimmer. I remembered locking eyes with it. Or maybe I just imagined I did. Its eyes were nothing like ours. They held no judgment, yet no empathy either. They were just the black marble orbs of a predator's eyes.

Spoiler alert, the shark didn't bite.

I should have prepared myself for fear to show up. Because it did. Around the ten-minute mark, something primal in me twitched. Not panic, but a deep awareness. An electric sense that something in me had shifted.

A bull shark passed beneath me. Bigger. Thicker. The kind they warn you about.

I held still; my heart kicked against my ribs like it wanted out. Like it knew what I was asking for. The bull shark wasn't like the others. Its presence shifted the water, made it heavier, and lifted the hairs on the back of my neck, even though they were soaked and cold. There was a new awareness in the silence around me. The kind that wraps around you right before something explodes. The calm before the storm, or so they say.

For a second, I thought the next moment would be it. The GoPro caught me adjusting my posture, opening my arms a little, as if asking: *Are you coming for me? Is this where I get to let go?*

I thought about what my body might look like when it happened—limbs drifting down through the blue green, my blood a ribbon curling behind me, mouth slightly open. Would anyone find the footage? Would people pause it at this exact moment and say, "There. Right there is when he died."

But the shark swerved. Swam past me like I was kelp.

It was the first time during my two stunts that I felt truly disappointed in real time.

Fifteen minutes in, I started to shiver. Not from cold. From something else. From the absurdity of all of it. This wasn't bravery. This wasn't facing death. It was offering myself up and being ignored. Like the ocean itself was saying, not you. Not yet.

Another shark passed. Then another. I counted eight in total. Not one touched me.

The footage started to shake a little then. My breathing got faster. Louder.

So, I gave up and resurfaced, gasping as I let the regulator fall from my mouth. I didn't know if it was because I needed more fresh air... or if I was protesting the unfairness of it.

Either way, I didn't get out of the water right away. I wasn't ready yet.

Instead, just like in the swamp, I floated on my back after releasing air from my BCD, buoyant in spite of myself. Watching the sky. It was pale and hazy. The kind of sky that hides the sun just enough to make you think you're safe from a sunburn, but you end up with one anyway. I didn't know how long I floated out in the water. The captain hadn't called me back. Maybe he was watching from the boat. Maybe he thought I was dead already.

I kind of hoped he did and had left. Not because I wanted him to worry—but because for a second, it might mean I'd have no choice but to let go. Drowning hadn't been on my list, but there was no way I'd be able to swim back to the shore, the remaining air in the tank wouldn't last long. Eventually, I'd lose strength and would have to let the depths take me. The ocean would finally be forced to do what I'd been begging it to.

But no. The boat was still there. And I was floating around like a pathetic piece of driftwood. Waiting for something that clearly wasn't coming. The longer I waited, the more absurd it felt. I had offered myself. Not in fear. Not in some desperate flail. But quietly. Willingly. And still, I was refused. Rejected. Like even the wild wanted nothing to do with me.

What eventually got me out of the water wasn't fear. It was boredom. That was the part that pissed me off the most. I didn't crawl back onto the boat trembling, or weeping in frustration, or overwhelmed by survival. No, I climbed up dripping and annoyed.

I tore the GoPro off my chest. Then pulled the scuba suit off, growing even more frustrated as the wet material seemed suctioned to my skin. Finally, I sat there in my wet shorts, water pooling at my feet, and stared at the blinking red light.

I was still recording.

I was still here.

I was still alive.

THAT NIGHT, I watched the footage three times.

First, to really see the sharks. Second, to revel in the silence. Third, to get a good glimpse of the moment I thought I might die —but didn't.

And I remembered saying it out loud, to no one, sitting on my motel bed with the shitty air conditioner rattling, "Does the next life not even want me?"

It wasn't a dramatic observation. It was just... factual.

Although I hadn't gotten what I really wanted, the footage was good. Clear and vivid. A perspective different from the one you saw in documentaries where the cameraman's job was to get some interesting shots to show you how strong and scary these predators were. My video was much more realistic and in your face. The sharks were beautiful in a way people didn't usually admit out loud. I was the inconsequential component on screen. They were the main characters.

I uploaded it at 1:45 a.m., half-expecting the algorithm to ignore me just like death had.

But I had gone viral by sunrise.

Chapter Five

Session One

Die Trying 

@dietrying

20m Subscribers • 22 Videos

SUBSCRIBE

December 2025

C arter had texted me two days ago.

CARTER

> I found you the perfect life coach. No therapy. Just a sage-waving, crystal-wearing lady who can give you some advice. I booked you an appointment. Wednesday at 3 pm. She only takes cash. If you don't go, I won't send you the final edit of the chicken video.

I left him on read.

Not because I didn't want the edit, I did want it, but because I hated that I'd let him in enough for this to be possible. I'd slipped. Accidentally attached the letter with the final footage. The one that gave away my deeply kept secret. And now he thought he had a right to interfere. Even before that, I had let him in. I had made him think we were friends. That I was somehow someone he had a right to care about.

He didn't.

But here I was anyway. Not because I suddenly wanted

help. Or because I'd had a revelation. I was here only because I needed that file. And I needed my channel to stay online. I had unwillingly come to the realization that the only thing I cared about before dying was making sure all the footage of my attempts stayed up, keeping my memory embalmed forever.

And maybe, just maybe, I was mildly curious what kind of woman signed up to coach people, when I presumed most of her clientele were just crawling through life on bloody knees. How could she enjoy the depressing conversations that I was sure occurred in her office?

The Uber pulled up to the address that Carter had texted me. It was a clean storefront with a simple sign and a green door. Inside, the waiting room was too quiet. There was no receptionist. Just a table with a sign that said to wait to be called in, a few houseplants that looked too alive, a curated stack of inspirational self-help books on a white oak shelf, and a tea station that looked like no one had touched it today.

I had barely lowered myself into a soft, fluffy chair when the door in the back opened and a woman stepped out.

"You must be Danny. I'm Iris. Welcome."

I stood, already regretting being here.

She was younger than I'd expected—late twenties maybe. She wore big glasses, with no detectable makeup on her pale skin, and her hair was pulled up in a loose, practical knot. She wore a cardigan with a scarf twisted around her neck. And sensible boots. They were almost nerdy.

But she was beautiful.

Not the obvious type of beautiful. Not the influencer kind that was splashed all over social media these days with exposed flesh and bright lips. No, her beauty was the kind that snuck up on you. It wasn't flashy in a way that made you notice it all at once. It was delicate; it forced you to take a second glance. She had a defined jawline. Long dark lashes. A full mouth. Lips that showed signs of smiling way too often for my liking. It was annoying, the way she didn't seem like the type that spent too much time on the way she looked, yet she looked even better because of it. I was irritated to have noticed it at all. I looked away quickly, like that might have helped me unsee it.

"Sure," I said, stepping past her into the room without waiting for an official invitation.

Her office smelled like lavender and old books. The couch looked soft. I made a point to sit in the chair instead.

On the wall behind her desk was a framed print that said, "You are exactly where you need to be." The sentiment made me want to toss it out the window so I wouldn't have to look at it again. Everything from the throw blankets to the reed diffusers looked like it had been curated to say 'calm' without using words. I hated it. Not because it was offensive but because it was sincere.

"You don't want to be here," she said as she sat down across from me. I got a faint whiff of her perfume as she passed. It was floral and woodsy, and I turned away from it as if it was bothering me. It wasn't.

"Gold star for noticing," I muttered, feeling the resentment of Carter forcing me to be here begin to bubble to the surface. "Guess you earned your degrees."

She smiled. Not tight, not fake. She just... smiled, even though my attitude was awful. Like she'd expected the jab from me.

"I did, actually," she said. "Several of them."

She opened a notebook but didn't write anything in it yet.

"ICF-certified. Co-Active Coaching through CTI. Trauma-informed training, even though I'm not a therapist. My under-grad was in behavioral psych. I specialize in working with people who aren't sure what their purpose is here."

My eyes narrowed. "Here as in... Earth?"

"Here as in this room." She cocked her head. "But Earth works too."

I huffed out a breath that might have been a laugh if I still had any of those left in me.

She didn't ask me anything right away, so we just sat there. Me silent and irritated, her with her ankles crossed and a faint smile splayed across her lips.

"I'm not interested in fixing myself," I finally said, growing uncomfortable.

"Good," she said approvingly. "I don't fix people."

"Carter thinks I need to be saved," I continued, voice low. "You should know that up front. He's on some savior kick."

"And you?"

I leaned back, eyes on the ceiling.

"I'm just here, waiting to collect a video file."

Her silence stretched again. Not uncomfortable this time— just still. Curious. Non-judgmental.

"I don't want to be helped," I added as if that wasn't already clear. "I don't want to be changed. I don't want to journal or set goals or talk about my feelings."

"I'm not here to make you do any of that," she said.

I glanced over. "Then what are you here for?"

"To help you ask better questions than the ones you've already been asking yourself."

My throat tightened. I didn't like that answer.

"Fine," I said. "You want a question?"

She nodded. I let the silence crawl around her for a moment just like she had done to me.

"Why is it that people who want to die have to be talked out of it... but people who want to live don't have to justify that?"

Iris blinked. I worried that maybe my question hadn't made sense.

"Do you want to die?" she finally inquired.

I didn't answer her question; instead, I just kept talking. "You get in a car and tell someone you want to drive across the country, they wish you luck," I said. "You tell them you want to get on a rocket to Mars; they call you a visionary. But you say—I think I'm done here—and suddenly everyone needs to hold an intervention."

Her eyes didn't waver. "You feel like you've done your time?"

"I feel like I've seen enough. Gone through enough."

There was a pause as we both processed what I had just said.

"Or maybe," I added, "I'm just sick of existing this way with nothing that can be done to change it."

She folded her hands in her lap. "And yet... you're here."

I looked away. I was, but I had also lost count of the nights where I'd woken up sweating, thinking I was twelve again. I'd spent three decades trying to be okay, and I was tired of it. Not the kind of tired that a nap or a life coach session could fix. The kind of exhaustion that sank into your marrow and stayed there.

She didn't fill the space of my silence. She just let it hang until I was ready to speak again.

"Maybe because I had no choice," I said finally. "Maybe because Carter forced me. Maybe because I need that damn edit."

"Or maybe," she coaxed gently, "you're here because some part of you wants someone to witness the ending."

That one got me. I sat up straighter, jaw tight.

"You're not going to be the one to save me," I reminded her again, firmly.

"Then it's a good thing that's not my job," she replied perfunctorily.

The timer on her phone went off. A soft chime. Releasing me from the torture. She reached over to silence it.

I stood. She stood, too.

"See you next week?" she asked.

I shrugged. "Guess we'll find out."

I turned to leave but paused by the door.

"Seriously though... why do people have to be forced to stay alive?" I asked quietly, not looking back. "Why is choosing not to live the worst thing a person can do?"

She didn't answer right away. When I glanced back, she looked like she was deep in thought. Not dramatically. Just enough to make me smirk. It made me feel like I'd somehow won this session.

"We're out of time, Miss..."

"Marlowe," she said, recovering quickly. "Iris Marlowe."

"Right." I tugged open the door. "Well, Miss Marlowe. Seems we'll have to unpack that next session."

And with that, I walked out—already unsure whether I wanted to or not.

Chapter Six
Tesla Coil

Die Trying 

@dietrying

20m Subscribers · 22 Videos

 SUBSCRIBE

(Uploaded: July 25, 2024. 11:13 p.m.)

Looking back, I wasn't sure how I'd seen Carter's message amongst the thousands of notifications that were bombarding my phone every day since my videos had gone viral but somehow, I had. The irony wasn't lost on me that the boy who had never gotten attention until now was suddenly the internet's latest sensation.

His message said,

Carter

Yo. Let me edit the next one for free. You're onto something here.

I remember I stared at that message for a good twenty

minutes, unsure if I was hallucinating from sleep deprivation or if someone had, genuinely said something kind to me. It took me a few days to respond, and I had to scroll back quite a few times since it was buried under a mountain of unread DMs, interview requests, sponsorship offers, and just a multitude of messages from people who didn't know me beyond my thumbnails. It was all noise to me. They didn't matter. The messages made me feel like the world thought I was trying to build something versus trying to undo it. Like the companies messaging me didn't realize that they were watching a potential funeral procession, not a rebrand. And it made me sick to my stomach that my mental health issues were getting mistaken for a call to be an influencer. That I was being offered product sponsorships instead of help.

But something about the tone of his message felt different.

"You're onto something."

Like he believed in it. Like he saw a purpose in what I was doing that I didn't. I worried if I said yes, I'd owe him something more than money. Vulnerability, maybe. Or, worse, honesty. That's what kindness did. It poked holes in the darkness. Made you squint because you weren't ready to look at something so bright.

And yeah, maybe that messed with my head a little. I wasn't supposed to be making something. I was supposed to be testing fate until fate finally tested back.

But I let him do it. Not because I trusted him or cared to, but because I was tired. And it was easier than trying to pretend I gave a shit about color grading or captions that would clickbait people into watching me almost die.

So, I messaged back:

Die Trying 

Sure. Knock Yourself Out.

And then I headed to the next attempt on my life.

Utah.

Not the first place that would usually come to mind when you thought of the usual death traps around the country. But out in Grantsville, tucked behind flat roads and faded red dust, there was a research facility that ran live Tesla coil demonstrations.

Most people went to take pictures or see the amazing scene in person. I went to stand under it.

The coil itself looked like something ripped out of a Frankenstein fever dream—metallic, humming, shooting blue arcs into the sky. It was beautiful in an almost unworldly way. I'd emailed ahead, pretending to be a science influencer who wanted to film some B-roll shots for an upcoming video on electromagnetic fields.

Which wasn't technically untrue. I was planning to record. I was also planning to stand close enough to get singed if it misfired. I obviously didn't tell them that part.

I suddenly had money to take any flight I wanted and book a nice hotel room. If my good luck so far was an indication of anything, maybe today would finally be my day.

I rigged the GoPro to my chest, strapped tight to a fire-retardant hoodie—a safety protocol that they ironically insisted on. And then I walked into the zone.

The sound hit me first.

It wasn't the static buzz you'd expect. No. This was deeper. Almost... alive. The crackling was thick, like the sky was splitting open, and the electricity danced in jagged halos above my head. It roared like it was a godly thing trapped in a cage. Arcs snapped up like lightning coming from the ground, not the sky. My molars buzzed. My skin prickled.

And for a moment, I felt it again. That flicker. The one I hated. The one that whispered, maybe I could do more with this than just disappear. But I quickly shoved it down and stepped closer.

The heat rolled in waves across my arms, tiny hairs sizzling at the edges. The coil flared, the surge fired toward the air, and I felt the impact not just on my skin, but in my chest. It was like the world was trying to reach inside me, rearrange my atoms, and decide whether or not I deserved to come away with it.

One second. Two. Three. My hands began to shake.

I willed myself to stay. My brain screamed at me to back up. Just a step. Just enough for it to know that I acknowledged that I was a fragile human, not a lightning rod. But my feet stayed planted, defying instinct. I was either going to leave this place as ash or live through it like I always did. Half-changed, half-ruined.

Four. Five. I kept counting.

My knee buckled slightly, and I thought maybe, just maybe, this would be it. But then the operator saw what I was doing, panicked, and shut it down.

The field collapsed. The air went dead.

And I was still fucking alive.

Again.

I walked back to the parking lot with my not so fire-safe

hoodie scorched at the sleeves, one palm stinging from where I'd instinctively reached for balance and scraped across hot metal.

It wasn't enough to be considered a real injury that needed to be documented or looked at, but it hurt just enough to piss me off.

I sat in my car and stared out at the horizon where the land bled into the sky. When I got done with my moping, I played the footage back. The arc. The sparks. The crackle of electricity kissing air. My face lit up blue and pale. The moment my leg gave out.

It looked... incredible. It looked like I was fearless. Which was a lie.

I wasn't fearless. I was actually tired of living in fear all the time. Now every time I survived, I felt like I was being punished. Like the universe was holding me hostage. Making me sit in the aftermath of my failed plans, watching the reruns of my pain, just to prove a point. No matter how close I got to the edge, fate pulled me back by the collar. *Not yet*, it whispered in my ear. *When?* I wanted to roar back. But I stayed silent.

I sent the footage to Carter without a message, letting the files speak for themselves.

He sent it back a few hours later, perfectly edited, better than I could have ever done myself.

I opened YouTube and uploaded it. No explanation. No long caption. I didn't give a shit. The views exploded, and the comments came in fast.

"THIS DUDE'S GOT A DEATH WISH FR."

"I HOPE WE GET TO SEE IT HAPPEN. THAT WOULD BE SICK."

"HOT AF. (FIRE EMOJI) WHO IS HE???"

"HE'S KINDA CUTE THO."

"NEW FAVORITE CHANNEL. THIS GUY IS NUTS."

"I'D LET HIM ELECTROCUTE ME (WINKING EMOJI)."

And just like that, I hated everything again. I didn't know what it was about those kinds of comments that made me sick to my stomach and uncomfortable in my body. Maybe it was the way they made something dangerous into something sexy. Maybe it was the way they made me into a joke, a fantasy, a screenshot for their group chats. What was it about the world that a pretty cover distracted people enough that they didn't see the pain screaming in my eyes? Being tall, broad, and conventionally good-looking was more important to the viewers than the fact that they had now watched me try to commit suicide three times and hadn't really noticed. My defined jawline, pretty eyes, and pouty lips were more important than the fact that I was very clearly, very obviously not okay. But as long as the masses were entertained, they didn't care. I imagined if I had died, they would have commented how good my hair looked mid sizzle.

That night, when I got to the point way beyond exhaustion, I finally let myself sleep. I literally passed out on the hotel bed, still smelling faintly of ozone and burnt cotton. Unfortunately, I wasn't exhausted enough to keep the dreams away.

I was twelve.

Back in that room.

The one with peeling wallpaper and the door that never locked properly.

And he was there.

Smiling like this was normal. Like this was love.

"You're so quiet, Danny boy," he said, voice syrupy slow. "That's how I know you want it."

My chest froze. My feet wouldn't move. The room was too warm, and his breath was too close.

"You're a good boy, right?"

I wanted to scream. I wanted to disappear into the floor. But in the dream, like in real life, I just lay there.

Frozen.

Waiting.

Enduring.

I woke up drenched in sweat, my nails digging half-moons into my palms. I sat up with a gasp, and collapsed against the headboard, fists still clenched as I stared at the ceiling, heart hammering in my throat.

It was just a nightmare. It hadn't been real in so long.

But the voice. The name. Danny boy. That felt real even now.

Even after I got up. Even after I showered. Even after I packed up my charger, checked out of the hotel, and started driving toward the next potential death, it followed me. Like a ghost I couldn't bury. Like static that wouldn't fade.

Chapter Seven
Session Two

January 2026

I was ten minutes early. I didn't know why. Maybe because it was either I came here early, or I sat in my apartment with the smell of dirty dishes and existential dread hovering in the air. The waiting room had a scent like someone had tried to cover up sadness with a citrus essential oil blend. It puffed out, every few minutes, from the bamboo automatic air freshener on the end table on the opposite side of the room. It didn't work. It just made the sadness taste fruity and bitter.

I didn't bother knocking when she called me in. The door was slightly ajar. Iris sat in the same damn chair with her legs crossed the same damn way, her little notebook in her lap. Her hair was mainly tucked behind one ear, though some had escaped and curled around her temples in wayward wisps. She smiled when she saw me.

"Hi, Danny."

I sat down across from her, collapsing a little too hard. My annoyance came off a little dramatic. "Hi."

The chair felt smaller than last time. Or maybe I just felt more obvious. Like my body took up too much space in this room meant for healing, for hope. I hated how my knee bounced. I hated that I couldn't stop it. It was like my nervous system was not down for this session even though my body was here.

Her eyes had that look when she observed me again—kind, too kind—and I hated how it made my chest feel itchy. I hated, even more, that I noticed the way her cardigan matched her lipstick, soft and plum-colored and somehow... it looked perfect on her. I hated that I noticed her lips at all.

God, I needed to stop noticing things.

"How's your week been?"

"Fantastic," I said dryly. "I only googled new ways to commit suicide twice."

Her mouth twitched, but she didn't flinch. "Progress."

"Joking."

"Still progress."

She was quick with her comebacks, and she seemed to exist so effortlessly, like she had no idea what it felt like to be uncomfortable in your own skin. I hated that too.

Like last time, we sat in silence a little too long, and I regretted not bringing something to fiddle with. My hands kept twitching in my lap like they didn't know what to do when they weren't researching places to die or holding a GoPro.

"You left us with a big one last session," she said eventually, flipping open her notebook.

"I did?"

"You asked, why do people have to be forced to stay alive?"

I leaned back in the chair. "Yeah, well. I didn't mean to ruin the vibe or whatever."

"You didn't ruin anything." She studied me. "Would you like to unpack that?"

I shrugged. "What's there to unpack? The world loses its shit over someone wanting out. We act like death is the worst thing that could happen. You're alive. You should know. This world and living in it is a shit show."

She nodded slowly, not writing anything. "Go on."

I blinked. "That's it. Life sucks. It's taxes and heartbreak and trauma and traffic. And then you die anyway. So what's the point of all the crap in between? If we're all going to die eventually, why is it so bad that I choose to go a little earlier than the rest of you?"

"You think life is mostly bad."

I snorted. "No. I think life is inherently bad."

"Why?"

I could tell she wanted me to talk. I could also tell she was good at not pushing too hard. But the thing was, when someone actually wanted to listen—it was weirdly harder for me to stay silent. I sighed and let myself talk.

"Because it's all pain, Iris. It's waking up tired. It's knowing people don't care, or worse, it's knowing people hurt you and then people still didn't care. You go through shit you never asked for, and then the world expects you to just... move on. Smile. Forgive. Try again. Why? For what?"

"For connection. For meaning."

I laughed without humor. "Connection? People don't connect. They comment. They repost. They call it inspiring so they don't have to look at their own lives too hard. They say, "so relatable," and then scroll to some influencer making pancakes for her golden doodle. It's not real. None of it is real. I have millions of subscribers who 'love me,' and not one of them truly cares how miserable I am. None of them will think about it that long when I die."

"I doubt that's all true."

"It is. You know how many comments I get every time I almost die on camera? Hundreds of 'you're so brave,' and 'God damn that was close.' You know how many people messaged me to ask if I needed to talk? If I was actually okay? Two. Out of millions."

She tilted her head. "And those two?"

I waved it off. "Some dude in Denmark who just wanted to trauma bond and an eighteen-year-old girl who thinks I'm cool because I stood under lightning."

"That sounds like a possibility for connection."

"Yeah, well. Not enough to keep me tethered. Not enough to make me care."

She looked at me carefully, like she was searching for something behind my cynicism.

"Why do you think other people are afraid of death?"

"Because they don't have the balls to admit that they're miserable. They think there is something here to miss. But I think nothingness has got to be better than... all of this." I waved my hand around her cozy office as if it represented the shit show that I said the world was.

I hadn't meant to say that. I hadn't meant for it to come out with that much venom. But it did, and now it sat there alive and buzzing between us.

Iris leaned in just slightly. "What if they're not miserable? What if they love someone? What if they're excited to be alive for their children, or their partner, or even for hope? Curiosity of what tomorrow will bring."

"That's great for them," I said. "I don't have any of that. And I don't want anyone to try to convince me that I do. I don't. I never did. Maybe life is nice for someone like you. You probably have a husband and two kids at home. A cat. A hobby other than driving me crazy. My life isn't like that." I almost laughed but I didn't. She kept her eyes solidly on me as if she could see what my intestines were doing. I squirmed.

"What would it be like if you did have someone?" she finally asked.

I hesitated. What would it be like? Probably like trying to breathe underwater. The idea of someone touching me without hurting me... felt laughable. Unattainable. Dangerous even. Connection felt like a gamble I couldn't afford to lose. I shrugged.

"I don't know. But it doesn't matter. I don't trust anyone. I don't want anyone. I don't... do people."

She didn't respond right away. She just watched me again. Not with pity, but with a kind of silent curiosity that made me feel like a museum exhibit.

"I think you do people more than you realize," she said softly.

I looked away. There was a clock on the wall, and I stared at it for longer than I needed to. The second hand ticked like it was mocking me.

"You're over time," I muttered eventually.

She smiled. "I don't mind."

"Well, I do. You're wasting your time."

"You're not a waste of time."

I closed my eyes for a beat, letting the silence swell. I didn't want to feel that thing blooming in my chest. This thing that felt dangerously close to... being affected by what she had said. Finally, I opened my mouth to end it. To say something cutting or cold. But she beat me to it.

"I watched your videos," she informed me.

My head snapped toward her. "What?"

She had the decency to look sheepish. "I wanted to understand. I figured if I am going to be your life coach, I should know what dying means to you."

I stared at her. "What about HIPAA or whatever?" I mumbled.

She held up her hands. "I'm not a therapist, Danny. I'm a life coach. I can watch whatever I want."

I blinked. "That... doesn't feel legal."

She laughed. "It's not illegal."

"Still weird."

"Still helpful."

I shook my head. "Okay." I said it with finality, like I didn't care what she thought of them, although I did. It sickened me that I did.

"I think..." She paused. "I think you've lived more in a year and a half than most people do in a lifetime."

I didn't say anything. Because something about that sentence made my throat tighten.

"And I think," she added, "you don't want to die as much as you want someone to understand why you don't want to stay."

I hated that she was probably right. I hated it so much. I stood up abruptly. "Cool. Well. That's enough soul-probing for one day. I'm gonna go shower all this woo woo stuff off me."

She stood too, brushing her skirt down, bringing my attention to her legs. I quickly looked away.

"I'll see you next week?"

"Unless I get struck by lightning."

She didn't laugh. Instead, she looked at me and said, "I'm glad you're still here."

I wanted to tell her to shut up. Instead, I muttered, "Thanks," and turned toward the door.

As I opened it, she added, "By the way... your Tesla coil video? It was a lot. But also kind of beautiful."

I froze; my hand tightened on the doorknob. I could practically feel the way the air had vibrated around me that day, like God himself was deciding whether or not to take me. I didn't look back. Because I hated that I wanted to know what she meant by beautiful. I hadn't been called beautiful since I was a kid, and back then, it had been the opposite of safe. But I hated, even more, that I was looking forward to next week.

After my session, back on my couch, I opened my laptop and created a new document. I thought about writing a new letter. A second one. A backup. Maybe to Iris, maybe to no one in particular.

I typed the words "still here." Then backspaced. Then typed it again.

There was nothing else to say. That was it. Because it wasn't a confession or a cry for help. It was a report. A fucking status update. I'm still here. And why? Well, I already knew that answer. I'm here because the world hasn't killed me yet.

But it's trying.

And so am I.

Chapter Eight
Bonneville Salt Flats

Die Trying 

@dietrying

20m Subscribers · 22 Videos

 SUBSCRIBE

(Uploaded: August 9, 2024. 7:03 p.m.)

They say the Bonneville Salt Flats look like another planet. That it's just sky and space and salt and silence—like Earth gave up trying to be beautiful and natural and decided to be something else entirely. I didn't come for the views, though. I came to die. Or maybe, to tempt death harder than I ever had before.

Standing on top of a car while it barrels through a desert at seventy miles an hour is not the kind of thing you can half-ass. One wrong shift in balance, one gust of wind, one unnoticed crack in the salt, and I'd be face-planted into the hard earth with nothing but a GoPro and a viral legacy. And smashed brains. Hopefully.

The plan had been simple. Get a rental car, find a closed section of the flats, and a driver who I paid enough not to ask too many questions, which I appreciated. I didn't need concern, I needed speed. After all, I had my ass strapped to the roof with a harness I'd pretended not to double-check three times.

I was going to film the whole thing with two cameras, one mounted near the front windshield and one on my chest. I'd climbed onto the roof like it was an altar. The horizon looked endless from up here. I adjusted the strap once, twice. The metal was warm from the sun and smooth in my hands. I sat down first, knees tucked under me. Once I was situated, I tapped the GoPro twice to confirm it was rolling. Red light: on. Then I gave the signal.

The car started slow. Just a crawl. The wind caught in my hair and teased at my shirt. My fingers curled tighter against the roof. And then—faster. Thirty. Forty. Fifty. The salt flats blurred. The landscape flattened. There was no depth, no sense of motion, only the rumble beneath me and the wind clawing at my ears. Sixty. I stood. It wasn't graceful. My knees wobbled, but I stood up anyway. Arms out. Like some kind of suicidal Jesus on top of a Dodge Charger.

The wind screamed past me, flattening my shirt against my ribs, turning my throat dry, and my lips numb. The sun blazed above like it knew I didn't belong here. Like it was trying to burn me out of existence. I welcomed it. My eyes watered instantly. Every breath tasted like heat and dust. My heart hammered—not with fear exactly, but with something ancestral. Animalistic.

The speedometer mounted on the hood of the car told me that we had hit seventy.

I was a human lightning rod on a rolling death trap.

And it was... beautiful.

Terrifying, too. I couldn't lie. Every cell in my body screamed that this was the end. That one wrong movement, one patch of uneven ground, and I'd be airborne—my body twisting in the sky before shattering against the salt crust. I imagined the headline. The slowed-down footage. The comment section full of kids saying, "RIP Legend." And for a heartbeat, I felt at peace. Finally.

It was a gentle acceptance. For a split second, I didn't feel broken or held together by sarcasm; all the times the world had failed me oozing out between the stitches. I just existed as a speck in the universe, a quick inhale in the chaos, a body defying gravity and consequences. It was the closest thing I'd felt to belonging. Not to people, a place, or a movement. Rather to the moment. But the moment didn't last.

The car began to slow, like the driver sensed the invisible line I was about to cross. I dropped back to my knees as the wind died around me, my hands pressed to the hot roof like it might keep me grounded in some other way. My muscles shook. My throat burned. I was still alive. Of course I was. I always fucking was. It was really starting to piss me off.

WHEN I REPLAYED the footage that night, there was this one frame—my arms wide, shirt flapping, face turned toward the sky —and I looked very much happy to be alive. Which was ridiculous. I paused on that frame. I was laughing. I didn't remember laughing, but there I was, head back, mouth open like I was joking with the sky. It infuriated me because it made me worry that a part of me thought I may have made peace with the world and was okay enjoying it, but I hadn't. Not even close.

After exporting the footage, I started a new email to Carter. As usual, I didn't type anything in the body, just attached the file and hit send. Less than ten minutes later, he called me.

"I'm sorry," I said, already anticipating a rant. "Should I have added a note that said, 'No, I didn't die. Yes, I'm still annoyed about it'?" He thought it was a joke. He had no idea my flirting with death was a real goal and not just me doing crazy things for the views.

"You're a fucking lunatic," he said.

"Do you know what kind of messages I get every time I upload? I had to block a woman named Sunflower_Moon_-

Mommy because she said she wanted to adopt me as her adult son." I changed the subject.

"That's beautiful. I hope she knits."

I laughed.

"You stood on the roof of a moving car, Danny." He brought our attention back to the insanity.

"And?"

"Barefoot."

"I wanted to feel the salt beneath my feet."

He groaned. "You could have felt your bones snap on impact, you dramatic bastard."

"Touché."

I named the video "Riding the Edge: Standing on a Moving Car at 70MPH" and uploaded it without fanfare.

The views started pouring in almost before the thumbnail finished rendering.

Carter texted me around midnight.

CARTER

3M views in 5 hrs. Congrats, Grim Reaper's apprentice.

DANNY

Tell that to my future grave.

CARTER

Working on your merch line: 'Still Not Dead.'

DANNY

Put it on a mug.

I laughed. Like, actually laughed. Then sat there wondering what the hell was so funny.

THE MONEY truly started coming in after my fourth almost brush with death. Stunt number four. The comments started stacking, views exploded, and brands were even more seriously sniffing around like flies to a carcass. Someone even asked me to model for their workout clothing line. I had to spit out my water when I'd read their message. By the time my car video hit forty million views, I had four sponsorships lined up—two adrenaline junkie gear companies, one sketchy energy drink brand, and a GoPro knockoff with a name I couldn't pronounce. It felt like the biggest joke of all. Companies were paying me to film my death wish. Influencers were making TikToks about "The guy who should've died by now." Someone even made a prayer candle with my face on it and tagged me. Meanwhile, I woke up every morning wishing I hadn't.

Sometimes I'd lie in bed and think about all the times the world had failed me. Not the big, headline-type stuff. The small stuff. The invisible stuff. The time I called the police because my foster father locked me in the garage overnight because at fifteen, I'd finally hit him back when he tried to pull my pants down and they said, "Maybe you should just listen better." Or the time I got a perfect SAT score but didn't apply to any colleges because I didn't think I could make it happen. Or the time I called a help line and told them I wasn't okay and they said, "We all feel that way sometimes." Or the time I bought myself a birthday cake because I knew no one else would. The summers I'd waste rotting in my room because I couldn't find the energy to want anything better. The time I got a thousand messages saying, "You inspired me to stay," because of how beautiful they found my videos to be but didn't know what to say because that had not been my intention. I wasn't trying to show the world how beautiful life was, but somehow my death wish videos were doing exactly that.

The problem with me was that I'd never felt safe. Not

really. Not anywhere. Not in my own skin, my own bed, my own head. And I didn't think I'd ever really felt happy either. Just moments of less pain. Numbness with better lighting. People thought rock bottom was one moment of despair, but it wasn't. It was a thousand quiet falls until one day you looked up and realized you'd been living in survival mode your whole life. That realization was rock bottom.

Chapter Nine

Session Three

Die Trying 

@dietrying

20m Subscribers · 22 Videos

 SUBSCRIBE

January 2026

In complete contrast to last session, this week I accidentally, and shockingly took a nap, and slept past when I should have left to make it in time. I woke up to sunlight bleeding through the broken blinds, my chest clenched and my brain jumped to feeling disoriented, before I even fully opened my eyes. I thought about skipping. About texting Carter that I didn't care anymore. To do what he wanted with my videos. But then my body got out of bed as if on its own volition, and I got dressed robotically, grabbing the first hoodie I saw and tugging it on. I shoved my phone and wallet into my pockets and left my apartment without even being fully awake yet.

I wasn't completely through the doorway to her office before she said, "You're late."

"No hello?" I muttered, as I shoved my hands into my hoodie pockets. "What if I brought you a muffin or something? You don't know. Maybe I was being nice."

"You didn't," Iris smirked. "But now I know you're capable of kindness, so I'll be expecting muffins next time."

I didn't smile, but I also didn't roll my eyes. Progress. Maybe.

I dropped into my usual chair. It had some loose stitching along the arm. I'd noticed it last time, right after counting how many freckles dotted her right cheek. Nine. I'd told myself I wasn't going to look at them again.

"You seem agitated," she observed, settling across from me with the notebook she never wrote in.

"I'm here, isn't that good enough?"

"Physically, sure."

I shifted in my seat. "You want to know why life sucks today, or are we pretending this is about growth and healthy change this time?"

She studied me. "Actually, I thought we could veer to unpacking what is the point of being alive."

I raised an eyebrow. "That's a big one. Do you think you can handle it?"

She didn't even blink. "I've been thinking about it."

"Well, don't hurt yourself."

Iris didn't flinch. "Tell me, Danny. Why do you think you're still here?"

"No reason," I said. "That's kind of the point."

She crossed her legs, her skirt rustling softly. I hated that I noticed the shape of her knee beneath the draping material.

"If there's no reason," she said, "why keep showing up to these sessions?"

"Carter said I had to."

"He said you had to come. You could just sit here in silence."

I shrugged. "Maybe I like annoying you."

"Or could it be that you don't want to be alone with your thoughts?"

That hit a little too close to home. I looked away, focused on the small stain her coffee mug had left on the wood of her desk. She waited. She was good at waiting.

"Okay," I finally said. "Let's pretend there is a point to life. Enlighten me. What is it?"

"I don't know," she said simply. "But like I told you last week, I think we're meant to strive to live a life of meaning, and meaning comes from connection."

"Ah. The 'you need people' argument. So original."

"Have you tried it?"

"Define tried," I said.

"Have you let someone in? Shared yourself with anyone?"

I gave her a long, deadpan look. "I'm talking to you, aren't I?"

"You're deflecting."

I tapped my foot, slow and rhythmic. "Look, I've met people. I've existed in groups. Had teammates. Coworkers."

"Friends?"

"No."

She blinked. "Ever?"

"No."

Iris didn't push, which made it worse.

"Do you date?"

The silence hung between us like a thick fog. Something in me froze. My mouth dried till my tongue was stuck to the back of my teeth. My shoulders tensed. My lungs and stomach seemed to fuse till I almost felt like gasping for air. It was like her question had spun around inside me and reached up to press a hand to my throat. My first instinct was to make a joke. My second was to lie. But I didn't do either; instead, I just sat there, feeling like she'd opened a door I'd nailed shut a decade ago. All my thoughts scattered as the memories surfaced in painful, sharp fragments. These were things I didn't touch in the daylight. Things my mind only pieced together in my nightmares.

"I don't," I said finally, thickly, practically prying my lips apart to force the words out.

"Why?"

"That's not really your business."

"I'm not asking who the potentials were. I'm asking why. You brought up this running theme of disconnection in your life. I'm just following the thread."

I felt something sharp build behind my ribs. "I don't date because I don't want to. Not everyone has some tragic love story, okay? Some of us just skip the whole thing altogether."

Her voice was gentler now. "Some people don't trust it; doesn't mean they don't want it. Or don't need it."

I hated how right that sounded. I shrugged again. "It's exhausting. The pretending. The interest. The performance. Besides—"

"Besides?"

I waved a hand at myself. "Come on. I'm not exactly... the warm and fuzzy type."

"You're not," she agreed. "But you are—"

She stopped. I narrowed my eyes. "What?"

"Nothing."

"No, come on, you were about to say something."

She bit her lip.

"What?" I repeated.

"I was going to say... you're right, you may not come across as approachable, but you are—good looking. Surely someone has wanted to date you at some point."

My breath caught. It wasn't the compliment itself, although the delivery had left much to be desired; it was the way her words landed. Like a slap and a balm at the same time. I despised it. Hated the heat that crawled up my neck. I suddenly didn't know what to do with my arms. They hung awkwardly at my sides. I folded them against my chest. I felt my jaw clench. I had never felt like someone could want me for me. Only for my body. Only as something to be used. Her words lodged in that soft, hidden place inside me that I never let anyone see. I wanted to get up, leave, and never see her again. I wanted to scream at her for saying it. I wanted to thank her for treating me like I wasn't a fragile grenade always on the edge of exploding.

She immediately looked down, flustered. "That was—sorry. That was unprofessional."

I let out a hollow laugh. "Wow. I can see the headlines now. Life coach flirts with depressed, suicidal client because he's really not much of a commitment if he doesn't plan on staying here long."

"I wasn't flirting."

"Sure."

Her cheeks flushed. She didn't look up. "It was purely an observation."

"Well, thank you for the observation, Iris."

We sat in silence.

I hated how aware I was of my body ever since she'd made her observation. My skin. My face. I didn't like being seen. Not like that.

"You say you don't believe in much," she said, finally moving on. "But you did those stunts. You threw yourself into situations most people would never risk. You clearly believe in yourself."

"Yeah. Because I didn't care if I made it out."

"But you did make it out."

"Unfortunately."

She paused. "Why do you think that is?"

"I told you. No divine plan. No cosmic reason. Just bad odds."

"Do you think it's bad luck to be alive?"

That shut me up.

"I think," I said slowly, "it's bad luck to feel the way I do and still wake up every day."

She wrote something in her notebook then. Her first note.

I hated that I wanted to know what it was.

"I want to circle back," she said. "You said life has no point. But yours has been making a huge impact on people lately."

"By accident."

"But it happened. Millions of people saw you. They were moved by you. It's been fascinating to see just how much of an impact you've had without even wanting to."

I stood. "Great. So, I'm just your little case study now?"

"That's not what this is."

"No? What is it then? Some passion project? Fix the broken boy?"

"You're not broken."

I stared at her. She said it again, quieter this time. "You're not broken, Danny."

I hated the way my throat suddenly felt. Like something had lodged itself there. A sob that wouldn't come out, a scream I couldn't let free. I wanted to throw her words back at her. Tell her not to say things like that. Not to offer me hope that I couldn't hold. But I didn't. I just stood there, fists curled at my sides, every muscle bracing for the moment I might shatter.

"I have to go," I said.

"We still have time—"

"No," I said firmly. "We're out of time." I turned toward the door but didn't move right away. My feet felt heavy. Like part of me wanted to stay and ask her to say it again. That I wasn't broken. Even though I didn't believe it. But I couldn't, so I forced my body to move, one foot in front of the other until I got to the door and pulled it open. She waited.

"Bye, Iris." I said it without turning around.

"We'll talk about it more next time?"

"Don't count on it."

Chapter Ten
Burning Man

(Uploaded: September 2, 2024. 10:42 p.m.)

Burning Man was exactly what I thought it would be: chaos dressed as freedom, dust wrapped up as revelation. A place where people abandoned their clocks, names, clothes, and sometimes their dignity. It was August 28th, and the desert didn't care who I was or why I'd come. That was the appeal.

Carter didn't know where I was. I hadn't told him about this plan. If I made it through my dance with the angel of death, I would tell him about it after. It was like some part of me knew, not just hoped, that this one would be different. That it came with a higher risk.

By the time I arrived, the temporary city was already in full swing. The air smelled like beer, weed, sunscreen, and grilled meat. Neon bikes zipped by, ridden by men wearing only goggles and a grin. Music pulsed like the heartbeat of an alien planet, and people smiled like they had it all figured out. I didn't have a plan. That was the point. I'd promised myself that if the gators didn't get me, the sharks didn't bite, the electricity didn't strike—then maybe strangers high on God-knows-what could succeed where nature had failed.

I'd brought my camera, of course. My GoPro was already rolling. This was still another potential episode, as well as being another attempt after all. As the sun went down, I began my path to illumination or dissociation—I wasn't picky with what they called it. I didn't ask what was being given out. I didn't check what I was taking. I let people hand me drinks, tabs, pills. Someone smeared something minty under my nose. Someone else gave me a glowing jelly shot and told me I had "divine shoulders." I played Russian Roulette with unknown substances till my veins buzzed inside of me, and my brain finally shut the fuck up. The mushrooms made my insides crawl with snakes telling me my time was coming, and the molly had the lights melting around me. The music wasn't just a sound anymore; it had substance, and it moved through me like a current. The shame from my past softened, and I almost forgot how broken I was because the drugs told my brain we knew what love felt like. My pain muffled so much that it almost, dangerously, felt like peace.

I couldn't feel my face anymore. The sand beneath my feet was so hot, and I realized that I'd lost my shoes. The small grains felt like shards of glass against my skin, then morphed into feathers, and then became nothing at all. I felt like I was everywhere and nowhere. All the light bent sideways feeling disorienting and euphoric at the same time. My heart beat so loudly in my ears that I wondered if everyone around me could hear it too.

I stumbled about, weaving from stage to stage, unaware of how my legs were even moving. Where I was going. What I was doing.

A guy with a long, greasy pony took a break from getting head behind the stage to hand me a small white pill.

"This one will make you forget you're human. I think. I can't remember. Don't worry about it. Just let it."

I laughed harder at that than I had in years. The pill dissolved in an sour burn on my tongue.

And then I stopped laughing.

I remember the sky folding in half. Not literally, but in that way your brain panics when it can't make sense of what your body's doing. I remember collapsing in the middle of a circle of people singing about the sun. I think someone tried to keep me awake. I think someone screamed. I think someone walked away.

Then everything went black.

When I woke up, I couldn't open my eyes at first. It was like my brain turned back on, but my eyelids hadn't gotten the memo. I still wasn't sure if I was dead, and the afterlife involved oxygen tubes in my nose or if I had made it out alive, yet again.

It turned out I was just in an ER in Reno. There was no bright light. No welcoming at the pearly white gates. No song of the angels. Just the constant beep of a heart monitor and the familiar ache of disappointment settling into my bones.

A nurse with pink scrubs told me I was lucky. "You flatlined for about a minute," she said. Apparently Narcan had brought me back. She said it like I'd won a prize

My mouth tasted metallic. My arms were covered in medical tape, IV tubing, and track marks from where they tried to get into my collapsed veins. The gown I wore made my skin itch. The noise of the machines was relentless. The nurse watched me like I was a miracle. Or a burden. I couldn't decipher which.

When it came time to be discharged, I couldn't bring myself to say thank you. I should have. But the words got stuck on my tongue.

I retrieved my camera from the security bag that they returned to me, but I could barely move, let alone think for three days, so it wasn't until September 1st that I rewatched the footage—partially out of curiosity, mostly out of masochism. The angle was skewed, but you could see the moment my pupils blew wide. You could hear someone asking, "Is he breathing?" You could see a stranger kneeling beside me with panic and regret in their voice. Someone else shouted, "Get a medic!" Then static. Then nothing.

I didn't know if uploading the video would break community guidelines. Probably. But Carter said he'd take care of it.

His email to me was short:

I didn't respond.

THE NIGHTMARES CAME BACK that night.

My old house. My foster mother gone on a women's church trip. The television humming in the background. And him—holding a soda in one hand and calling me "Danny boy." Telling me I was a good boy. He asked if I wanted it. He said I did. He said I always did. I was thirteen. I had no idea what wanting it even meant. But I remembered the way his fingers closed around my wrist. The cold condensation from the soda can that had dripped down my skin. I remembered the color of the carpet. The sound of the ice maker in the kitchen. The way my body became something else. When I woke up, my sheets were soaked in sweat, and my throat was raw from screaming. I didn't go back to sleep.

Later that day, Carter sent me the final cut of the Burning Man footage. He'd softened the visuals, blurred out my face in the worst moment, and added a quiet piano track in the background. I watched it once. Then again. Then a third time. It didn't feel like me. But it was perfect. It felt like a whole fucking experience, and it made for a great story. Telling what? That I wasn't sure.

The thumbnail read: "Russian Roulette at Burning Man–Die Trying Ep. 5."

By the time I uploaded the episode, my fingers were shaking. Not from fear but from resentment. I hated that the world would watch it and call it inspirational. That people would DM me about how "brave" I was. That strangers would tattoo quotes from my videos on their bodies and call me a survivor. They didn't know me. They didn't know the sweat-soaked nightmares. The memories that were stitched into my skin. The way my own name made my stomach twist. They didn't know that I didn't want to be saved. They just saw a story. And they clicked "like."

The comments flooded in instantly:

"HOLY SHIT, I THINK HE ACTUALLY DIED FOR A MINUTE!"

"THIS IS THE CRAZIEST ONE YET."

"I'VE NEVER CRIED WATCHING A YOUTUBE VIDEO BEFORE."

"THIS GUY NEEDS HELP."

"IS IT WRONG TO SAY HE'S SO HOT???"

That last one made me slam my laptop shut.

Fuck.

Carter called me after midnight.

"You okay?"

I'm breathing, I thought. *So... no.*

"Stop worrying about me. It's giving overprotective Dad."

"You scared the shit out of me." He ignored my sarcasm.

"I'm fine."

"You could have not been fine."

I didn't know what to say to that. I didn't know how to straddle a world where I didn't want to be fine and experiencing what it felt like for someone to worry about me for the first time in my life.

"You know you've got four brands waiting on sponsored videos," he added. He was answering all my emails now, especially the ones from companies.

I blinked. "They still want me?"

"Yeah. You're a fucking phenomenon now."

"Even though I literally almost died?" The word almost burned in my throat.

He sighed. "I guess they don't mind."

I shook my head. "Crazy world. Companies paying an almost corpse."

He laughed bitterly. "Whatever makes them money I guess."

That night, I sat in my dark apartment and made a list of all the memories I had when the world failed me. I needed to drown out the warm feelings Carter's worry had planted inside of me. I reminded myself of the times I had felt the unkind hand of the universe giving me the middle finger.

1. Age four: Told to be quiet when I cried. I had been

crying because I was hungry and had gotten spanked for saying so.

2. Age seven: Called "dramatic" when I said I didn't feel well and couldn't go to school. I ended up having 103 fever and was sent home.

3. Age ten: Got sent to a new foster home and was abused that way for the first time.

4. Age eleven: He threatened to starve me if I told anyone. It got worse

5. Age twelve: No one noticed what he was doing to me.

6. Age fourteen: Tried to tell someone. Was called a liar. He beat me bloody. I ended up in the ER. I kept quiet when they asked if I was safe at home.

7. Age fifteen: I finally hit him back. He broke three of my ribs. CPS did nothing.

8. Age seventeen: Ran away. Slept in a Walmart parking lot.

9. Age twenty-one: Woke up next to a stranger, not remembering how I got there.

10. Age twenty-six: Got mugged on the walk home from work. Found out that seventeen people had walked around my unconscious body before someone finally stopped and called 911.

11. Age thirty: I was completely alone, and the world was just fine with that. I had nothing to live for. All I did was run away from my nightmares. I had never experienced love, safety, or kindness. The world had kicked me down and kept me there. And I was done.

I'd tried the ocean. The swamp. Electricity. Now the desert.

And I was still here. I'd started wondering—half-joking, half-desperate—if I was cursed. If I had nine lives like a cat. But if I did, I wasn't grateful for them. I was exhausted by them. Waking up again and again when all I wanted was permanent silence. I'd realized something tonight, it wasn't even that I wanted to die per say. I just didn't want to be here anymore. If I could just will myself out of existence without all the drama and fanfare. I would.

Chapter Eleven

Session Four

Die Trying 

@dietrying

20m Subscribers · 22 Videos

 SUBSCRIBE

January 2026

I hated how quiet it was in her office. The silence pressed against my ears like a cotton wrap. Not heavy, not oppressive, just too quiet. My whole life I'd learned to brace for quiet because it had never meant something safe was coming my way. It meant everyone else in the house was gone and he was ready.

Every time I walked in, I felt like I was stepping into some sort of alternate reality where people gave a shit, and the walls hadn't been scuffed by rage or time. Everything was soft and muted. The bookshelf wasn't just full, it was curated with titles I'd never heard of, journals with leafy patterns, and a goddamn candle that smelled like vanilla and optimism.

It pissed me off. But I kept showing up. I told myself it was because I wanted that footage from my last attempt posted. Carter said he would stop toying with me and would post it after today's session. But he was still holding the threat of deleting my entire channel over my head if I didn't complete every session. So, he knew I'd sit through sixteen more of these bullshit appointments to keep my account safe.

Iris was sitting in her chair as usual when I walked in, her legs crossed, her notebook resting lightly in her lap like she was born for this shit. She looked up with that same unreadable expression, all calm and open and interested. Her hair was pulled back again today; a few dark curls escaped like they always did and brushed her jawline. She wasn't wearing her glasses today. That shouldn't have mattered; it didn't, but of course my brain noticed. I wished it would stop, but it kept cataloging things like the angle of her jaw and the faint mark on her cheek from where she had rested it against her hand as she concentrated on something.

"Hey, Danny," she said. "How's your day going?"

"Objectively or existentially?"

Her lips twitched. "Let's start with objectively."

"Well against my better judgement I'm here."

"You are." She scribbled in her notebook. Probably something like: Patient remains a sarcastic little shit.

I dropped into the chair across from her and sprawled out like I owned the place, like I didn't care. That was the performance, anyway.

"You know," I said, "this whole setting is a little deceptive. I keep waiting for a camera crew to pop out and tell me I'm in a documentary that you're making."

"No cameras," she said. "Just me. Although your paranoia is duly noted."

I snorted. "Paranoia is just pattern recognition." I looked up at the ceiling.

In my peripheral, she nodded slowly, like she was actually considering it. "Interesting perspective."

"I just think it's funny," I said suddenly, still staring up at the ceiling. "How people don't care about you until you want to off yourself. And then when they've fixed you, and you don't want to off yourself anymore suddenly, they don't care again."

"That sounds like something that frustrates you."

"No shit." I glanced at her. "You know, if I had to guess, I'd bet half the people on this planet are miserable and pretending they're not, and the other half are trying to sell something to numb the misery."

"What happened to you, Danny?"

I scoffed and looked at her. "Weird how fast this turned into almost feeling like therapy."

"It's a fair question."

"What happened to me made me the kind of person who doesn't belong anywhere. I didn't grow up safe. I didn't grow up wanted. I'm not built for this world, and it's not built for me. Yet, I'm being forced to participate. Against my will."

We sat with that for a bit. The weight of it. The honesty of it.

"You ever think about what comes after this?" she asked. "The after life?"

"Sometimes," I said. "Usually when I'm daring the next moment to kill me."

"And what do you think?"

"I think it's nothing. I hope it's not worse than this."

"That's bleak."

"Reality tends to be."

"But you keep searching. You keep testing the edges. That says something."

I narrowed my eyes. "What do you think it says?"

"That part of you might still be hoping it's not all bad."

I let out a breath. "Or maybe I'm just stubborn. Or bored."

She smiled softly but didn't push further. I shifted in my seat, suddenly needing to knock her off her axis. "Can I ask you something?"

"Of course."

"Why do you do this? Sit here with broken people, trying to duct tape them back together."

"I don't see people as broken," she replied. "And I do this because... helping people find direction, makes me feel like I'm putting something good into the world."

"Sounds noble."

"It's not about being noble. It's just about doing what is right."

I tilted my head. "Who gets to decide what is right?"

There was a beat—one of those tiny pauses where someone decides whether or not they're going to lie.

"My dad's a reverend," she said finally. "I try to emulate his teachings as my moral compass."

I raised a brow. "A reverend's daughter?"

"Mhm."

"Explains the modest skirts and the Superman complex with a need to save the world."

She gave me a look, amused but unfazed. "It also explains why I understand the difference between faith and fear."

I leaned forward. "So, what? You're one of those no-sex-before-marriage types?"

She didn't flinch. "I was raised that way, yes."

"But you still live by it."

"I choose to, yes."

"That's convenient framing." I sat back. "You ever consider that your whole abstinence thing is just your own trauma response dressed up as virtue?"

Her eyes met mine. Still calm. Still open. But her faster-than-normal blink gave her away. I had finally rattled her. My dark obsession with death couldn't do it, but my mention of sex did. Noted. It shouldn't have affected me, but it did. That tiny flip-flop in my stomach as the power dynamic shifted slightly between us. It scared me more than it excited me.

"Maybe," she admitted. That surprised me. I'd expected her to push back, to defend it.

"But," she continued, "I've done the work to understand where my choices come from. Can you say the same?"

I barked out a laugh. "Touché."

Silence again. But this time it didn't feel combative. It felt like... recognition, acceptance, maybe even mutual respect somehow.

"I think people just want control," I told her quietly. "We make rules to keep ourselves from falling apart. Doesn't mean the rules make sense."

"And you don't want control?"

"Not anymore. I just want out."

She nodded like she could respect my honesty even if she didn't agree with what I wanted to do and why I wanted to do it. Iris leaned forward slightly, resting her elbows on her knees. "You say life is bad. That it's not worth staying for. But you've also done things most people couldn't even dream of. You've stood in the path of death more times than I can count. Is it possible that was also brave?"

I scoffed. "And what did that get me? Some viral videos and an inbox full of brand deals?"

She tilted her head. "No. It got you proof."

I blinked. "Proof of what?"

"That there's still something in you that thinks you're worthy of being seen. Even if it's through the lens of destruction."

I looked away, jaw tight. Her words were too close to something I'd been trying not to think about. She didn't let the silence grow comfortable, not this time.

"You say you don't want connection, but I wonder if you do but you're afraid of what might happen if you ever let someone actually see you."

I flinched internally. Not because she was wrong but because she kept skirting way too close to the truth.

"That's rich coming from someone who hides behind modest clothing and affirmations."

She grinned and threw my word back at me. "Touché."

I shook my head, laughing bitterly. "You're exhausting."

"You're fascinating."

I stood up, brushing imaginary lint from my jeans. "Yeah, well. Fascinating doesn't keep people around."

"I'm still here."

That stopped me. I glanced at her, unsure of what to say.

She didn't wait for an answer. "Same time next week?"

I smirked. "Guess we'll see if I make it till then. Miss..."

She raised a brow. "I think by now you and I can both agree that it's just Iris."

"Alright, just Iris." I headed for the door.

"I agree with you, you know. I don't think you're afraid of death, Danny. I think you're afraid of being alive and it not meaning anything."

I didn't turn around.

"You ever think that some of us were just made wrong?" I volleyed back. She had this knack for saying the most profound things right before I left. Did she do it on purpose to keep me coming back? There was a beat of silence. Then her voice, quiet but clear, "No, but I think some of us were made to feel that way."

I laughed once, sharp and hollow.

"Same result either way." I opened the door, the knob cool against my overheated palm. "See ya around, just Iris."

For once she didn't say anything.

Chapter Twelve

Hurricane

(Uploaded: October 15, 2024. 4:12 a.m.)

I'd always thought hurricanes looked beautiful from afar. From the safety of satellite images, the swirl of clouds, the eye in the middle looking like a cosmic target. But being in the middle of one? That was a different kind of truth. One that screamed in your ears and clawed at your skin and made you wonder if maybe this time—just maybe—you wouldn't make it out. That was the point, of course, but it still sucked in the moment.

I'd picked South Carolina because the news said it would be getting hit head-on. Hurricane Isa, a Category 4. The storm was expected to make landfall by mid-afternoon. I'd found the treehouse on a weird little forum for adrenaline junkies—it had survived two previous hurricanes and was built in a towering old oak out in the middle of nowhere. I figured if the wind didn't take me out, the fall that had to be coming definitely would.

I'd arrived while the sky was still only whispering threats. The clouds didn't roll in all at once. They crept. Heavy and low, like they were stalking something. The air smelled heavy, like metal and wet earth, thick with warning. The animals had fled.

Birds were gone, not a chirp to be heard. Even the cicadas had shut up. I was surrounded by the kind of stillness that made your skin tingle with anticipation. The kind of quiet that made my instincts rear back, clawing at my brain, telling me I still had time to get out. Instead, I parked a half mile down a muddy road and hiked in with my gear, a harness I didn't plan to use, two GoPros, a flask of whiskey, and a steady resignation crawling through my bloodstream.

Climbing the tree was simple. The bark was slick, but I'd done worse. The wind picked up as I climbed, my hands slipped a few times, and I had to grip till my fingers bled. Maybe I'd fall before I even got to the top. The video, if anyone found it, would definitely be lacking fanfare but at least it would be quick. Just a snap of my neck and then nothing. But I got to the top, and the treehouse creaked as I finally stepped onto its floor, swaying just enough to feel like I was truly flirting with the end of my life. I strapped a camera to an exposed beam along the wall of the treehouse and aimed it toward me. In the time it had taken me to climb to my final resting spot, the wind had picked up and was howling through the branches like it had a bone to pick with the world. *Same,* I thought. *Same.*

I remained there for hours as the storm approached. The first hour passed slowly. The treehouse creaked with every gust. I sat cross-legged on the floor, watching the horizon disappear. I kept thinking I heard the wind calling my name, making my existence up here, defying nature, even creepier. Every time a branch hit the roof, I flinched. I took a swig of my whiskey, but it didn't help. I was still cold. And way too fucking alive.

The rain began to pelt sideways. Trees bowed like they were praying. The world turned gray and then even darker than gray. I couldn't see the ground anymore, just sheets of water and wind and movement. I thought about turning the cameras off but then concluded that it didn't matter. Either I'd die on film, or I wouldn't. Either way, whatever happened would hopefully find its way to Carter to be uploaded. I'd left instructions on a paper in a Ziploc bag inside my camera bag. I'd never done that before, and it unnerved me because it felt like I gave a shit. I didn't want to give any shits.

The treehouse suddenly shook, and I couldn't catch my breath. Every time I tried, I felt like I was drowning from the unrelenting downpour of rain. I crawled out onto the edge, gripping the railing as the wind tried to peel me off its surface. Below me, the ground was a blur of moving water and whipping branches. I screamed into the void—something animalistic cracked inside me. It wasn't just a scream. It was everything I hadn't said in years. Rage. Loneliness. Desperation. I was vomiting emotion out with the sound, as if my ribs would shatter if I didn't let it out, but maybe I wanted them to. I swear the wind screamed back. *Fuck you, Danny boy.*

Then the roof tore clean off. I ducked instinctively, but a piece caught my arm. Blood mixed with the rain as it dripped red down my skin. The wood cracked beneath me. I crawled back toward the center, and for a second—just one stupid, weightless second—I stopped. I could let go. It would be so fucking easy. Just uncurl my fingers. Let the wind take me. No pain, no fallout, no need to send files or write letters or keep pretending I was okay when I wasn't.

I imagined the fall. The silence right before impact. The way no one would know until the next morning, when Carter checked his inbox and found nothing. My fingers ached to end it, but I didn't move. The wind was howling around me. Telling me to do it. *Let go.* It promised me it would be quick. I wondered if I'd feel regret right before it was over. I wondered if I would know how much it hurt. One thing I hoped was that I wouldn't shut my eyes. That I would be brave enough to watch it happen. I wanted to know the truth of what I'd done until the last second.

I looked down again. And then I didn't do it. I held on. Not out of hope. Not because I wanted to live. But because I couldn't figure out if it was fear or habit or some pathetic thread of unfinished business still clinging to my ribs that had me holding on. Whatever it was, it forced me to crawl back inside and sit there, shaking as the walls breathed and bowed with the storm. I waited. And waited. And when the wind finally died down enough not to be a danger to my life anymore, I packed up my cameras and climbed down. My cut arm ached with every movement.

Once I got back onto solid ground, the mud swallowed my boots with each step. All around me trees had been torn apart like paper. The sky above me looked like it had been scrubbed raw, devoid of any color at all.

After a wet and difficult hike back to the road, I got into the rental car and drove slowly toward town navigating the flooded roads, still shaking the whole way. Half from the cold, half from whatever had kept me from letting go.

I stopped at a gas station. I needed caffeine and something salty. A quick glance in the mirror told me I looked like I'd been chewed up and spit back out by the hurricane—and maybe I really had been. The bell above the door jingled as I walked in; the cashier gave me a weird look but didn't say anything. I grabbed a small bag of olives, a pickle in bright red liquid and a Coke.

When I stepped back outside, bag in hand, I heard a voice call out.

"Are you... wait—holy shit. You're him."

I turned slowly. A group of teens stood near the ice machine, their phones held up, pointed at me.

"The YouTube guy! From the Tesla coil video. Dude, that was insane."

I blinked. They weren't screaming and running away. They weren't scared. They were acting like they'd just spotted a Marvel superhero out in the wild instead of a deranged, death-hungry lunatic.

"Can we get a picture with you?" one asked. I stared at them for a long second. My shirt was soaked in blood and rain; my eyes were still foggy from what I'd nearly done earlier. From what depraved, deep part of the universe I'd touched inside that storm. And they wanted a selfie.

"No," I said flatly. "You have me confused with someone else. I'm nobody."

Their smiles dimmed, confused. I walked past them and got back in my car. What the hell was wrong with people? I was not someone to idolize. Definitely not someone you'd want to memorialize in a photo. How did they not get it? How were my videos not making it clear that I was honestly not someone teenagers should be watching at all?

Back at the motel, I reviewed the footage. My hands shook when I watched the part where the roof got blown off. I saw the moment I looked down. Saw the moment I didn't let go. Saw how close I had gotten to the jaws of death. Closer than I ever had before.

I uploaded the video to our shared folder and emailed Carter with the subject: "Hurricane. You're gonna shit yourself. I think I might have."

His text reply came within minutes.

CARTER

Jesus Christ. You okay?

I didn't answer. I lay down on the bed, still damp and aching.

The heater rattled like a heartbeat, grating in my ears. I stared at the ceiling and tried to feel something. Anything but what I always felt... Relief. Regret. Anger. But all I felt was... I'm still here.

Like I'd missed the exit again. Maybe the afterlife really didn't want me. But neither did this world, and ultimately that was the problem.

"BRO WHEN THE ROOF CAME OFF I GASPED."

"THIS GUY IS STRAIGHT UP INVINCIBLE."

"I HAVE ONE QUESTION. WHY?"

"PETITION TO GET THIS MAN A @NETFLIX DOC."

"HOW IS THIS ACCOUNT STILL MONETIZED LMAO."

"THIS MAN REALLY LOOKS DEATH IN THE FACE
AND SAYS "NOT TODAY."

"THAT SCREAM THOUGH... GAVE ME LITERAL
GOOSEBUMPS."

"THAT MOMENT WHEN HE ALMOST FELL. THAT
ONE HIT DIFFERENT."

Chapter Thirteen

Session Five

Die Trying 

@dietrying

20m Subscribers • 22 Videos

🔔 SUBSCRIBE 

January 2026

I hadn't planned on sitting on the couch. It just happened. One second, I was walking in with the same steel resolve I always brought to these sessions—and the next I was sprawled across the cushions of her cloud-looking couch. Usually, I took the chair across from her desk, not the one closest to her, but the one behind it. I deliberately chose the hardest looking one. But today, something about the way the sunlight caught the dust motes drifting through the window, or maybe the way my whole body hurt from last night's insomnia-fueled spiral, made me collapse onto the couch. The cushions folded around me, as if in an embrace. I should've stood back up. Reclaimed my distance. But I was too tired to pretend I wasn't seeking a little comfort today.

Iris noticed, of course. She always did. But she didn't say anything. Just gave me that annoying little half-smile of hers and jotted something into her notebook.

"Please don't write 'subject willingly took couch,'" I muttered.

She glanced up. "I was actually writing that your shirt is on inside out."

I looked down. It was.

"I'm starting a new trend," I said. "It's called unhinged couture."

Iris tucked her legs under herself on the chair opposite the couch. "I like it. Very Brooklyn."

"Very 'I'm a grown ass man who can't even dress himself properly,'" I shot back.

We sat there for a moment, the silence more loaded than usual. I didn't trust it. She was planning something. She was probably going to pull out finger paints and ask me to draw my inner child.

Instead, she said, "So. Do you believe in God?"

I let out a bark of laughter. "Wow, no warm-up? No gentle seduction into spiritual trauma? Just straight into the deep end."

She tilted her head. "You've alluded to it in previous sessions. In a few different ways. So, I'm curious."

"Right." I crossed my arms across my chest. "Okay, I'll play. Do I believe in God? Maybe. If I do I believe, there's some bearded jackass up there watching us like it's a reality show and placing bets on who breaks first."

"That sounds like resentment, not belief."

"No, no." I leaned forward. "I believe in God the way you believe in a landlord who never fixes anything but still cashes the rent checks. He's likely there, I just don't think he deserves a fan club. He either doesn't give a shit or he's asleep. Or maybe he's sitting back, popcorn in hand, skipping past the cries of the hurt and the sick to get to the juicy parts like who's cheating on who, and the drama happening in our government."

She didn't flinch. She never flinched. Did I sound bitter? Hell yea I did, but I had every right to. If there was a God, he owed me answers, not the other way around.

"What do you think when people say things like, 'we don't always understand God's plan'?" she asked softly.

My jaw clenched. "That's my favorite line. Right up there with 'everything happens for a reason.'"

Iris waited. I sat up straighter. This couch was really comfortable. I bet I could fall asleep and not have a nightmare on it. "If there's a God with a plan, and that plan involves children with cancer not getting better unless enough people pray hard enough—then he's an asshole. If that plan involves a kid begging for someone to stop touching them and no help ever comes—well, what kind of God is that? One who says no? One who needs more convincing?"

Her voice was almost a whisper. "Did someone hurt you, Danny?"

And there it was. I looked at the floor. My tongue was like sandpaper in my mouth. My chest felt like it was full of wet cement. Every cell in my body wanted to run—but I couldn't even make my fingers twitch.

"I'm just saying," I said, voice flat, "that if there's a God keeping score, he's got a fucked-up sense of morality."

"That's not what I asked."

I looked over at her. She wasn't writing. She wasn't analyzing. She was just sitting there. Waiting. As usual. I gave her half a smirk. "What do you think?"

"I think you carry a lot of pain for someone who says they don't care."

"Pain's a side effect of being alive. Which is why I'm trying to remedy that."

She didn't answer. She just got up with a swish of her silky-looking skirt and walked over to the bookshelf to pull something off the top shelf. A coloring book. Then she tossed it at me.

"Color," she said.

I blinked. "Are you serious?"

"I'm very serious. Pick a page."

"You're going to therapize me with crayons?"

"I'm not a therapist, Danny. Pick a page."

I flipped it open. The first one was a mandala. The second one was a beach scene. I landed on a page of broken clock faces and thought, oh, well that's fucking poetic, and showed it to her.

"I'll take this one."

She handed me a box of colored pencils and sat back down. I didn't want to color. I didn't want to feel anything. But my hands moved anyway. Red. Brown. Gray. Slow at first, like I was testing the weight of my surrender. The pencil scratched softly against the paper. Not making art, no I was bleeding out my emotions without making a mess.

Somewhere in the quiet, Iris spoke again. "Can I ask you something?"

I gave a theatrical sigh. "You always do."

"Why *do* you think bad things happen to good people?"

I laughed. Not because it was funny—but because it was so damn typical. The kind of question people asked when they were still pretending life had rules. Cause and effect. Do good, get good kind of thing.

"You mean like karma? Divine punishment? God working in mysterious ways?"

She didn't offer a rebuttal. I leaned back, colored pencil in hand. "It's random. That's the answer. The world's just a roulette wheel. Spin it, and maybe you get a vacation in Hawaii. Or maybe you get molested by your foster dad and spend the rest of your life trying to breathe through it."

Silence. Iris didn't move other than her hands shifted as they folded in her lap a little tighter. I looked down at the page in my lap.

"And the worst part? People try to make sense of it. They say things like, 'maybe there's a bigger picture' or 'everything happens for a reason.' But if this is the only shot we get—if this is our one life, why does it hurt so much? Why do the good people get chewed up and spit out while assholes keep climbing the ladder? Tell me what fucking *good* reason was there for a little boy to get raped and no matter how much he begged; it didn't stop." Spittle landed on the page in front of me and for a horrifying second, the picture I'd been coloring blurred as tears sprang to my eyes, but I swallowed them back down before blinking, lest any moisture fall.

I heard Iris shifting in her seat and then, very gently, she asked again, "Did someone hurt you, Danny?"

I didn't answer. Just went back to coloring. I pressed the pencil down too hard, breaking the tip. She silently handed me a new one; her finger ghosted against mine for just a second, sending a tingle blasting down my spine. I put the broken pencil down.

"I watched the car chicken video," she finally said, changing the subject.

I stiffened.

"Is it your last one?"

I looked at her, annoyed. "Did Carter send you that?"

"No. I saw it on your channel."

That stunned me more than it should have. I guess the video was finally posted, and he hadn't told me. He had promised to post it last week and hadn't. I guess now he finally did it. That bastard.

"It felt like a goodbye," she added.

I leaned back on the couch. "It was."

She nodded slowly. "So, you're not planning on making more?"

I looked up at the ceiling. "I'm not planning to be here to be able to make more."

She didn't gasp. She didn't argue. She just nodded.

"That's what I thought," she said.

We were quiet again. Then she smiled sadly and whispered, "Well, in case no one's said it to you today... I'm glad you're still here."

I stood. "You really need better boundaries."

She laughed softly. "You really need to realize that people care about you."

I grunted. She looked up at me, like she saw something under all my mess. "Same time next week, Danny?"

"Only if you let me color a scene with a dragon."

"Deal."

As I walked out of the office, the coloring page clutched tightly in my hand, I wondered why the hell it felt like something had shifted. I didn't know what it was, but it made the air around me a little thicker with awareness. Like I'd let my guard down somehow without realizing it. Like I'd taken a step forward, toward something warm and stupid, and now I couldn't reverse it. And that terrified me more than dying ever did.

Chapter Fourteen
Jellyfish Swarm

Die Trying 

@dietrying

20m Subscribers · 22 Videos

 SUBSCRIBE

(Uploaded: November 1, 2024. 11:11 p.m.)

I put this one on my list because it seemed poetic. A Jellyfish swarm: soft, lovely, and probably fatal. A death that sounded delicate. Nature has always had this way of seducing you into forgetting it can kill. It shows you a pink sky and makes you forget about lightning. It brushes your ankles with warm tidewater and doesn't mention the sharks. It fills a bay with drifting, glass-bodied creatures so translucent they look like spirits—and then reminds you their sting can stop your heart.

I found an article about them in one of those clickbait posts. "Thirteen Things That Can Kill You at the Beach (and You'd Never Expect #Five)."

Number five was sea nettles. Commonly found in the Chesapeake Bay. There could be thousands of them, sometimes more. All floating silently like a collective ghost. It sounded more than perfect.

I'd called the marine center under the guise of a documentary project. Told them I was filming a short piece on climate change and species migration. They confirmed that the jellyfish bloom had started early this year, making it prime conditions for my next attempt.

"Bring a drone," the guy said. I nodded into the phone.

"Sure. I'll bring a drone." What I didn't say was that I'd also be in the water.

It took me two days to plan the shot. I scouted the bay. I picked the angle. I rented a kayak I wouldn't use. I charted tide patterns, sun angles, and wind speeds. I needed it all to line up: the time of day, the reflection on the water, and the swell of the current. This wasn't something I could do twice. If I lived, I'd only have one chance to get this footage. And if I died? Well. Then it really needed to be beautiful.

I got there at 6:17 a.m. No one was around. All I could hear was the sound of water lapping gently against the dock. I could see the slow glide of something translucent just beneath the surface. I watched it. It pulsed like it was its own heartbeat. Like it was breathing, and maybe it was.

I stripped off the sweatshirt I'd worn in case someone saw me walking in, revealing the GoPro already strapped tight to my chest. I wore a bathing suit and nothing else. No wet suit. No shoes. No gloves. I wanted skin to jellyfish contact, and I wanted the sting to be immediate.

The sun crested the edge of the water like it was daring me to enter. So I stepped in. The temperature shocked me at first. Not just that it was so fucking cold—but it also felt so alive. Almost too alive. It was brisk and biting in a way that woke up every nerve ending in my body that I thought I'd dulled over the last five months.

And then I felt them. They were slippery and silken. Wrapping and unwrapping like living ribbons.

The thing about jellyfish is, they don't hunt you. They don't chase or bite. They just are. And if you float too close to them or they float too close to you, the result is a mistake you will pay for. They don't even know they're hurting you. Their sting is automatic, like a defense system wired into their flesh. It's not done with malice. It's a pain they don't even mean to cause. I found that to be fascinating.

The first sting got me behind my knee. I flinched. The second wrapped my forearm. The third hit the back of my neck like a kiss.

My breathing sped up, but I stayed in place, arms drifting, body treading lightly. The camera on my chest recorded everything—the shimmer of light through their bells, the eerie elegance of them curling through the water like dancers in a slow-motion film.

I counted fifteen around me. Then twenty. Then I stopped counting. My skin burned. Not like a fire. More like an itch buried under the skin, getting more frantic as time went on.

The stings built, layered on top of each other. Some sharp. Some lingering. My body trembled from the growing discomfort, but I didn't get out. I wasn't bleeding. I wasn't seizing. I wasn't drowning. So, it wasn't done.

The beauty of it somehow became the worst part. The way they lit up under the sun. The way they glided past me, brushing against my ribs and wrists like they were trying to offer me comfort. The water around me rippled with light, and for a second, it looked like heaven, even as I burned.

After six minutes, I started to feel dizzy. Not enough to black out. Just enough to know it was working. The dizziness crept in like a fog—soft, cloying, almost gentle, until I began to feel disoriented. I tilted my head and blinked, and for a second, I couldn't tell which direction the dock was in. My chest started to tighten, not from panic exactly, but from the slow realization that this may be it.

But then my body took over. It jerked me away from the jellyfish, and swam me over to the dock, somehow knowing where to go. My movements felt graceful but in reality, they were probably awkward and clumsy. I pulled myself up and collapsed on the wood, coughing up bay water, my throat raw and my legs blotchy with welts. My whole body buzzed like it was short-circuiting.

But I was still alive. Again. I was too disoriented to lament it.

I showered at a nearby state campground under freezing metal taps that stung every place I'd been touched. I hadn't brought any cream or vinegar or other forms of medical care. I just scrubbed my skin until I felt a semblance of being human again and then limped back to my rental car, wet hair clinging to my forehead.

By the time I got to the hotel, the itching was unbearable. I took a Benadryl and collapsed on the bed with my laptop open next to me. I didn't even bother rewatching the footage. I already knew it would look... magical.

Which had kind of been my goal this time around. I'd wanted to give my viewers a glimpse of something subtly dangerous but also gorgeously delicate at the same time.

I sent Carter the files with one sentence:

"Chesapeake Bay. Stung by jellyfish."

Ten minutes later, a text buzzed on my phone:

CARTER

Bro. U walked into a jellyfish BLOOM??

CARTER

I am crying. Who needs therapy when you can just French kiss nature's ghosts? I'll get this edited asap. Also, sidebar you ever watch Friends? Cause I feel like you're Ross but like if Ross did really stupid things and had no one to pee on him.

I blinked at my screen. Was he high? He made it sound like

I was just doing normal, everyday things. Like this was some weird and wild version of being alive.

I'd never seen Friends. I'd missed that whole cultural wave because I was too busy trying to survive, and now I felt like I was too old to catch up. But Carter had this thing where he brought up random shows or references to pop culture, and I usually just rolled with it, pretending I had made time to enjoy things while I was living out my trauma. This time, though, I pulled up Netflix and searched for Friends. I turned on season one and let the theme song play. It was catchy; I found myself tapping along to the beat, which was embarrassing if you wanted to pretend you didn't give a fuck. But maybe if I watched enough episodes tonight, I'd forget that my body still itched like a thousand bees had loved me a little too much. The discomfort was a constant reminder that I had failed at my one goal yet again.

LATER, after finishing half a season of the show, I checked the comments under my latest video.

"BRO'S FEARLESS."

"DUDE'S HOT AND DEAD INSIDE. THAT'S EXACTLY MY TYPE."

"IMAGINE BEING THIS SEXY AND THIS INSANE."

"I'M OBSESSED."

"CAN WE GET A FULL-FACE REVEAL?"

"HE SHOULD COLLAB WITH MR. BEAST."

"WHAT'S THIS GUY'S DEAL? DOES HE WANT TO DIE OR IS THIS, LIKE, PERFORMANCE ART?"

I stared at that last one for a while. Performance art. Maybe it was. A performance of pain. A choreography of almosts. A series of rehearsals for an ending I still hadn't figured out how to write. I couldn't shake it. Was that what this had become? An endless dress rehearsal for an exit I couldn't quite commit to? That didn't make me fearless, and I wasn't trying to make a point. But I most certainly wasn't trying to make art either. At least it hadn't started out that way.

I opened a new document on my laptop. "Dear Internet," I typed. "Thank you for noticing. It only took seven near-death experiences for you to wonder if I might not be okay." I didn't save it. Just closed the document on my laptop and let the Friends' theme song play again.

Chapter Fifteen

Session Six

Die Trying 

@dietrying

20m Subscribers · 22 Videos

 SUBSCRIBE

January 2026

I was early. Not by much, just a few minutes, but enough to second-guess every step on the sidewalk toward her building. Enough to wonder why the hell I was holding a muffin and a paper bag with a stupid little ceramic mug tucked inside.

The muffin was blueberry. Not because I knew her favorite flavor or anything stalkerish like that—but because it was the first option I saw when the girl at the coffee shop asked me what I wanted, so I blurted out blueberry. That, and it looked fresh. Unlike me; I was still in the t-shirt I had fallen asleep in last night.

Iris opened the door before I could knock, like she'd been waiting. Her smile caught on her face for a second, confused by what I was holding.

"I brought you something," I said flatly, offering the bag like it was evidence. "For... putting up with me."

"Is it poisoned?" she asked, grinning as she took it.

"No promises," I muttered.

She pulled out the mug first. It was yellow, big enough to wrap two hands around, with Not All Wounds Are Visible written across it in messy script. It felt dumb now as I watched her examine it.

"I thought it fit the whole life coach aesthetic," I explained. "Or whatever."

Her fingers ran over the words like they meant something. She acted like it was normal to get a gift from an emotionally stunted man like myself. I, on the other hand, had never bought something for someone before. Not for a teacher, a friend, and certainly not my foster parents. Giving her this gift, simple as it was, felt like giving her a piece of me, and that made my skin crawl.

"It's perfect," she said softly, then peeked into the bag again. "And carbs? Be still, my heart."

I smirked. "Just trying to soften you up before I ruin your day."

She waved me inside, and I followed her into the familiar room. This time, instead of collapsing on the couch or slinking into the chair further back from her desk as usual, I sat near her desk. Not directly across from her. Closer to the side of it.

She noticed. Of course she did. But she didn't comment. She just opened the top drawer of her desk, pulled out the colored pencils and a blank sheet of paper this time, and slid them toward me. No dragon in sight, but I didn't mind.

"Care to color again?" she asked.

"You know it's a little patronizing, right?" I said as I picked up a pencil anyway.

"Not if it works."

She was right. It did work. Coloring gave my hands something to do. The motion of dragging color across paper helped keep my thoughts from spiraling into existential static. It helped me go from, maybe I should step into traffic today, or when I ask for help from above, I'm hoping for a sniper, to feeling more grounded. Like the chaos had taken a break from harassing me, which was nice, even though it was just temporary.

"I like this view better," she said after a beat.

I looked up.

"I can see your eyes from here."

I rolled them instinctively, but my lips twitched at the edges. "Lucky you."

She didn't answer; she just kept her own eyes on me for a second longer than necessary. People always said that eyes were the window to the soul, but I hoped that was bullshit. I didn't want her seeing the inside of me. It was dark and bleak, and I almost felt bad if she were to sully herself with my decrepit energy.

Iris settled back in her chair and picked up her notepad, the muffin still untouched on her desk beside the new mug.

"So," she said, "we've talked about what might come after this life."

"You mean death."

"Sure."

"And you want to follow that up with...?" I prompted dragging the green pencil across the paper in messy, unspecific swirls.

"I want to talk about fear again," she said.

I froze. She noticed.

"I want to know if you're afraid," she continued. "Not of death, but of the life you haven't lived yet."

I scoffed. "You make it sound like I've got some fairytale future waiting for me right around the corner."

"I'm asking a real question, Danny. Are you afraid to die?"

"You already know I'm not."

"Okay. So, are you afraid to live?"

I didn't answer. Not immediately. My pencil scratched across the page again. Sharp movements. Angry lines. Because yes, fuck yes, of course I was. But how many more times could I tell her without sounding more pathetic than I already was? I didn't want to sound like I wanted help. I didn't want her to think there was a chance of saving me. The question sat between us like it was alive. Like I needed to snare it. Crush it. It made my stomach twist. Living meant trying. Meant risking wanting things. Meant failing. And I'd failed at the most basic of things. Like keeping myself safe. If all I had left was a life of being reminded of that, well I didn't want it anymore.

"Are *you* afraid to die?" I shot back, more aggressive than I'd meant to be. She nodded without hesitation.

"Yes."

"Why?"

"There's so much I haven't done yet," she said, voice calm and honest. "There is so much I still want to do."

I didn't mean to laugh, but it came out bitter. "Like what? Pet a dolphin? Travel to Paris? Get an Instagram-worthy brunch?" For a moment, I wanted to be cruel. Wanted her to feel what it was like to be torn apart and taped back together with whatever pieces you had left. Maybe then she'd stop expecting so much of me. But I didn't say anything else—not because I suddenly felt like being kind, but because I was a coward. And even cowards didn't kick dogs or crush butterflies. They left beautiful things alone.

"No," she said, unaware of the war my mind was at with itself. "Bigger things. And smaller ones."

I tilted my head. "Like what?"

Her cheeks flushed. Not dramatically—but enough. "You're going to laugh."

"Probably."

She took a breath. "I've never been kissed."

I blinked. "Seriously?"

She nodded. "Seriously."

"I just assumed… I said the husband and the cat thing…"

"I don't have either," she said quickly. "The cat was your guess and a wrong one at that."

"Tragic."

She smiled. "I grew up in purity culture. Remember my dad's a reverend. I was raised to believe that kissing led to other things and those things were meant for marriage."

"And you still believe that?" I asked.

She looked thoughtful. "I believe in honoring my boundaries. But lately, I've been wondering if some of those boundaries were handed to me out of fear, not faith."

"So, I was right, it is a trauma response," I said, raising a brow. She tilted her head.

"Maybe."

I stared at her, unsure what I was feeling. Respect? Pity? Annoyance that she'd made herself vulnerable when that was supposed to be my role? Something had shifted in the air between us. I almost felt like I had listened in on a private conversation and wasn't supposed to know this about her. It felt weird. And it made me try to imagine what it felt like to be untouched. To have a body that was so completely yours that even a kiss still belonged to the future.

"Let's each make a list," she said suddenly, interrupting my stream of consciousness.

"What kind of list?"

"Five things we want to do before we die. Just five."

"Why?"

"Because you said life sucks. I want to know what, if anything, you'd still want to try before giving it up entirely."

I hesitated. "Fine. You go first."

She picked up a pen and began writing.

1. Have my first kiss.

2. *Publish a non-therapy coloring book.*
3. *Dance barefoot in the rain in another country*
4. *Learn to surf.*
5. *Fall in love.*

I raised a brow. "You're cornier than I thought."

"Your turn," she said, handing me the pen.

I didn't want to do it. Didn't want to see my thoughts on paper like they meant something. But I wrote anyway.

1. *Try sushi.*
2. *Watch a movie in the theatre.*
3. *Confront my foster father.*
4. *Sleep an entire night without a nightmare.*
5. *Get a hug.*

I stared at the list. How pathetic. Embarrassing. Something a seven-year-old would write. But there it was. Ink to paper. The ugliest truth I'd written since my suicide note. I wanted someone to wrap their arms around me and mean it, simply because I existed. I felt sick just reading it. I looked up to find Iris watching me. Neither of us said anything for a long moment.

"I didn't mean to give you hope," I said finally. My voice cracked sharply on the word *hope* like it was foreign to my mouth.

"You didn't," she said, voice soft.

But we both knew I had.

Chapter Sixteen
Royal Gorge Bridge

Die Trying 

@dietrying

20m Subscribers • 22 Videos

 SUBSCRIBE

(Uploaded: December 14, 2024. 1:12 a.m.)

They said a storm was coming. I wasn't worried. That was precisely why I was here. Wind advisories were already blinking red across every digital road sign from Pueblo to Cañon City, warning drivers to stay home, shelter in place, not to be stupid. But if I was anything, I was consistent with how stupid I was. I had accidentally made a full-time income out of being foolish on purpose. I planned my attempts with calculated recklessness. I had grown a following by being artfully suicidal.

The Royal Gorge Bridge stood like some defiant relic of time, suspended over nine hundred feet of jagged nothingness. It wasn't just the highest bridge in America; it was a damn tightrope stretched over the mouth of the Earth. And tonight, it groaned in the wind like it was yelling at me to leave, that it didn't want me here. Good. The feeling was mutual.

I parked my rental car at the edge of the closed gate, shouldered the GoPro, and climbed the perimeter fencing like a man with nothing left to lose. Because I was. The bridge swayed under my boots before I'd even made it ten feet in. It wasn't raining yet—but the air smelled with the promise of it. Damp and full, taking a breath made me feel like I was inhaling water. That's how ripe the air around me was. A rising panic swelled in the dark clouds. The kind of sky that made animals hide and old people say shit like, "it's in God's hands now."

I kept walking. Because that was the deal, right? Keep going until something stopped me. Each step clanged against the metal slats. The wind howled with continued warning, ripping through the gorge below and then up—straight through my clothes, my skin and my bones. I welcomed it. Maybe if I stood still long enough, it would just pick me up and fling me off. But that would be too easy, wouldn't it?

I paused at the center of the bridge. The storm had arrived in full force now, wild and uncontained. Lightning split the sky in the distance, thunder followed close behind, getting louder. The rain was blowing at me sideways. My hoodie clung to me like wet skin, the fabric growing heavier each time I took a breath.

The footage was going to look insane; the thought burrowed its way into my mind. Blurred lenses. Gusts loud enough to drown out my voice. A silhouette of a man alone, standing in the center of a suspended wire, as the heavens quite literally opened above him.

I didn't know when I started screaming. Maybe it had been building. Perhaps it began as a sob I refused to let out that turned into rage because that was safer. But suddenly, just like last time, I was leaning over the railing and howling into the storm, like it was some ancient god I was trying to piss off enough to strike me down.

"I'M RIGHT FUCKING HERE!" I shouted. "COME ON! WHAT ELSE DO YOU WANT FROM ME?!"

My voice cracked, ripped raw. My hands clutched the metal until they burned. I shouted until I couldn't anymore. The storm kept raging, yet it didn't take me. Lightning crackled across the sky, lighting it up like it was a sunny day. For a second, I felt suspended in time, everything around me buzzed with anticipation. And then it was gone. The flash of light vanished, leaving the sky dark and menacing once more. My heart began to beat again. *Da dum. Da dum.* The song of the living, whether I wanted to be or not.

I didn't die.

There wasn't a loose railing to lean against. No slippery missteps. No divine gusts of wind. No Hollywood-worthy collapse of cables. At the end, all that remained was me. Standing there. Alive. Fucking alive.

It was infuriating, but I felt it then, something I hadn't felt in so long it might as well have been a brand-new emotion for me. I wasn't numb. Not dead inside. Not aching or empty. I felt aware—of my pain, of my wonder, of my existence. I was soaked to the bone, my throat hurt from screaming, and I was alone on a bridge in the middle of a storm.

And weirdly—I felt grateful.

LATER THAT NIGHT I watched the footage back and saw it. Not just the rage, not the wildness in my eyes, or the way my chest had heaved. But rather, I saw the moment I gripped the edge of the railing like I was clinging to something real. If something chaotic could also look peaceful. I had done it.

The comments noticed it too.

"THIS ONE FELT DIFFERENT."

"HE'S NEVER LOOKED MORE INTENSE."

"THAT SCREAM HIT ME IN THE CHEST."

"HE TURNS STORMS INTO THERAPY. MIND BLOWING SHIT DUDE."

Someone even slowed the footage down and clipped the moment I threw my head back into the rain like I was being baptized in it.

Two DAYS LATER, I got a call. I still had no idea how they had found me and got my number, but they had.

They were calling from a Colorado newspaper, The Mountain Herald. Some feature journalist named Tamara Mikel wanted to interview me for their year-end spotlight.

"You've been selected as one of the most fascinating people of 2024," she said, sounding chipper. "We'd love to get your insight on what drives someone like you to do what you do. What makes a man walk into near-death experiences and come out laughing?"

I snorted. "Wrong guy. I'm not fascinating. I'm just bored."

She paused, like she was trying to decide whether I was being modest or just difficult. "Well, with respect, the world seems to disagree."

"That's the world's problem, not mine."

Another pause. "You make people feel something, Mr. Calloway. In a time where everything feels fake and filtered, you're raw. Real. Reckless, yes—but also unignorable. Maybe that's what we're all missing."

I stared at my laptop, her voice still in my ear. My inbox

pinged with more sponsor emails. A new brand offering ten grand to hold up their energy drink in my next clip.

In an instant, I had excused myself from the phone call and hung up. I didn't want to be rude, but I also didn't know what else to say to her. I was no hero. I wasn't an influencer. I wasn't fascinating. I didn't want people to like me for something I wasn't. But I did want them to like me. That realization jolted all my senses. And it hurt. Because when had I let myself start wanting things again? When had I gone from a man chasing oblivion to a man getting offered product deals and space in newspapers instead?

When I told Carter about the call, he nearly pissed himself laughing.

"The most fascinating man of 2024?" he wheezed. "You? You're the guy who used to think warming up SpaghettiOs counted as cooking."

"Still do," I muttered, sipping from a can as we spoke.

"Jesus, Danny. They're gonna make you the next Bachelor before you know it."

"Kill me now."

"I feel like if you're not careful, that's what's gonna happen, bro. Eight stunts and counting."

"Yet, here I am. You just give a fuck 'cause I've become your payday."

"You're a fucking asshole, Danny, you know that?"

I did.

We chuckled together.

"We still need to make merch," he said.

"Yeah, design shirts that say, 'emotionally unavailable' and 'hanging by a thread'."

He snorted.

"They'll buy them, Danny. I know they will."

I grinned into the phone even though he couldn't see me. It

was moments like these that pissed me off the most—when laughter felt easy, and my chest didn't feel so heavy, and I almost forgot that all of this was supposed to end. My brain would whisper that maybe—just maybe—I wasn't meant to die. And if that was true, then what the fuck was I supposed to do now? Because living was the scariest stunt of all.

Chapter Seventeen

Session Seven

Die Trying 

@dietrying

20m Subscribers • 22 Videos

 SUBSCRIBE

February 2026

Even though I wanted to die, ironically, I still had to pay my bills. I was sitting on the couch logging into my phone plan's website to pay the next month's charge when said phone rang.

Iris.

I stared at her name for a beat too long. I'd originally saved it when Carter sent it to me as **Shrink**. But then last week, I couldn't tell you why, I had changed it to **Just Iris**. Our session wasn't for a few more hours and now her name blinked back at me like we were... what? Friends? That thought made me want to throw my phone through the wall. I almost didn't answer. My thumb hovered over the decline button, trembling slightly. I didn't know why the phone call had unnerved me, but I wasn't exactly inundated with play date requests, so seeing my phone ringing from anything other than spam callers and Carter was weirding me out. At the last second I answered.

"Hey," I said, immediately regretting it. My voice sounded soft. Too eager. Too normal.

"Hey," she echoed, her voice had a smile in it. Of course it did. "So... I've been thinking about that list you made."

My stomach tightened. "You don't say."

"Yep. I think we should try to check it off. Being that you have so little time left and all."

Was she mocking me? Or did she think not stopping me with her words would somehow make me change my mind?

"Okay?"

"Let's get sushi for lunch. I'm out anyway. Can you meet me?"

I hesitated. "I don't do restaurants."

There was a pause. "Okay," she said simply. "Then I'll bring the sushi to you."

I blinked. "You're going to come to my apartment?"

"Well, I can't eat all this sushi on my own," she replied brightly.

"You already ordered it?"

"Yup. I spent $126 too. It's a lot of sushi. I practically got one of each option."

"I'm pretty sure it is emotional blackmail to ask someone if they want to do something, and then before you get a confirmation, they find out you've already ordered it, and then you tell them how much you spent." I shifted uneasily on the couch, looking around my pathetic apartment and for a second, a flicker of caring passed through me. But I shoved it away. Almost-dead men didn't care. I wasn't gonna start now.

"You told me you need to try something new. And you said you wanted to do it before—well—you know. So, what's your address, Danny?"

I didn't respond. She didn't let the silence deter her.

"You'll like it. I promise."

I grabbed a shirt from the pile next to the couch and tugged it on after giving it a quick sniff test.

"Fine." Why was I so grumpy? I could almost laugh at myself because my attitude was ridiculous. I was pretty sure I heard her clap her hands excitedly when I told her where I lived. I rolled my eyes. She was something else.

At 12:03 p.m. she stood in my doorway holding a brown paper bag in one hand and what looked like a six-pack of sparkling water in the other.

"You're late," I said, mockingly, but a grin had crept over my face, belying my moody tone.

"You're lucky I showed up at all," she tossed back at me with a wink, and stepped inside like she'd done it a hundred times before. Her eyes skimmed the apartment, which was admittedly messy but not disgusting; I had quickly cleaned up in the amount of time it took for her to get here. She made no comment.

"You brought enough sushi to feed an entire support group."

"Maybe I thought you'd get brave and invite your neighbors."

I didn't even have neighbors. And if I had, I assumed they would not be people who would take sushi from a stranger in pink sneakers and a galaxy-print hoodie. She wasn't wearing her usual attire of a skirt and business-appropriate top. She was in leggings, and I swallowed audibly when she unzipped her hoodie, and saw that she had paired it with a tight tank top. She smelled like she had rubbed wildflowers on her wrists before coming here. It was a scent I'd be hard pressed to forget. I forced my eyes back to the sushi that she was laying out on my coffee table, popping the clear plastic covers off each one.

She sat cross-legged on a cushion on the floor that she had grabbed from the couch, and I was startled at how out of place she looked. For one, I had never had anyone in my apartment other than Carter that one time, and he was most certainly not a woman. And two, she was too vibrant, too full of life for my apartment of dead ends and forgotten dreams. My den of depression looked even worse in comparison to her bright eyes and happy constitution.

"Are you just gonna stand there like a weirdo or you gonna come eat?" She held out a pair of chopsticks.

"I'm pretty sure therapists aren't allowed to call their patients a weirdo."

"I'm not a therapist."

I almost smiled.

"I don't know how to use those."

"Then you're in luck. I brought the easier version." She pulled a plastic fork out from her never-ending bag. I laughed.

We ate in silence at first. I watched her more than the food. She was too pretty in a way that didn't make sense. She didn't try like the girls I saw in the glossy magazines. Her face was bare. I was pretty sure her lip color was natural. Her hair was swept back. But she was the prettiest thing I had ever seen. And I couldn't tell you exactly why, but it annoyed me more than anything.

I picked up a piece of something orange and squishy.

"What is this?"

"Salmon."

"Raw?"

She gave me a look. "That's sort of the point of sushi, Danny."

"Right." I popped it in my mouth and immediately gagged.

She tried not to laugh, but I could see the effort failing in real time.

"You're enjoying this way too much."

"I really am."

I reached for the sparkling water and took a gulp. "This is what you consider fun?"

"I consider this a life experience. You're crossing something off your list. That's a good thing."

"Debatable."

"You're allowed to enjoy things before you die, Danny. It doesn't say in the handbook that the time you have left has to be miserable."

I stared at her. "What handbook?"

"The 'I Want to Die' handbook."

"You're stupid," I told her around a mouthful of rice.

She picked up a piece from a spicy tuna roll and held it in front of my face. "Try this one."

"That was wildly inappropriate," I said, eating the sushi directly off the end of her chopsticks. The chopsticks that she held.

"You need to eat off of chopsticks at least once to really get the whole experience," she replied nonchalantly, taking a piece for herself. Her mouth was right where my lips had just been. I looked away.

"Of course," I chewed, something nervous and excited flipped around inside of me, souring my stomach. "Is this like immersion therapy?"

She nodded seriously as if my sarcasm had gone right over her head. "It can be."

I smirked. "Iris... I thought you said you aren't a therapist."

That made her laugh. Really laugh and I felt it—like a rush of wind cracking open something that had been sealed inside of me for years. I'd made her laugh. God help me, I liked it. I wanted to do it again. I shouldn't want anything from her. Not her laughter or her presence. But there was that flicker of something inside of me again. Something ugly and hopeful at the same time. The kind of thing that could wreck a person if they weren't careful. But I was never known for being careful.

We kept eating, trying more combinations, until my

stomach hurt. As she introduced me to horrible things like wasabi and eel, she told me about other experiences that she was adding to her list, like skydiving, riding a horse, even eating funnel cake at a county fair. I hated that I wanted her to keep talking, I wanted to know everything else on that fucking list.

Then, somewhere between the introduction to miso and her telling me about a book she'd been reading, her arm accidentally brushed against mine. It was nothing. Just a quick tap as she moved to stop a small container of soy sauce from toppling over onto my coffee table.

"That was close," she said brightly, looking up at me.

My body responded instantly. A jolt of heat shot through me so fast I nearly dropped my fork. I hadn't... felt that in years. And never like that. In my primitive years, my brain had been all kinds of fucked up. I didn't even want to think about what had activated things.... down there. But then as I grew older and had left the abuse, I had sought out help at a local clinic for my intrusive thoughts. They put me on Zoloft, and I stayed on it for years. And stayed soft the entire time too. I hadn't cared. After going off it, I was too fixated first on survival and then on *not* surviving to think about anything else. Especially not sex. That sort of connection wasn't something I'd ever given thought to; I was too busy avoiding the nightmares of it in my sleep. But now here I was sitting next to a beautiful woman, my life coach, with more sushi than I knew what to do with, in my shit hole apartment, with a boner.

I suddenly felt like I couldn't take a full breath, and I tried to cough the panic out of my throat as I stood up abruptly. Forgetting that I should be hiding said erection, not standing up with it. I wasn't exactly well trained on what to do with inappropriately timed hard-ons.

She looked up. "Danny?"

"I need you to leave."

Her brow furrowed. "Did I do something wrong?"

I shook my head. "Just—go."

She rose slowly, carefully, as if she could see me beginning to unravel. She knew what crazy looked like after all. She saw it all day. "Okay. Um... I'll see you at the next session?"

I didn't answer. She hesitated in the doorway. "It was nice, you know? Crossing something off your list with you."

I gave a half-assed grunt as if it could possibly say: yes, it was. Thank you for spending all that money on sushi and introducing me to sashimi. I'm sorry I'm so bad at the people thing, and the littlest normal body reaction has me half insane. But I didn't say any of that. I just shut the door behind her before I could do or say something I'd regret.

Then I leaned against the wood, breathing hard, wondering what the hell had just happened. I felt like a creepy teenager who had just discovered boobs. My body had betrayed me and all she had been was nice. I hated myself for not knowing how to do normal. I had tried it and had ruined it, and she had just been acting... nice.

Die Trying 

@dietrying

20m Subscribers · 22 Videos

 SUBSCRIBE

(Uploaded: January 18, 2025. 5:12 p.m.)

I'd spent weeks scouting the building—the wing I'd chosen was twenty-eight stories tall, with barely secured rooftop access, and elevators from the late nineties that creaked like the bones of someone who'd lived too long and still refused to die. It was perfect. Serendipitous in a way. They also still ran on an outdated traction system with counterweights and a manual brake override. Meaning, if you wanted to try to die, it was a really good elevator to do it in. As always, I planned the stunt for a time when no one could stop me. It was a quiet night, past midnight, during a snowstorm, when most of the city was asleep or too high to care what I was doing.

The plan was simple enough. I wanted to ride the elevator on the outside of it; not beside it but rather on top of it. If my math was correct, the descent would stop just above the base-ment level. At the bottom was a pit, six feet deep, lined with concrete and buffers. When the elevator reached it, there would be less than two feet between the roof I'd be lying on and the ceiling of the pit. If my math was incorrect, and the safety failed, or the emergency brake didn't catch, that gap would vanish, and

I'd be squashed like a bug. I wouldn't be around to hear the "told you so," plus I didn't give a fuck.

Once in the elevator, I pried the doors open on the four-teenth floor using a screwdriver and a crowbar that I had stowed in my bag. I jammed the emergency brake to stop it mid-floor, then hauled myself through the access panel on the ceiling. Getting on top wasn't the hard part. Staying alive once I was up there? That was the experiment.

The shaft was so dark it made me feel deaf and blind. My GoPro caught only my face at first—lit by the weak flicker of the service bulb a few floors above—and the outline of the cables that thrummed with stored energy, vibrating with the weight of the whole damn system.

"Let's see what the universe wants to do with me today," I muttered, my voice swallowed by the echo.

I lay flat on the roof of the elevator, heart pounding against the metal like it was trying to shake me off and leave me behind. A thin layer of grime coated everything, and I knew one wrong move would send me sliding off the edge and into oblivion. But I wasn't afraid. I was wired, almost euphoric. Like this was finally the moment I'd been working toward.

The trick was starting the descent. From what I'd learned online, the brake release lever could be triggered manually from the top if you knew what to pull. I found the steel handle near the rear of the roof, half rusted and forced it down. I didn't count down. I didn't pray. I didn't say anything at all as the elevator lurched beneath me, and for a split second nothing happened. I just heard a creak. A whirring sound of the ancient cables above me. Then a small movement made the metal I was holding onto sway slightly, and my stomach dipped, not enough to make me call it quits, but enough to make me second-guess my whole plan for just half a moment.

The cables groaned louder, and suddenly they dropped. I

found myself surfing steel as it fought gravity. The metal roof rattled under my stomach, shaking my arms, sending vibrations up my spine forcing me to hold on. It wasn't too fast at first. Just a quick tug pulling me downward. Then came the acceleration. The cables whined, the shaft blurred, and my body yanked into freefall while lying down. My ears popped. My blood surged till my face felt like it was on fire and my teeth clattered together. The air punched out of me as the elevator gained speed. My hands gripped the lip of the vibrating roof so hard my knuckles tore open. My body shook with it. Dust flew in my eyes. I couldn't breathe. Couldn't think. Just dropdropdropdrop...

I couldn't curse or laugh or call out; my mouth was just opened as if in a soundless scream. My hands were wet with sweat; my busted knuckles protested as I held onto the edge, not letting go.

I didn't know how many floors I had flown past, but I thought I might be close to the end when at one point, gravity began pulling harder than my grip. If the system misread the weight differential, the safety would fail, and I'd be flattened like a pancake. I was almost there... The speed was so intense that the noise around me almost bled into silence. My body was pinned to the metal, and I braced myself for impact.

Then, out of nowhere, the governor cable engaged with a grinding groan that almost sounded like thunder. Sparks burst down the wall of the shaft as the elevator's safety jaws bit into the rails. The shrieking of metal against metal reverberated in my ears as the car jerked to a stop so hard that it nearly threw me off. My chest slammed against the edge, my ribs screamed. And then—silence. It had stopped inches above the kill zone.

I didn't move for a full minute. Not out of caution or shock but because of the adrenaline coursing through my body. I blinked as I stared up at the cable above me, now gone slack. I should've been dead. I'd wanted to be. That was the whole point. But somehow, again, life held on. I felt like clapping, as though applauding myself for surviving made sense.

I turned my head slightly, my cheek scraped against the gritty metal, and I felt it leave a smear of something on my cheek. I blinked again. I was still here. I almost couldn't believe it.

An emergency response must have kicked in because the elevator clicked back to life and slowly began to rise. I crawled back through the hatch, arms shaking so bad it took me two tries to drop back inside. I collapsed on the floor and laughed. I laughed so hard I nearly puked. I wasn't sure anymore if I was relieved or pissed. But I was still here. That much I knew.

Later on, Carter emailed me the final cut. The video was tight, edited perfectly, with just enough audio distortion and motion blur to stay within YouTube's community guidelines. In one frame, my face was caught mid-fall—eyes wide, pupils blown, mouth open—and the caption read: When your life flashes before your eyes but skips all the best parts.

I uploaded the footage four days later.

The title was simple: #7 Elevator Drop (Don't Do This at Home)

Within an hour, it was trending. Within two hours, Carter called me.

"Dude," he said, barely able to catch his breath between bursts of laughter. "What in the actual hell? That was like Mission Impossible meets every panic attack I've ever had."

"I almost died," I replied flatly.

"I know! I was freaking out! And your face when it stopped... I replayed that like twelve times. Did you see the meme of it rounding the internet?"

There was silence on my end. I didn't see any memes. I didn't even have social media other than my one YouTube account, and an old Facebook that brands used to reach out to me.

Carter went quiet, then said, "Hey... you're okay, right?"

"Define okay."

"I mean... not dead?"

"Yeah. I'm not dead."

He exhaled, clearly not yet processing what a stupid question that had been.

"Christ, Danny."

THAT NIGHT, I couldn't sleep. I tried. But every time I closed my eyes, all I could hear was the elevator shaft screaming, except this time my plan had worked. I was trapped between floors, my ribs were caving inward, my organs were slowly being crushed inside of me. I took one last gasping breath before my heart punched into my lungs and I died.

My eyes flew open, grateful for once, to see the crack in the ceiling above me instead of the never-ending dark hole of the elevator shaft. I sat on the edge of the couch, hands gripping the frame, my hands still raw and stiff. I opened my laptop and winced as the glow from the screen hurt my eyes. I dimmed the light and looked back at the empty document that I had opened. I titled it, 'why', and made a list of all the reasons I was still doing this. I felt I needed a reminder. I didn't want my resolve to slip. I was growing tired. My busted knuckles protested the movement, bruised and crusty with a freshly formed scab.

- Age 3: Left at a gas station.
- Age 6: First broken bone no one treated.

- Age 10–17: Everything.
- Age 21: Homeless for six months.
- Age 31: My editor thinks *Friends* is therapy and I'm still here.

I stared at the blinking cursor. My fingers hovered. The air in the room felt heavier as the weight of all I had been through filled the space around me.

Then I typed: I should be dead.

And underneath that: I don't know why I'm not.

"DOES THIS GUY THINK HE'S TOM CRUISE?"

"I JUST DON'T UNDERSTAND WHY??"

"HE LOOKS LIKE HE GETS OFF ON THE PAIN."

"GOD WHY IS HE SO HOT WHEN HE DOES THE STUPIDEST THINGS. HE'S SUCH A RED FLAG AND I WANT HIM ANYWAY."

"DID YOU HEAR HIS VOICE AT THE START OF THE VIDEO? OH, MY GAWD I JUST KNOW HE MUST BE AMAZING IN BED."

"I SWEAR THIS GUY IS GONNA KILL ME EMOTIONALLY BEFORE HE GETS HIMSELF KILLED."

Chapter Nineteen

Session Eight

February 2026

I had a hard time staying asleep since she left my apartment. I'd fall asleep, even get a few hours in, but every time I got close to true relaxation, my brain served up memories I didn't want, images I'd buried deep. Paired with the reminder of the heat of her arm brushing against mine, it had my mind busy activating those memories all night, despite my numerous attempts to fully scrub my brain of them.

By the time I showed up at Iris's office a week after our sushi lunch together, I was so sleep deprived that I was practically drunk from it. I was sure I looked like I'd been hit by a truck. I certainly felt like it; emotionally and physically.

She opened the door and tilted her head. "Are you okay?" She was a vision in her brown leather skirt and yellow blouse. Her dark hair was braided away from her face, accentuating her big eyes and freckles. I gulped and looked away. I laughed; it came out as a hollow, dry sound. "Am I ever okay?" Then added, "I haven't been sleeping well."

Instead of pushing back to inquire why that was, she

stepped aside and gestured to the couch behind her. "Lie down."

I blinked at her; my eyes burned with exhaustion. "What is this? Nap time?"

She smiled faintly. "Just lie down, Danny."

I walked in, too tired to argue. The couch was so comfortable. Just like I'd remembered. So soft that as I sank into the cushions, it almost felt like being held. A sensation I was not well acquainted with but one I could still think of fondly despite my visceral reaction to Iris's accidental touch the other day. Iris, who now stood before me and held out a folded throw blanket. I hesitated before taking it. Something about her quiet gesture, the gentleness that it held made the inside of my chest twist. But I took it anyway and wrapped myself in it, almost letting out a sigh as the thick, soft material enveloped my body. I turned my face away from her, practically burying my nose into one of the cushions of the couch, and my eyes closed of their own volition. Iris didn't have to tell me to do it. The blanket smelled of her. I breathed it in. It was a soothing scent, warm with a bite of sweetness.

I tried not to fall asleep, I really gave it a gallant effort, but it was next to impossible not to slip off into oblivion. I was surrounded by softness and warmth. Plus, Iris was here; she would watch over me. She would keep the nightmares at bay so I could finally get a break. One I'd been chasing after for so long. It was like years of keeping one eye open and watching my back fell away and, in an instant, I was dead to the world. Not the dead I so fervently desired but good enough for now. Then I truly slept. No nightmares found me in my slumber. It was just dark, quiet, peaceful, and nothing at all.

When I woke up, my brain went straight into fight mode. That twitchy, half-awake moment where you don't know if you're safe or if you should already be running. My heart was thudding, my mouth tasted like old pennies, and for a second, I didn't even know where the hell I was. Not until I heard the soft ticking of a clock, a clock I didn't have. I turned and looked at said clock, it was 4:22 p.m. The stupid clock reminded me where I was. I was still in Iris's office. I was on her couch, wrapped up in her blanket. I had actually slept. And not that half-sleep where your body jerks every two seconds because it's bracing for a memory. No, I had experienced real sleep, with no nightmares. That realization had me sitting up quickly.

"Shit. I slept through your whole day."

Iris was still at her desk, sipping something, tea maybe. A book sat in front of her. She looked up when I spoke, startled to find me awake and talking. "You needed it."

"I will pay you for the time." I rubbed at my face. I needed to brush my teeth; my eyes were still thick with sleep. "Or I'll pay double next session. Whatever you want. I'm so sorry."

She set her mug down. "Has no one ever just done something kind for you, without needing something in return?"

The question caught me so off guard I actually froze. I stared at her. "What?" Her words had knocked the air right out of me. The muscles in my neck clenched, my brain scrambled for a sarcastic one-liner to throw back at her, but I came up with nothing. All that reverberated within me was a growing and heavy discomfort. I sat there, frozen, my only movement was my eyes blinking, wondering if I had misheard her. I peeled my tongue from the roof of my mouth and pressed my lips closed, holding back the words that crawled up my throat.

"I mean it." Her voice was quiet. "Has anyone ever done something kind for you, just because they cared?"

I looked away. My throat felt raw, and when I swallowed, it burned like I'd chewed on glass.

"I feel like maybe I haven't been really clear with you from the start, and it seems like it's left some confusion on your part.

So let me spell it out for you, fully. My birth mother left me at a gas station when I was three," I said. "She told the attendant she'd be right back. She never came back." I hadn't planned on saying that today, if ever, but here we were.

"After that, from ages four to ten, I was passed around from foster home to foster home. I never stayed in one place long enough to really unpack a suitcase. Or have a place that felt like home. I never stayed in one school long enough to make friends. Some of the houses and families were decent, even okay. Some weren't. Then I landed in the one that kept me the longest, but it was the one I wished hadn't."

Iris didn't interrupt me. She just listened, like she always did.

"He was a church deacon," I said, and the words felt like poison on my tongue. "I was ten when I was placed there. I was forced to stay until I was seventeen. You can fill in the blanks however you'd like, because whatever you come up with, probably happened to me there."

She didn't move. She didn't look shocked or horrified either. She just sat still. A steady counterpart to my chaos. My voice cracked.

"He called me Danny Boy. Told me I was a good boy when I held still. He broke my ribs when I didn't. So no, *just* Iris, no one has done anything kind for me. No one has ever cared about me. And they certainly didn't do anything for me with nothing expected in return." I hadn't said that name out loud in years. I just heard it reverberating in my head in my nightmares.

I pressed the heels of my palms against my eyes as they burned with the pain of my memories. Hard enough that I almost saw pinpricks of light in the darkness. Like I was trying to shove everything back, deep where it belonged. I didn't want to cry. I couldn't let it happen. I had done such a good job of bottling it all up and packing it away, but it didn't work. To my sheer embarrassment, the defenses to the dam broke. I was horrified as it started, but once it did, I couldn't take it back. Couldn't make it stop. At first my sobs were silent; my body shook with tears that came harder the more I tried to stop them. Then my shoulders began to vibrate with all the emotion that burst out of me at once. Then the ugly sobs started, and they ripped out of me, having been stored in a place inside of me that I hadn't acknowledged in years. The burn of the pain, the yearning for something different, the wish that what had happened to me wasn't tattooed into my very soul—it all burst from me in such body wracking cries that I scared myself from the magnitude of them. I hated the noise, the snot, and the way my body shook like I was a little kid. Nothing I did would make it stop, so I let myself get swept away in the grief, the pain and the enormity of my feelings that had been buried so deep for so long.

Iris didn't speak. At least she didn't say anything that I could hear over the racket I was making. But I did feel her move to sit down next to me on the couch. Not too close, not touching me. She was just near me, and I was so aware of her. For the first time in my life another person's presence next to me felt safe.

"I'm not weak," I said through clenched teeth once the tears finally dried up and my body stopped shaking.

"I know," she said, her voice sweet and gentle.

More tears came at that. My nose was running, and I wiped it unceremoniously on the sleeve of my shirt. She could think I was disgusting; I didn't care. She already knew I was crazy; I may as well also be gross.

And then—a soft hand landed on my arm. So light I barely registered it. It was almost nothing, but I still felt a jolt run through me when I realized what was happening. I didn't have the energy to move away or make a joke or ignore it. Instead, I leaned into it. Just a little. We sat like that, me breathing in the aftermath of my heightened emotions, her breathing out comfort and safety.

Then she opened her arms a little more, and I shifted my body just a bit until suddenly I was wrapped up in her. She was warm, fragile, strong, and soft. It felt real. I may have sighed out a groan, I wasn't sure. I couldn't even summon up embarrassment if I wanted to, I was completely depleted of energy.

I had never been hugged like this before. The hugs I remembered all came with a price, and this one felt like the first human contact I'd ever had that hadn't cost me something.

My body collapsed against her, and my arms went around her waist, resting on her back. She didn't falter. She didn't try to fix it. Didn't say it would be okay. She just let me be, and it undid me all over again.

When I pulled away, I sat up and wiped at my face. "You're just trying to get through my list by checking off a hug for me." I was finally able to get out a joke, and I said it in an attempt to push away all this unfamiliar heaviness. It was like I knew if I didn't, I would collapse under the pressure of trying to gather all my secrets back up and push them back down to where they had come from.

She laughed, gently. "You're on to me, Danny."

We sat there in the quiet, just breathing. Right when the silence stretched on long enough to make me feel like I should go, she asked, "Do you think maybe this obsession with dying is because you're avoiding pain and anger?"

I snorted. "That sounds like something a therapist would say."

"Good thing I'm not one."

"I'm pretty sure you need to feel safe to experience sadness and anger. And I've never had that." I didn't answer her question. Not really. Because deep down I wasn't sure if she was wrong. Maybe I didn't want to die as much as I didn't want to sit with my pain. I didn't want to ponder why life had given me the hand it had. Why had other kids grown up with love, warm dinners and safety, and I'd been abandoned, forgotten and worse?

With a brief, "Thank you, just Iris," I stood and walked out before she could say anything kind again. Because the kindness was starting to hurt worse than the pain I was used to.

Chapter Twenty
Skid Row

(Uploaded: February 12, 2025. 7:01 p.m.)

I didn't pick Skid Row because it was edgy. I picked it because it was real. It existed with no pretense. It was the opposite of the curated chaos of Burning Man or the fake rebellion of storm chasing. Skid Row just offered pain. It was what hitting rock bottom looked like in all its raw and exposed truth, existing like an open nerve that the world tried its best to ignore.

I wandered there at dusk; the air was thick with the smell of piss, grease, and something sweet and rotting. People stumbled past me like ghosts in the dark, their eyes hollowed out from years of being unseen. Just like me, but they'd ended up on a different path than I had.

I wasn't scared as I stood there. I wanted to be. I wanted to feel—something—anything that would be more powerful than the numbness pressed against my ribs.

At the last second I decided to go shirtless. Maybe if I bared my skin to the chaos, it would also bare my soul. I pressed record knowing that the video would start with me framed on the screen in just jeans and quite literally nothing else but the shirt not on my back. No bag, no wallet. Just my body, a camera rigged on my chest, and a death wish.

The stench of life being lived on the street continued to assault me the further in that I went. Walking through Skid Row was like stepping into a world that time had abandoned. The sidewalk beneath my sneakers felt sticky in some spots and gritty in others. It was littered with the flattened remains of cigarette butts, bottle caps, broken plastic forks, needles, and paper cups long since collapsed in on themselves. The sour tang of ammonia hung heavy in the air, layered over the dull, acrid scent of burnt rubber and something sickly potent—like rotting fruit, or maybe vomit that had baked in the sun and then cooled under urine-soaked blankets.

Every few steps brought a new smell—feces, blood, garbage, weed, fried food, body odor—all woven together into a nauseating perfume that no one else around me seemed to notice anymore. I didn't judge them; at one point I had been them. I didn't really know what had propelled me to do better for myself, not that what I had was so much above this, but the fact was I had done enough for myself to have indoor plumbing and a place to sleep at night. Uncharacteristically, I was actually proud of my younger self for doing what I had to do so as to not make living on the street a permanent arrangement. I may be suicidal, but I wasn't stupid and I certainly wasn't lazy. I had built a life for myself despite the fact that the world had handed me nothing, and had kept its heel on my neck so that I was constantly gasping for air.

The noise around me was constant, but not loud; it wasn't at a volume that made me want to plug my ears, it was just a consistent undertone of sound that never stopped. A woman shouted scripture while standing on a crate under a street lamp. A man argued with someone I couldn't see. When I rounded the corner, I realized it was someone he couldn't see either. The tinny jangle of a shopping cart loaded with aluminum cans and other recyclables. Muted coughs. A baby crying. A distant siren that nobody flinched at. The community here knew the sirens weren't for them; society had long since abandoned those that lived on the streets.

The buildings around me were like skeletons—stripped down, graffitied, faded by the sun and beaten by rain, wearing the grime of age. Some had bars on the windows, others had no windows at all. Most had boarded-up doors or broken padlocks clinging to a door handle like an afterthought. One wall had the remnants of the words, "GOD IS WATCHING" spray-painted on it in angry red, but the letters were partially worn away, so it just read "GOD IS WAT." I didn't know if I should pretend it meant "waiting" or "wasted." It could honestly be both.

People lined the sidewalks in tents and makeshift shelters built from tarps, cardboard, and fading hope. Some sat on over-turned buckets, hunched over, staring at the ground. Some talked to themselves, or to the sky. Some just stared—at nothing at all; it almost looked like their eyes saw right through me. One man was cradling a small dog, gently feeding it a McChicken with hands so dirty it turned my stomach. A woman nearby painted her fingernails with a grimy bottle of nail polish while singing "My Heart Will Go On" in an off-key but confident tone. Her toes were turning blue from the chilly night air. Or maybe it was bruises, I couldn't tell.

Everything around me looked so temporary, so fragile—like these people's entire lives could all blow away with the next gust of wind. There was a heaviness in the air that felt like grief. Not simply sadness, but the kind of grief that settled into your bones. The grief that came from being forgotten. The grief that grew from being passed over by life. The grief of knowing that no one was coming to save you.

And yet, weirdly—impossibly—there were also sounds of

laughter. Two men were playing cards on a flattened pizza box. A little further down, a boy no older than seventeen sat cross-legged with a makeshift chessboard in front of him. His pieces were made from different color bottle caps that he'd attached together to represent pawns and kings. He played both sides, each one taking his focus and attention, playing with a strange kind of dignity, as if the outcome mattered. A girl with pink dreads danced to music only she could hear. Nobody told her to stop. In a fucked-up way there was a semblance of respect down here. Someone nearby was grilling something that smelled almost edible. Life, or at least the illusion of it, kept ticking by. They hadn't given up, not yet like I had. The guilt of my current predicament being self-imposed burned in the back of my throat like a sudden bout of acid reflux after finishing off an entire family sized container of jalapeno chicken poppers.

I walked through the controlled chaos like a ghost. No one stopped me. No one looked twice. Maybe I appeared like I belonged. Maybe they were too numb to care. Or maybe they could sense that I wasn't there to be saved either.

Somewhere deep in one of the alleys, a man stepped out from behind a dumpster. He was maybe my age, or maybe fifty, it was hard to tell. He looked wired—eyes darting everywhere, jaw clenched, hands buried in the folds of a tattered hoodie. He said something I didn't catch. I kept walking. He began to walk faster, muttering quickly under his breath. I could hear him growing closer, and I found that I had slowed down on purpose, defying my body's natural urge to put as much space between him and I as possible. Despite my better judgment, I turned just as I saw him pull out a knife. It was small and from what I could tell, the handle was rusted. The blade was jagged and dull like it had been sharpened on concrete. The thrill of someone finally being ready to fuck with me had me stop walking all together. For the first time in a long time—I hoped.

"Give me your money," he demanded, his tone low and gravely. Like maybe these were his first words of the day. His demand was futile though, as I had nothing on me.

"I don't have any," I told him as I realized that he was the first person I had spoken to in so long other than Carter. Oh, the irony.

"I'll stab you if you don't give it to me." He was slurring, likely on a substance that was rapidly wearing off, and he already knew that he had to find the funds for his next hit.

"Do it," I said, my voice even. I spread my arms like I was welcoming it. "Right here."

He looked shocked and he stumbled with it, putting space between us. I closed in on him. This time I was the one pursuing him. Turned tables and all that.

"C'mon my guy, don't offer a man a good time and then back out." I pounded on the center of my sternum, right above the camera. "Fucking do it. Give me a good one."

He hesitated. Stared. And then I said the thing that I think scared him more than if I had pulled out my own weapon.

"I won't fight you."

The words were barely out of my mouth when he fully backed up. I heard him mutter something about me being crazy and then he disappeared into the dark. I stood there for a long time, the knife-shaped silence vibrated in my ears. My heart thudded, loud and thick. I wanted it to stop. I wanted the world to cave in. I wanted to laugh at him for calling me crazy. But I didn't. Instead, I told the universe to fuck off. My words reverberated through the space and one of the women in the crowd behind me yelled back, "Yeah, fuck you too!"

I walked back to my shitty motel. My pulse wouldn't settle. My skin tingled from the lingering adrenaline and the cold nip of the air. Was I growing pathetic as I begged others to get done what I couldn't do myself? Did it make me a pussy that I kept imploring the universe to make a choice for me that I pretended to have already made? Because tonight I could solidly say that death hadn't just dodged me, it had laughed in my face.

Back in the room I showered before I emailed over the footage. I needed to wash the shame and the grime off me before I could face the video. It was another failed mission, but at least I knew the camera's angles were clear and crisp. I definitely had another viral episode in my hands. I didn't know when that started to matter, but it had.

Carter's email came back quickly.

Who the fuck in their right mind dares a homeless man to stab them!? I can't even think about the diseases that were on that blade. If I'm gonna catch something, I'd rather it be from a hooker than a knife.
Seriously dude, you're continuing to scare me.

I replied.

Just do your job and edit the footage.

Then, while I waited for him to work his magic, I watched the video back again. It was weird watching my own face as I stared down that blade like it was nothing. It could have been everything. If he had just done it. But he hadn't. Instead of wondering if I had finally crossed a line of desperation, I focused on uploading Carter's version of the video and then deleting the raw footage off my GoPro, making room for my next adventure.

As soon as the video was posted, the comments rolled in.

> "THE WAY THIS GUY STARED DOWN THAT BLADE, I WISH HE'D LOOK AT ME LIKE THAT. OOF. CHILLS"

> "THIS MAN HAS ZERO FEAR. ICON."

> "I KNEW HE HAD THAT BODY UNDER HIS HOODIES. GD BABE."

> "I'M CONCERNED. BUT ALSO... RESPECTFULLY THAT WAS (FIRE EMOJI)."

> "SOMEONE NEEDS TO GET THIS MAN A MODELING CONTRACT AND A THERAPIST STAT."

> "DID HE JUST ASK TO BE STABBED?"

Nobody saw it for what it was.

A man trying to die and being denied once again.

My audience cared more about my hint of abs than my absence of a will to live. More about the angles and the drama than the obvious ache in my soul. But, hey, the video was on track to break a million views in four hours. So, I had achieved something... I guessed.

Chapter Twenty-One

Session Nine

Die Trying 

@dietrying

20m Subscribers · 22 Videos

 SUBSCRIBE

February 2026

I was in a mood.

Not my usual brand of sarcasm and quiet brooding, but something far more chaotic—a sugar-spiked, caffeine-fueled kind of restlessness. My hands wouldn't stop fidgeting. My leg bounced so aggressively I was vibrating the fucking chair in the waiting room. I counted every ceiling tile; there were twenty-four in the perimeter. I tracked every time the air freshener puffed out its essential oil spray, it had made its mechanical noise six times before I was called in. Four people walked by me as I waited, one wore red heels, another wore a pair of tattered sneakers, the third a black pair of Uggs, and the fourth clomped by in dirty brown Timberland boots. I had begun counting how many times I heard a taxi honk when Iris called out my name.

As soon as I entered the room, I couldn't stop talking, couldn't stop cracking jokes, couldn't stop running from something that felt like it was boiling and writhing beneath my skin.

"Would you like to sit over here today?" Iris asked, nodding toward the couch with that sweet therapist smile she always wore. It was just how I referred to her at this point even though she insisted she wasn't one.

I narrowed my eyes. "That's the trauma spot. I've already cried over there. Stained the fabric with my manly disgrace. I can't go back there. How do I know it won't happen again?"

She tilted her head as if suddenly understanding the chaotic energy I had walked in with. "Then where would you like to sit?"

"Right here." I patted the chair that I had already collapsed into, the one closest to her desk and leaned back, smirking. "Close enough to throw myself out the window if things get too serious."

She didn't laugh. She just folded her hands in her lap and said, "Tell me about the anger, Danny."

Ah, there it was. Today's agenda bomb dropped in the first five minutes. I let out a slow whistle. "Wow, Iris, coming in hot. No foreplay? You're not gonna get me wet first?"

I was trying to goad her, trying to flare that little bit of discomfort that I had witnessed in one of our other sessions. I was trying to make her forget that I had cried in her arms. Maybe if I used dirty humor to deflect, she'd do anything other than softly pick at the freshly formed scabs of my unhealed wounds.

Unfortunately for me Iris didn't even give my words any attention, although I did notice that the tops of her cheeks reddened with a faint blush.

"You've been circling it for weeks. I see your anger under all the sarcasm. I can feel the rage under your humor, and I think you're ready to explore it."

I laughed. Loudly. "Define 'ready.' Because if you open that box, you need to really understand what you're asking for."

"What are you waiting for exactly, Danny? According to

you, you're running out of time." Her voice was gentle, but her words cracked in the air around me like a whip.

I didn't move. What she said hit me with all the subtlety of a freight train. I blinked at her. Looked away. Blinked again. My throat started closing in that way it did when I felt cornered. So, I did what any cornered animal would do—I detonated and struck back.

"No, see you don't get it," I said, standing up so quickly that the chair screeched and fell back behind me. "If I let that out—if I really go there—I won't come back the same. I won't be someone you can sip tea with while coloring cute little pictures and writing bucket lists of our hopes and dreams."

"Maybe you were never supposed to come back the same," she said quietly. "Maybe that's exactly what you need."

My hands curled into fists. My chest tightened like it was being compressed from the inside. My skin was suddenly stretched too tight over my body, like my bones, blood and memories were trying to punch their way out of me. The room tilted, not from dizziness, but from the kind of rage that made the edges of my sight blur. I could taste blood on my tongue from where I had bitten the inside of my cheek. For a split second I saw flashes—of him slamming the door in my face, the look on the social worker's face because she didn't believe me that an upstanding member of the church would do such a thing, the word liar reverberating in my brain. All of it rose at once like a tide I could not stop but one I also could not drown in. I sat there, trembling, jaw locked, hands in fists so tight my nails dug into my palms, the pain was the only thing grounding me. I didn't want Iris to see this part of me. I never wanted anyone to. But it was too late.

Maybe you were never supposed to come back the same.

"I don't want to be this fucking project for you, Iris!" I

shouted. "I'm not some jigsaw puzzle you get to feel good about putting back together!"

I saw her eyes flicker to the side, probably checking if the hallway was empty. Then she looked right back at me, calm and unfazed as ever.

"I've told you, you're not a project," she corrected. "You're a person."

I grabbed that fucking notebook from her desk, flipped it around, and then threw it across the room. It hit the wall and fell to the floor, flopping open to an empty page.

"I'm a fucking wreck, that's what I am!" I bellowed. "A science experiment gone wrong! Of course I'm angry. It's not like you have to be smart and intuitive to figure that out, Iris! Every person who was supposed to love me either fucked me over or left! I didn't deserve that! I was just a little boy."

My hand swept across her bookshelf. A small stack of books tumbled to the floor. One of them hit the edge of her potted plant, plopping a puff of dirt onto the carpet. And then—I didn't know what possessed me—I grabbed the mug. The mug I had bought her, and I hurled it at the wall. With all my strength and every furious feeling inside of me. It shattered into three separate pieces that skidded across the carpet, stopping only once they crashed into the opposite wall in a spray of yellow shards.

She didn't flinch. She just sat there and breathed. Her calm and solid composure tore me out of the red-hot haze that had taken over me. Her steadiness was the first thing I could ever rely on, and that realization was almost physical.

"I'm so sorry," I said instantly, hands up, stepping away like the shards might attack me back. "Shit. I'm so—I didn't mean— fuck." I got onto my hands and knees and tried to clean up the mess I had made both literally and figuratively. My hands were shaking, and I found I had sliced little cuts into the tips of my fingers as I tried to gather up the pieces of the mug, as if fixing that could somehow heal my shame.

"It's okay." She was on her knees beside me, cradling my hands away from the sharp pieces of ceramic.

"No, it's not," I said, gasping as if I had just run a marathon. "I broke it. I broke the goddamn mug." I felt as though I had broken way more than that. Maybe the flimsy bit of respect that she may have had for me. Or some feeble semblance of trust.

"Let's go buy a new one." She stood and somehow, in what felt like just a moment, she had gathered up the pieces of mug and threw them out with a soft clink into the small garbage can beside her desk. The books had been put back in their spot on the shelf, and her notebook had been retrieved, no worse for wear, as far as I could tell from my spot on the floor, where I was still crouched, my throat aching with shame. My legs were tucked under me, and I didn't want to stand. I didn't want to face it, how unhinged I had been.

"Come," she urged softly.

I blinked up at her. "What?"

"Let's go. You'll buy me a new one. We'll call it a field trip."

"You're serious?"

She smiled. "You broke it. You fix it. Seems poetic, doesn't it?"

I couldn't argue with that. It all just seemed too easy, to have a space to flip out in and still she came out unfrazzled, as if nothing crazy had just happened. Still, she felt safe to be around me. Her lack of judgment left me almost bewildered.

"I'm so proud of you for getting angry." She smiled as if she could read my thoughts. *Huh.* Pride in myself curled within me, wispy and fragile like smoke, but there all the same.

As we stepped outside, the air was cold against my skin that was still heated from my meltdown. The silence between us was heavy but not suffocating. My boots scuffed against the pavement; each step rang in my ears. I stole glances over at Iris, who walked beside me to the little gift shop down the street, her hand curled neatly around the strap of her purse like she hadn't just watched me come apart in her office.

Once we got to the shop, I held the door for her. She murmured, "thank you" as she walked in. A bell tinkled, announcing our arrival. The owner called out that she was here if we needed anything. Iris drifted over to a shelf of mugs. I looked around and found that they sold overpriced candles and cutesy mugs with sayings like, "But First, Tea" or "This Might Be Wine." The air smelled of freshly ground coffee, vanilla candles, and something citrusy. It was a little too clean and perfect in here for a guy like me. I was a bit too tall and a tad too broad for all the delicate china and shiny crystals on the shelves around me. I was almost worried I would accidentally break something. I gently trailed my fingers over a bright blue mug that read, "Fixer of Everything." Iris laughed when I showed it to her and then she picked up a pink one and held it out. It said, "Chaos Coordinator" in bold purple letters. We finally settled on a turquoise handmade mug that was a little lopsided and had the words, "I told my therapist about you," painted on the side of it. I almost made a joke about it being messed up, just like me, but the words got stuck in my throat as I watched her hold it up to proclaim how much she loved it and admire how cute it was. The sound of her voice wormed its way into the little pockets of my heart. I didn't even have the energy to try to stop it. The sun chose that moment to drift its rays through the window, framing her perfectly, warming her skin and glinting off her hair. I stood there, watching her, and the moment felt like it meant way more than it should have.

Once we were ready to pay, I watched as the woman at the cash register wrapped the mug in shiny gold tissue paper and placed it into a black gift bag. Iris took it with a soft smile and a warm thank you. I handed the woman a twenty and turned when I heard the man behind Iris comment on how expensive a silly mug was. I didn't say anything but seeing Iris's smile when she had examined the mug and embraced all its imperfections made me feel like it was worth every penny.

Back outside, the cold air hit us again like a slap. My head was still buzzing. The broken mug and its replacement felt like a metaphor.

"So," I said, stuffing my hands in my jacket. "If you had all the money in the world, what would you do with it?"

She gave me a sidelong glance, looking surprised at what I could only assume came across as a very random question but one that had come to my mind from the man's comment on the cost of the mug. "Why do you ask?"

"I just wondered. You give off 'I'm really-responsible-with-my-money-vibes'."

She laughed. "I'd buy a house. Pay off my student loans. Start an organization that helps people deal with their past and learn to embrace living in the present. Maybe start a scholarship fund for kids in the system." She barely had to think about it. Big thoughts and plans about her future didn't seem hard for her to come up with.

"Damn," I muttered. "That's almost too wholesome."

She nudged me with her elbow. "What would you do if you got a lot of money?"

"I have a lot of money," I mumbled, rummaging around in my pockets just to give my hands something to do, acting almost embarrassed by it. Or maybe it was the shame of how I had acquired the money. "But if I'd actually do something big with it, I'd buy a billboard that said, "Live fast, die whenever the hell it finally works.""

She stopped walking and I almost bumped into her. "That's not funny, Danny."

I looked over at her, surprised. I had never been able to get anything out of her other than calm questions, real happiness, and empathy. But I finally heard something else in her voice, and it sent a thrill through me. Her face was soft, almost sad. And it was obvious to me that she really cared. Probably more than she should.

"I'm joking, just Iris," I lied and shoved her gently with my elbow. She stumbled and I caught her with my hand before she fell.

"Jesus, I should not be allowed around people," I joked, flushing.

"You're doing just fine." Her smile was forgiving. Much more forgiving than I was of myself.

We parted ways on the corner, Iris to her office, and me to pick up dinner before going to my apartment.

"I'm sorry for today," I mumbled as she walked away.

"Don't be. I'm not," she called without turning back around. I watched her go, a smile playing on my lips.

When I got home, I sent Carter a message.

DANNY

Can you find me a lawyer? I need to do some paperwork.

CARTER

Not if it's to plan your funeral fucker.

DANNY

Already did that. Envelope with instructions is in my dresser drawer. So you know.

CARTER

(Middle finger emoji).

I didn't say what the paperwork was for. I wasn't even sure

myself yet. But something inside of me had shifted and I finally felt peaceful with my decision, versus the frantic feeling I sometimes got when I thought about... the *after*. I finally had a plan other than just wanting to die, and it felt right.

As I fell asleep that night, I heard Iris say, "You're not a project, you're a person." It was the closest I'd ever come to feeling seen.

Chapter Twenty-Two

Lake George

Die Trying 

@dietrying

20m Subscribers • 22 Videos

 SUBSCRIBE

(Uploaded: March 19, 2025. 8 p.m.)

Lake George stretched out like a mirror someone forgot to hang up on a wall. A frozen expanse of what had once been a beautiful lake before the temperatures had dropped, its surface glassy and pale beneath a sky that was so blue it caused everything to feel too bright. It was the kind of blue that looked fake in pictures—cloudless and endless.

The mountains surrounding it stood like ancient sentinels, their peaks dusted with snow. Trees lined the edge of the lake; bare branches bowed under the weight of winter and its never-ending snow. Not a bird, not a ripple, not a single sound, but the quiet groan of the ice shifting could be heard through the stillness.

There was beauty here—yes—but not the comforting kind. It was the beauty of solitude. The kind that doesn't invite you in so much as dared you to stay. And I stayed.

When I sat down on the ground to put on my ice skates, the cold was more uncomfortable than I expected. I wasn't new to pain. But this was different—sharp and crystalline. The kind of pain that crept in with the wind, and pretended to be clarity yet ended up biting at your skin. My fingers went stiff as I laced up the skates, the material ached against my foot. The chill gnawed at my ankles, at the thin bit of skin where my socks and pants didn't overlap. For a second, the absurdity of the moment had my stomach tightening. I was sitting half frozen by the edge of a lake because I couldn't figure out a better way to stop existing. My breath fogged out in front of me and then drifted sideways, taken by the breeze.

When I finally looked up, I had to squint my eyes for a moment; the sun was so bright as it reflected off the sheen of the ice. The lake spread out in front of me, wide and patient. It was deceptively solid, but I was sure that it was beginning to thaw. I'd done enough research to know when the water below the surface would wake up after its long winter slumber. Not all at once—but just enough to whisper promises of hairline fractures spiderwebbing across the surface like veins under translucent skin, each one a slow exhale from beneath the ice. The kind of thaw that didn't scream danger, just murmured it—soft, seductive, patient.

The ache of shifting ice sounded like bones cracking after sitting too long, almost like they had grown bored. Water moved beneath—just barely—but I could feel it, see it. Lurking and waiting. I'd imagined this moment. The quiet surrender; it would happen without a splash, with no scream—just the ice giving way, opening its arms, and me slipping through. I wouldn't fight it; I wouldn't call out a farewell. I would just let the cold take me whole. I'd float down into the silence where no one could reach me. Where nothing could hurt.

The lake didn't care about cameras. It didn't care about followers or sponsors or the lie of forced bravery. It only offered one thing: danger disguised as peace. Or maybe it was the other way around. And I wanted it. God, I wanted it. It would have been poetically beautiful here today, if I wasn't planning on potentially dying.

I adjusted my GoPro and stepped onto the ice. The first crack sounded like a gunshot beneath my skates. Good. That meant I was doing it right.

I didn't want easy. I didn't want safety. I wanted that line— that razor's edge where life ended, and something else began. I skated slowly, pushing forward as the wind slapped my face, and my breath curled around me in puffs of smoke. The ice groaned in protest, low and guttural like it knew what I was planning. For a while, it was just me and the ice.

My blades sliced into the frozen lake like I'd done this a thousand times before. My breath came out again in more steam trailing behind me as I gathered speed. The air bit at my cheeks, but I welcomed it. It made everything sharper. Realer. The blades hissed across the surface, carving long silver scars into the ice. My lungs burned from the cold; my thighs ached from the movement. It was ironic how alive I always felt right before I tried to tease death into taking me.

There was something reckless about skating on wild ice. Not the smooth, curated kind where you rent skates at a city rink. No, this rink came with no crowds, no railings, no fees; this was just a wide, endless sheet of unpredictable terrain stretched beneath the sky. And it was perfect.

I found myself almost flying across the ice, then skating in circles, then attempting to do a figure eight, then I switched to spirals that made me laugh out loud. Real laughter, the kind that startled me. I twirled until I got dizzy, let my arms fly out like wings; the wind got caught in my coat as if even it wanted to lift me off the surface and hold me in its embrace.

For once, I wasn't staging anything. I had no props, no planned storms or chaos. It was just graceful movement with no destination. I chased my reflection on the ice and for a heartbeat, I forgot. I forgot I was broken. I forgot I had a list. I forgot about the ending I thought I wanted. I was just a man skating across a half-frozen lake, grinning like an idiot, pretending I had nowhere else to be.

If this weren't a ride to my death, I'd have admitted I was having fun. I let myself have a few more twirls before I forced myself to focus. Some spots were thick and solid. Others glittered with thin fractures, fissuring out like they were daring me to test them. So I did. Each push of my skate was a question. Will it hold? Or will it break? I'd researched the weather patterns, the depth, the risks. I knew the weak zones, and I aimed for them anyway.

About twenty feet from the shore, I hit one. The crack was instant, like a whip that echoed against the mountains surrounding me. My leg plunged through the ice, and in a breath, everything changed. The water was hell—pure arctic agony. It clawed at my skin like a thousand needles. I screamed without realizing it. The sound reverberated around me, swallowed by the vastness of nature that didn't care. I didn't move right away. At first, I couldn't. The cold had stolen my ability to think. But then I realized how easy it would be to just let go. To kick out the rest of the ice and slide the other leg in. I'd quickly disappear beneath the surface. I hoped I'd pass out before losing all my air. The idea of knowing I was drowning beneath the prison of ice had my heart hammering against my ribs. My fingers dug into the frozen surface, and my nails scratched at the ice, leaving little half-moons; evidence that I had been here. My heart continued to slam inside of me. I was existing between two realities—above and below. Air and water. Wanting to live and wanting not to.

A voice in my head whispered, *finally,* and another, older, and louder voice pushed back, *not yet.* That muscle memory of survival that hadn't completely decayed within me, twitched.

Just like it had when I held on in the treehouse and when I had swum back to the dock with the jellyfish. My body refused to give in without a fight. Even if that meant fighting me.

I planted my hands onto the freezing cold ice, and with every bit of strength that I had in me, I heaved, forcing my body up and out even as I stopped feeling my leg. The water grew so cold it made my limb fall numb. The broken edges of the ice scraped across my shin as I pulled myself out. I almost lost my grip and slipped but at the last second I heaved again and got my leg out of the water. Like a baby learning to move, I crawled back. Soaking, freezing, my pants started to solidify with ice to my skin.

After what felt like a torturous eternity, I made it to the lake shore and lay flat on the ice where it was still thick and unmoving until the burning in my body dulled to a numb ache. Above me, the sky stayed blue. As if it couldn't give two shits at what had transpired below it.

WHEN I GOT BACK to the cabin I'd rented, I took a one-hour shower, scalding hot, as if I could rid myself of what a loser I was that I hadn't just let go. But that voice in the back of my head reminded me that it had to fully be an accident, or as accidental as skating out on literal thin ice could be. If I were going to help nature along, I could just as easily stick a gun in my mouth. I pretended that my logic made sense and that I wasn't just skirting around the obvious, that maybe I wasn't as brave as I thought. Or maybe I didn't want to die. That last thought scrambled my brain more than I cared to admit.

Begrudgingly, I sent the footage off to Carter. I was almost embarrassed to keep sending these to him. How many fucking times could one man do so many stupid things and still survive? His email pinged back almost immediately.

Did your dick shrink when you hit that water? Careful, my guy, you want to use that thing again.

P.s. I will never unhear you shriek.

P.p.s. You're fucking insane. Thank you for letting me monetize on your trauma.

I laughed even as my leg throbbed. I didn't care about my dick, but he didn't need to know that. I just emailed back.

Glad I can help.

Despite me beating myself up, I uploaded the video. I later found that everyone in the comments was enthralled by my latest episode of stupidity. So much so that I found myself squirming at the extreme fan fair.

"THE SOUND HE MADE WHEN HE FELL IN. SOMEONE AUTO TUNE IT AND TAG ME."

"I SWEAR THAT MAN'S NIPPLES COULD CUT GLASS AFTER THAT."

"IS IT BAD OF ME THAT I GOT HORNY WATCHING HIM CRAWL OUT OF THE HOLE LIKE THAT?"

"AT THIS POINT I THINK DEATH IS GHOSTING HIM. #SAD."

"THIS IS WHAT BRAVERY LOOKS LIKE. I SAID WHAT I SAID."

Chapter Twenty-Three
Session Ten

Die Trying 

@dietrying

20m Subscribers • 22 Videos

 SUBSCRIBE

February 2026

"I want to try something a little different today," Iris told me, as she leaned forward in her chair, her elbows rested on her knees.

I was already slouched deep into the couch like I was trying to melt into it, arms crossed and eyes narrowed. I was pretending I hadn't thrown a massive temper tantrum in here last week. I had tried to push down my shame and embarrassment as I walked in. I had even brought Iris flowers and handed them over with a quick, "Sorry." Her eyes had lit up and she had asked, "For what?" as if she had forgotten all about me yelling at her and smashing a mug against the wall.

"You're not going to make me do breathwork, are you? Because last time I tried to meditate, I ended up obsessing over whether I could choke on air."

The corners of her mouth lifted.

"No breathwork. But I do want to switch things up."

I eyed her suspiciously. "Define 'switch.' Define 'up.'"

"I've been thinking about last week's session," she continued. My stomach lurched uncomfortably. So, she *did* remember.

"We've done a lot of talking, a lot of opening up, and time spent discussing all the world's issues, and I realized—you've done all these extreme things in the last year and a half. Stunts most people would never even think about let alone do. Ironically, you've lived a very full life recently with your escapades, but your circumstances caused you to skip over the middle. The normal."

"The middle," I echoed. "Is that something between electrocution and shark diving, or between ice skating on death traps and elevator surfing?"

She let out a soft laugh. "The middle is what happens between chaos and peace. Between surviving and actually living. You've missed out on the normal stuff. Going grocery shopping. Watching a movie in the theatre and making yourself nauseous from eating too much popcorn. Making dinner. Baking cookies."

"I'm not Julia Child." Excitement that turned into unease gnawed away at me. I shifted in my seat; my shirt suddenly felt two sizes too small.

"You don't have to be. That's kind of the point." She let out a giggle. I sat up straighter but kept my arms crossed protectively against my chest.

"You're seriously suggesting we turn our therapy sessions into a cooking class?"

"I'm suggesting we try something grounded. Not dangerous. Not deep. Just experience something that doesn't get your adrenaline pumping but something you still enjoy. Something... normal." Her voice softened. "It might help more than you think."

"There's nothing you can do that'll change my mind," I reminded her. And yet, even as I said it, I felt something flicker under my ribs. A quiet betrayal of my own words. Something I wished I hadn't noticed. But she noticed. She always did.

"You say that," she murmured, "but your eyes just blinked in Morse code for 'maybe.'"

I stuck my tongue out at her.

Once I agreed to go grocery shopping with her, we left her office and walked side by side to the Whole Foods down the block. The air was cold on my cheeks, and I almost tripped over a pigeon at one point which made her crack up, but we made it to the store in one piece and entered through the automatic doors. The fluorescent lights hit me like a punch to the face. It smelled like smoothies and overripe bananas.

"I hate this already," I muttered.

"We just need five minutes," she assured me, grabbing a cart.

We meandered through aisles, passing a toddler crying over the color of his juice box, a woman trying to hand out samples of flax seed crackers, and a man comparing two brands of toilet paper with intense concentration, as if he wasn't going to just wipe his ass with it.

Iris paused by the shelves of pasta. I had no idea there were so many different kinds, shapes, and colors.

"What's your favorite meal? Let's make that." She looked up at me. I shrugged. "I don't know. I don't really have a favorite meal."

She looked back at me, surprise flooded her expression, a box of curly pasta in her hands. "Really?"

"I mean, I've never really had the chance to find a favorite. When I was young, I ate when there was food offered to me, and it didn't matter what it was. When I grew older, I ate what I could afford, and now I eat whatever is easily available or will be delivered the fastest because I don't care anymore."

The way she looked at me then made me uncomfortable— not in the usual way, but in a softer, quieter way. Like I'd just revealed something deeply personal without meaning to.

"That's... really sad, Danny."

I grabbed the box of spaghetti that she kept eyeing and deposited it into the cart. "Then let's change that. Make me your favorite food and I'll see if it becomes my favorite food."

She beamed at me like I'd said something groundbreaking. I pushed the cart after that and followed her around the store while she bagged vegetables, got some cans and spices, and chattered the whole time. People smiled at us as we passed them in the aisle and when we checked out. People usually barely looked at me when I was out alone but with sunshine and happiness next to me, I suddenly came across as wholesome and someone to smile at. She didn't seem to realize it was happening or that it was different for me, but I did.

Her apartment smelled like vanilla and cedarwood. It was warm and glowing and looked like a Pinterest board had thrown up in here—in the best possible way. Soft throws were over every armrest. Candles flickered on the windowsill. A tea kettle whistled on the stove like it was personally excited we were home.

"You live like a fairy who pays her bills on time," I muttered, staring at a row of tiny potted succulents on the windowsill. I ran a finger over one of them. It tickled me and made me grin.

She laughed. "I like cozy things. They make me feel safe and happy."

I wanted to say that I wouldn't know what that felt like, but I bit it back. I'd already given her enough pieces of me for the day. Iris handed me a cutting board and a red bell pepper. "Let's start with something simple."

I looked at the vegetable like it was a small alien. "You want me to cut this up?"

"Yes."

"What if I chop off my finger and bleed out?"

She gave me a look. "Then you'll get your wish, and I'll have to figure out how to discard your body."

"Woah, Miss Morbid. Calm down."

She giggled as she took the clip out of her hair, and I finally saw it fully down for the first time. It was shiny and rested around her shoulders in soft, dark waves. I wanted to touch it to see what it felt like. I didn't feel worthy of touching her though, so I curled my hand around the handle of the knife and shuffled in place.

She flitted around the kitchen in her white cable knit sweater that almost came to her knees, the black edge of her skirt peeked out from the bottom. I watched from where I stood at the small island as she pushed her glasses up into her hair, and I got a good look at her big eyes and strong brows. The kitchen smelled of garlic and butter, and the longer we cooked side by side the quieter the static in my chest became, like someone was slowly turning down the volume on my ever-present panic.

I didn't think she realized it, but she hummed as she deftly cut up sun dried tomatoes for the sauce of the pasta. She said it was called, "marry me chicken pasta," and then laughed when I got uncomfortable.

"Calm down, Danny, I can say 'marry me' without you acting like I'm proposing to you."

I gave a hollow laugh back and said, "I don't expect anyone would want me like that. I'm too crazy to marry."

Her face clouded and I distracted her by dropping the knife and then moving behind her to go wash it off. I copied her wrist movements and cut a second pepper into big, clumsy pieces which she told me were perfect. I beamed under her praise even though I knew she was lying. Then when I was done mutilating the vegetable and making a mess of the seeds, who knew peppers had so many little seeds in them, she had me make a salad dressing from scratch. Apparently, balsamic vinegar does not taste good on its own, but it was delicious mixed with honey, a little mustard and some oil. Then we pretended to bake cookies from scratch when really, we just peeled pre-made dough from the package and laid them out onto a cookie sheet and popped them in the oven.

She even let me eat a piece of raw cookie dough.

"Don't blame me if you die of salmonella," she warned.

"I'd consider it an honorable death. If I would have known how easy it was to die by cookie dough, I could have saved myself a lot of money in flights and a lot of fucking time," I tossed back. She couldn't help herself and even though I was joking around about death, she threw her head back and laughed. I basked in the glow of it; my skin prickled as she moved behind me, carrying plates to the coffee table in her small living room.

We ate dinner on the couch with mismatched plates on our laps. The food was delicious. She told me my peppers were the best part. I rolled my eyes and told her that this was officially my new favorite food.

"Marry me chicken is perfection," I announced. I caught her eyes watching my lips as I spoke. When my gaze met hers, she looked away and reached for the remote to put on some indie movie I'd never heard of. I didn't really watch it. Instead, I watched her giggle at the silly parts and listened to her talk over the serious ones. I learned that she picked her lip when she was thinking, and she curled her toes under the blanket like a little kid.

There was a moment—just a sliver of time—where I felt... not happy, exactly, but not empty either. Like I could maybe exist in this moment without dragging my thousand-pound past around with me.

The next thing I knew, I was waking up. The light was

different, dim and hazy. A blanket had been pulled over me, and the scent of her lingered in the material around me. Lavender, maybe. And something smoky-sweet.

When I looked up, I found her sitting in the chair across from me, book in hand. She watched me as I stirred.

"You fell asleep."

"I didn't mean to."

"I know."

"I didn't mean to enjoy any of this either," I murmured.

"I know that too."

I sat up, the warmth of the blanket slipped away a little too quickly, almost telling me that this sliver of happiness was complete. My cocoon away from the harsh world was over. I didn't know what to say, so I said nothing.

"You can stay," she offered quietly. But I knew I couldn't, so I stood and pulled on my jacket as I tried to dampen the feelings that were blooming in my chest. Then I thanked her for the life experience and the delicious dinner. She followed me to the door.

As I reached for the handle, she said, "We'll try another one on my new list next time. And maybe a haircut for you?"

I hesitated. "You and your lists."

She shrugged. I ran a hand over my hair.

"I don't like when men touch me. I usually just cut it myself."

"I can do it," she offered quickly, too quickly.

I stared at her. "Is looking good before I die also in the 'I Want to Die' handbook?" I asked, half amused, half undone.

"No," she replied, glancing up at me with a small smile. "I wrote that one myself in the margins."

Chapter Twenty-Four
Tornado

(Uploaded: April 22, 2025. 1 p.m.)

I went to Kansas and waited two weeks for a tornado to show up. I'd been there so long, the hotel clerk stopped asking me if I wanted to extend my stay and just did it for me. Two weeks of flat highways, hotel lobby coffee, and watching the sky like a gambler watching the card dealer. My phone notifications were all weather updates. At least it had given me time to drive around and find a lot of good empty fields that I could set up shop in, so to speak. I had almost given up; the boredom had finally gotten to me, when they announced that a storm was coming. The news warned us it would be a big tornado and that it should be taken seriously; no one should chase it, but I wasn't chasing it, I was waiting for it.

I'd found Kansas to be too flat and too quiet, like the Earth over here was permanently holding its breath, forever waiting, bracing itself for what was to come. But I appreciated how flat the horizon was when I parked my rental car on the edge of a field in the middle of nowhere—miles from the nearest town, with nothing but telephone poles and silos in the distance. I could see everything for miles around me because no hills blocked my view.

I'd upgraded my recording equipment and set it up for the first time on my new tripod with my fancy camera, quite literally drilling it into the ground in hopes that if I didn't make it through this, at least the footage would. I checked the angles twice and then waited some more.

The shift wasn't dramatic at first. It started as a weird thickness in the air, filled with a metallic smell of lightning and wet stone. The birds had vanished; the insects had gone underground. Then the sky went from blue to green in under five minutes. A sickly, haunting shade of green I'd only ever seen in storm documentaries. Then the wind picked up. Grass bent like it was bowing to something larger than itself. The horizon rippled, and the clouds churned with a violence I felt in my bones. It was coming. My hands shook just slightly with that knowledge; my mouth filled with too much saliva, and I had to spit out my nerves.

I left the camera recording and walked further into the field; each step had the wet earth sucking at my boots. The wind whipped my jacket and the gusts felt like they were trying to spin me around. I kept walking. The telephone wires above me thrummed overhead and debris started to fly by. A grocery bag, a cardboard box, something that looked suspiciously like a strip of metal from the bumper of a car. My body wanted me to crouch or run. I was no stranger to this moment. The moment my body vehemently protested what I was doing, but my mind told me to stay. It had happened every single time that I welcomed the inevitable instead of fighting it. While every instinct in me screamed at me to hide, I kept walking. Slow, deliberate; my boots crunched over dried stalks and then more soggy earth. My heart thudded like a drum in my chest. As always, I couldn't tell if I was terrified or thrilled—or if the two had merged and had become the same thing by now. They blurred so closely in my brain and felt so similar that they may as well be.

The air was charged with electricity. Every hair on my body stood up like I was being hunted by something otherworldly and furious. The roar built in the distance, low and growling, like a monster waking up or a freight train barreling toward me with no brakes. And then I saw it. A wall of rotating darkness touched down just beyond the tree line. It spun like a goddamn black hole—pulling the sky into its fist. The tornado.

I stood there. Arms open. Wind screaming in my ears. I screamed back. Just like I did on the bridge. Just like I had in the hurricane. I was surprised I still had anything left inside of me to let out but somehow, I had more feelings built up, and they exploded out into the chaos of Mother Nature.

This time I had no words. Just sounds. Raw and broken animalistic sounds. For every unwelcome touch. The stench of mildew on my thin blanket. Every snicker from my classmates because I smelled. Every broken bone. Every hungry night. The words "Danny boy." Each gust ripped a memory out of me and hurled them into the spinning dark. I let out so many pieces of myself into the wind I could almost see them getting carried away.

The tornado moved with impossible speed, carving a path of annihilation across the fields. It ripped a barn apart like it was made of paper. Metal shingles flew past me like shrapnel. I dropped to my knees and screamed again, so hard it tore at my throat.

I didn't move. I didn't run. But instead of hoping another shingle would fly by and slice my carotid artery, or that a tree would fall and cover my lifeless body under its branches, I found myself enjoying what it felt like to be so close to chaos and live. I vibrated with it. The intensity of the moment. The knowledge that people didn't do what I was currently doing. I was standing here in the face of God's madness and telling him to fuck right off.

The funnel veered—missing me by maybe half a mile—but the outflow of wind hit me hard enough to knock me backward into the mud. I landed flat on my back, choking on dirt, teeth rattling, rain spraying down on me, almost drowning in adrenaline and something close to euphoria. I stayed down for a long time. The roaring of the tornado faded away, the howling wind died down, and the rain eased up, and I just lay there.

Finally, I rolled over to my stomach, retched up some bile, and then stood up. I was shaking, soaked in sweat and rain, and covered in mud. My hair was plastered to my skull. My palms were bleeding from the force of my nails clawing into my skin as I clenched my fists. All around me the field was shredded. A section of fence lay twisted in front of me like a pipe cleaner. One of my tripods had toppled over, but the other one miraculously still stood upright, light blinking. I stumbled toward it, grinning like a lunatic. I gathered everything up, even the broken pieces, and returned to my car without looking back. The smile never faded.

CARTER

Bro. What the actual fuck was that?

DANNY

A field trip.

CARTER

Are you INSANE? You almost got turned into a human lawn dart.

DANNY

But I didn't.

"Die Trying #12: Tornado Season"

"THIS MAN JUST WALKED INTO A TORNADO LIKE IT WAS A SUNDAY STROLL. WHO HURT YOU, DUDE??"

"AS SOMEONE WHO LIVES IN KANSAS... YOU'RE LUCKY TO BE ALIVE. THIS IS NOT A JOKE. THAT EF2 RIPPED THROUGH SO MANY FARMS."

"IS IT WEIRD THAT I CRIED? THERE WAS SOMETHING ABOUT THE WAY HE SCREAMED INTO THE STORM THAT FELT... FREEING."

"THE MAN IS ON HIS 9TH+ LIFE, AND I DON'T THINK HE EVEN WANTS IT."

"HE SAID "YOLO" AND THE TORNADO SAID "BET."

"WAIT... DO WE... DO WE NEED TO CALL SOMEONE? LIKE A HOTLINE OR NASA OR SOMETHING?"

"NOT THE WAY THE WIND WRAPPED AROUND HIM LIKE IT KNEW HIM. THIS BROKE ME."

Chapter Twenty-Five
Session Eleven

Die Trying 

@dietrying

20m Subscribers · 22 Videos

 SUBSCRIBE

March 2026

Iris had texted me the night before telling me not to come to her office, that she would be coming to me. I'd asked why but she hadn't responded. I busied myself for the majority of the morning cleaning my apartment and showering. I'd even put on my shirt the right way, double checking that the tag was in its proper place, before she showed up at my door holding scissors in one hand and a grocery bag in the other like this was a totally normal thing for a life coach to do.

"I told you I'd cut your hair," she said as I looked pointedly at the scissors, stepping inside without waiting for an invitation. "You're beginning to look like a sad rockstar who gave up halfway through the tour."

"How sweet," I muttered, shutting the door behind her.

She set the bag down on my coffee table and pulled out a black barber cape. "Sit."

I obeyed, settling onto the old wooden chair that creaked beneath me. She stood behind me; her fingers skimmed the back of my neck as she adjusted the cape, and goosebumps sprung up on my skin like my body hadn't gotten the memo that I was supposed to remain chill and unaffected. She ran a comb through my hair with surprising gentleness. I tried to ignore how good it felt. She brushed it, sprayed it with some water, and then used an electric clipper to tidy the edges and sides. Once she was satisfied with what she saw, she took out the sharp, silver scissors and got to work. The snip of the scissors echoed louder than it should have in little gasps of metal and air. A mess of my hair littered the black cape that I had tied around my neck. It tickled my neck, and I fought the need to reach up and scratch. As she moved around me, I caught the scent of her shampoo—it was floral and fresh; nothing like the chemical scent of the cheap shampoo that I used. Once she finished cutting the back, she moved around to stand in front of me. She was suddenly too close. I stared ahead, pretending that the wall behind her was more interesting than the fact that her body was just mere inches from my face. I hated that I noticed it. But no more than I hated that I didn't want her to move away.

Her chest brushed my arm, and something in my brain short-circuited. My body reacted instinctively, uninvited, unwelcome, but real. I froze. Not now. Not for her. Not again. But I didn't panic this time. I didn't shove her away. I just clenched my fists and stared at the scuffed floor while she kept cutting, oblivious—or pretending she hadn't heard the hitch in my inhale or noticed that my pulse pounded in my neck.

When she finally stepped back, I let out a breath.

"All done," she said. "You look... surprisingly decent."

"I'll try not to let it go to my head."

She laughed and held up a mirror. I hesitated. I didn't look at myself much, what was the point? Looking in the mirror was like shaking hands with a stranger I'd never wanted to meet. My reflection couldn't lie—it was a mashup of the people who made me and left me. My birth mother's cheekbones, my father's tired eyes and his strong jaw. The way my mouth curled in that slight, traitorous lift it always did—like I was seconds from a laugh that I didn't feel. But I didn't want to hurt her feelings, so I looked in the mirror. My hair was neat for once. My eyes weren't hollow. The lift around my mouth was almost believable, like the beginning of a real smile. For a second I didn't look like a man planning his exit; I looked like a man who had somewhere to be tomorrow. I looked up to find that she was watching me.

"I like it."

She grinned. And then simply to piss her off I said, "It's a good haircut to die in."

She hit my shoulder playfully. It was the first time I hadn't meant it. I wasn't dying. Not today.

After she cleaned up and warmed up the lunch she brought for us, I told her that I had started watching Friends. She gasped like I'd confessed to a felony. "What season are you up to?"

"Two."

"Wait till season five. It's the best."

We ate lunch on paper plates because I didn't own anything nicer. We watched two more episodes while sitting on my couch. I found half the jokes to be too corny for my dark humor, but Iris found all of them to be funny, and I found her joy to be infectious. She laughed with her whole body; her shoulders shook, and she pressed a hand to her stomach. It was the closest thing I'd ever had to a date. Except it wasn't a date. Obviously. But it was what normal people did. They ate burritos, sat a tiny bit too close to each other on the couch, while watching a sitcom and didn't feel like the walls were closing in on them. A normal person probably didn't analyze every single breath he took or notice how cute her feet looked in her plain white socks, but it was a start.

When Iris finally stood to leave, I walked her to the door because it felt wrong not to. She wrapped her scarf around her neck and smiled at me like she always did—like she saw something in me that I didn't. I wanted to say something, but the words got stuck in my throat. My chest ached with the knowledge that she wouldn't give up on showing me the softer side of life. I didn't know how to hold it.

"Don't forget to water the plants," she told me as she disappeared down the hall.

"What plants?"

But she was already gone.

When I came back in, confused, I found that she had left three tiny succulents in mismatched ceramic pots on my counter, a throw blanket—gray and soft—draped over the back of my couch, and a small wooden tray bearing three vials of essential oils. Lavender. Bergamot. Peppermint.

I stared at the setup like it had materialized out of thin air. Like her kindness was a trick of the light. And I guessed it kind of was. The blanket was softer than anything I'd ever owned. I ran my fingers over it and then texted a picture of it to Carter before wrapping it around my shoulders. I uncapped each bottle of oil, sniffing them, almost overwhelming my senses with the strong scents.

DANNY

Is this normal?

DANNY

Or should I fire her? It's weird right?

CARTER

Bro. DO NOT screw this up.

CARTER

This is some rom-com level shit.

CARTER

PLANTS, Danny. She left you PLANTS. That's a declaration of love.

I stared at the text for a long time.

Then I watered the succulents. I needed to keep them alive. They were relying on me.

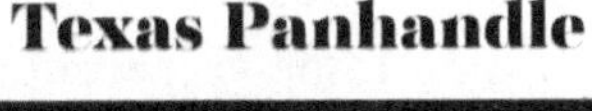

Chapter Twenty-Six
Texas Panhandle

Die Trying ✓

@dietrying

20m Subscribers · 22 Videos

🔔  SUBSCRIBE  👍

(Uploaded: May 3, 2025. 6:05 p.m.)

I hadn't intended on trying my luck with yet another weather event, but the news promised a lightning storm, and I couldn't stop myself. The sky in Texas had been brewing something electric all afternoon. The clouds had a mood to them— low, brooding and thick with the promise of violence. I chased them West in my rental car, a rusted-up Chevy with a bad tire and worse brakes, watching the clouds swell across the horizon like a fresh bruise. I figured if the lightning didn't get me maybe a car crash would. Either way, I wouldn't complain.

I parked on the side of the road somewhere near Amarillo. When I got out of the car, I walked into a field of dry grass that came up to my knees. I left the car door open as if I'd be right back. I confused myself because wasn't the point to *not* come back? But I chose not to get too caught up in that because all around me the air buzzed. The humid static wrapped itself along my arms like a second skin. Everything smelled like ozone and adrenaline. It felt like something big was coming.

The storm didn't just arrive; it assembled. Like an army ready to take on its counterpart. Lightning split the clouds open and tore across the sky like a net of fire. It had started as a gentle flicker, then another, and then it began to look like someone was playing with magic up there. Each flash cast my shadow against the ground, and each time I hoped it would be the last thing I ever saw. Thunder cracked around me in delayed fury. The storm hadn't started with rain; it was almost eerie to stand out here with just the sound of thunder crackling and lightning flashing across the sky. Gusts of wind kicked up out of nowhere, slapping my face with sharp dirt and wet heat.

When the first bolt hit a tree a few fields over, I flinched, but I didn't move. This was what I had come for. The wind whipped across the open field like it had teeth, biting at my skin. I took my shoes off and chased the storm barefoot through the grass, wet blades sliced at my ankles. The sky pulsed above me like it was alive—furious and breathing. Lightning forked across the clouds in rapid succession, illuminating the world in stark white flashes. Each bolt struck somewhere in the distance like the sky was marking targets. The air crackled with static, buzzing beneath my skin like a live wire had threaded itself through my veins. I ran toward the sound of it, toward the thunder that rolled like a voice I thought I'd heard before. "Come on," I whispered, breathless, "I'm right here." If this was judgment day, I wanted a front row seat.

A bolt hit a telephone pole less than thirty feet away, and the explosion of light and sound stopped my heart for half a second. It was like God had gotten distracted with his show and missed, forgetting to kill me. The air shattered around me and my ears rang from the explosion. Something came flying through the air and hit me. My chest throbbed from the impact, but I was still standing. Still breathing. Still me. I dropped to my knees in the wet grass and laughed—hysterical, wrecked, and alive. Not because it was funny, but because it was beautiful. Because at that moment, I wasn't thinking about dying. I was feeling—really feeling—everything. Fear. Wonder. Rage. Awe. The kind of wonder they say children have before they realized the world was cruel. The kind of wonder I had lost early on. The kind of awe that makes you want to believe in something, anything, even if it's just in a sky that keeps refusing to take you home.

I stood there, arms out; my body trembled but remained upright, defiant. I knew it wasn't taking me today. I'd accepted that. So, I stayed for the beauty. I stayed for the experience.

The wind knocked me back, and I stumbled to the ground, gravel embedded in my palms. I watched the lightning pass over me from where I sat in a praying form on my knees. It left the sky cracked open, looking exhausted. Storms were selfish that way; they came, wreaked havoc, and then left without so much as an apology. The rain finally bothered to show up, and warm, fat raindrops began to fall, soaking me.

I walked back to where I had left my camera and began to pack up my equipment. I found myself looking forward to watching the footage back. For the beauty of it and the experience versus trying to find the moment the gates of heaven had said no to me. I was fluid and loose in my movements as I broke down my tripod, feeling at ease with existing for once.

Then, from behind me came a voice, too close to just be my imagination. "Hey."

I spun, blinking rain out of my eyes. A girl—maybe in her late twenties, dark hair soaked to her scalp—stood behind me in a yellow poncho, gripping her phone. "I saw your car. I thought maybe you got stuck."

I didn't answer. She stepped closer. "You were just... standing in it. Why?"

I shrugged. "Why not?"

She squinted at me. Taking in my bare feet and my camera

equipment. Then she walked even closer to stand near me. Close, but not too close.

"You okay?"

"Are you?" I volleyed back. She laughed.

"Funny you should ask 'cause I almost wasn't. I had thought about ending it. This morning. I almost... you know. But something about this storm... It's—it's stupid, but being out here, watching the sky throw a tantrum, made me feel like maybe I'm not the only thing falling apart, and that maybe I'll be okay."

We stood in silence for a few seconds. The gravity of what she had just said weighed heavily on me. On one hand, I wondered why she would tell a stranger that, and on the other hand, I recognized the moment of no longer giving a fuck of what anyone thought because tomorrow it might not matter.

"You changed your mind?" I finally asked.

"Maybe not for forever. But for today, yeah."

"Yeah," I said. "I get that."

We let her words sit there, rain pouring down our faces. We didn't ask for more details. Didn't put words to the questions we probably both had. Her wondering why I was out here in a dangerous lightning storm, me wondering how she would have done it if she had gone through with it. We didn't need to. We were just two idiots who had gone out today looking for different kinds of endings and wound up here with an odd kind of beginning instead.

She hugged her arms around her, puffing out the yellow plastic of her poncho and we continued to stand there, on the steaming grass, dripping wet. The storm still flashed off in the distance. Her face was pale, all sharp angles and deep-set eyes. But they didn't look hopeless, at least not to me; she still had fight left in her. I could see it. I wondered if she knew.

We didn't exchange names. She still didn't ask about the camera although I saw her look at it multiple times as I put it into the trunk of the car. Eventually, she stepped away. "Take care of yourself, okay?"

I nodded. "Yeah. You too."

She walked down the road, and I watched her until she became a yellow dot on the horizon. Then I got into the car and left.

The drive back felt different. The storm had broken apart, and the sun shone through the tears in the clouds. I still had the windshield wipers on, and they squealed across the glass just making the mud splatter worse. Her words, *for today*, kept replaying in my head. Like remaining alive was an agreement you signed one day at a time.

I came across a gas station, and I got out to pump some gas and buy myself chocolate milk. I stood there soaking wet, adrenaline still alive in my veins. I wondered if I'd see her yellow poncho in my dreams tonight or if I'd be plagued by my usual nightmares. When the pump indicated that my tank was full, I got back in my car and drove off. I forgot the chocolate milk.

"THIS IS SOME GOD-LEVEL CINEMATOGRAPHY. TERRIFYING AND BEAUTIFUL."

"NO WAY THIS GUY MADE IT THROUGH THAT UNTOUCHED."

"I FEEL LIKE HE'S NOT CHASING STORMS—HE'S CHASING SOMETHING INSIDE HIMSELF."

"I NEEDED TO SEE THIS TODAY. THANK YOU."

March 2026

The time between sessions had never dragged before. I always had plenty of bullshit to keep myself busy with. For someone who already had one foot out the door, so to speak, I certainly had time on my hands, but I always found things to do. But since my haircut last week, I couldn't stop wishing, hoping, willing time to move a little bit faster.

I was looking forward to seeing her and that knowledge sat there in the pit of my stomach all week, churning and reminding me of how foreign a feeling it was. I found myself staring at the time on my phone more than usual. Wondering what she was doing. If she'd worn that big hoodie of hers again or if she was baking something in her cozy little kitchen.

I kept admiring my haircut. The sides were crisp. I could see the clean taper in the mirror when I tilted my head just right. She'd done a good job. Too good. I ruffled it slightly with my hand to mess it up and walked away before I could start staring at my face again.

I had slept under that stupid blanket she had left me. I loved it. And I kept moving the plants around, trying to find the perfect spot for them to bask in whatever sunlight the crisp March weather had to offer. It was pretty ridiculous, but I couldn't stop myself.

Wednesday finally crawled around, and a text pinged on my phone at 2:03 p.m. Fifty-seven minutes before our next session was scheduled to start.

IRIS

Meet me at the theater. We're watching a movie. I'm buying you popcorn. Don't be late or I'll eat it all on my own.

I stared at her message for a minute, mildly annoyed at the late notice, and also... weirdly pleased. We were going to watch a movie. Yet another thing I had missed out on during my childhood. By the time I had the money and the time to go to the theater by myself, I had lost interest and had just never gone. This was not a date I reminded my brain. This was just Iris doing her normal life-immersion therapy crap again.

Despite all my confusing feelings and resistance to her non-therapy methods, I showed up. I wore a sweater over my shitty t-shirt, and I even brushed my hair. Fuck, she was getting to me.

As I walked in, I spotted her standing just outside the entrance, her coat half-open over a soft green sweater, and a huge tub of popcorn already tucked under her arm. She smiled when she saw me, the kind that crept up slowly and took over her whole face.

"You're early," she noted, handing me a soda.

"You threatened to steal my popcorn. That's psychological warfare."

She laughed. "Fair."

We picked seats in the back row—her choice, not mine. The seats were way fancier than I had imagined they'd be. Little buttons let you recline, so your feet were up, and your body was relaxed back. She helped me figure out the buttons, set my chair exactly how I wanted, and shone the flashlight on her phone once the room grew dark so I could see where to stick my soda. My entire body was acutely aware of her presence beside me. I felt the heat of her arm resting near mine. Heard the way she licked popcorn salt from her fingers. At one point, our fingers touched as we both went in to grab more popcorn at the same time. Neither of us moved. It was too dangerous for me to acknowledge her touch. Dangerous in a subtle, silent yet still meaningful kind of way.

The movie was fine, but forgettable. I couldn't have told you what it was about if my life depended on it. All I could think about was how close her leg was to mine. How her laugh hit a little too hard during the funny parts. How she hadn't looked away when she caught me looking at her.

When the lights came up, she blinked slowly and turned to me. "Thoughts?"

"I like these seats. That's my only thought."

"Put it on your list of things to buy," she teased.

"What am I gonna do with a theater seat in my apartment?"

"Anything you want." Her eyes gleamed in the darkness as I followed her out of the theater. My imagination conjured up all sorts of things one could do in a theater chair, and I flushed as my mind went to a place it usually never did. I wondered, wryly, what would Iris think of me if I put *that* life experience on my list. Would it make her blush? I wanted to make her blush again so much that I felt a blush of my own stain my cheeks.

As we walked out, the city met us with its usual chaos. Horns blared. People walked around us without looking up from their phones. It wasn't pretty or calming, but it was New York, and it was perfect. It was always the one thing I never hated about my life. I figured if there was any place where my traumatized self fit in, it was right here.

A man walked by a little too closely to us and bumped into Iris, jostling her roughly while she dug around in her purse for something.

"Excuse me," she said, not unkindly—just startled.

"Maybe look where you're going, sweetheart," he said back, mocking her. It was the word sweetheart that activated me. He said it with the same slick tone that my foster father had used when he spoke to waitresses. It was a slimy form of disrespect that made my skin crawl.

"Back the fuck up." I was in his face before I even realized what I was doing. My fists were clenched at my side. He sized me up. I was taller than him, but not by much. For a split second I wanted him to swing first so I could have a reason to let all my buttoned-up rage spill out. My vision tunneled and all I saw was Iris's eyes widening when she heard him call her something that sounded a lot like 'fucking bitch.'

"What did you just say?" I got even closer to him. "Say it again."

His gaze flicked to Iris, then back to me. "Whatever, man. She ain't worth it."

I stepped even closer. "She's worth a hell of a lot more than ten of you."

There was a beat where the guy considered saying or doing something else, but he must've seen it in my eyes, the fact that I didn't care what happened to me, which meant I'd just keep going. Like a pitbull. He backed off with a sneer and disappeared into the crowd. I turned around, heart pounding, jaw tense, adrenaline winding up my spine. Iris touched my arm gently.

"Are you okay?" I asked, my voice sharper than I intended. She nodded slowly.

"Yeah. Are you?"

I looked away. "I was gonna hit him for you," I said finally.

Her hand rested on my arm again. We walked in silence for a while. She didn't say thank you. I didn't say sorry. But something shifted in the space between us. Something fragile and a little terrifying.

And for once, I didn't want to run from it.

She tugged her coat tighter as we walked; the air had grown a little awkward as the tension from earlier dissipated and all that was left was everything we hadn't said. I cleared my throat.

"I'll walk you home." I tried not to sound like it meant anything, but she smiled anyway, like she was on to me. We didn't talk much on the way; our steps echoed on the pavement, and we tossed a few jokes out to fill the quiet. Every so often her shoulder brushed my arm, and it made me imagine turning the corner and walking straight into her apartment again. Into that warm air that, tonight, smelled like cloves and citrus and live plants. Into the soft light and colorful rugs and the faint sound of music playing from another room. Into her. Not physically. Just... into whatever made her make me feel like this. But of course, I didn't. At the door, she thanked me. I shrugged.

"It was no big deal."

She made a noise in the back of her throat as if to say, *sure it wasn't, Danny. Keep lying to yourself.* But instead, she just turned the key and stepped inside. The golden glow from her apartment flooded the hallway, and something in my chest ached. She waved and then shut the door. I stared at the closed door for a second too long, harping on the bruised emotion in my chest. Then I turned away, reminding myself that I had an expiration date.

Chapter Twenty-Eight

Electric Fence

(Uploaded: June 15, 2025. 2:35 a.m.)

There wasn't a private property sign. No gate, no chain, no barking dog to keep me out. Just the blue sky and open land and a fence that hummed with a painful promise.

I'd walked a mile off the gravel road; my feet crunched over half-dry corn husks and soft dirt, feeling more like a ghost than a trespasser. I hadn't even checked for security cameras to see if anyone could be watching. That was the point, wasn't it? If someone stopped me, maybe I'd get what I'd come for. If they didn't... well, maybe the fence would do it.

I found it along the far edge of the field. It was all metal posts and thin wires, a livestock fence, probably running with a decent jolt to keep cattle in and coyotes out. I could hear it buzzing faintly, sounding like a rattlesnake was curled up nearby. I stared at the wire. It didn't look dangerous. In fact, it kind of looked like it would do nothing. But it was like all the other invisible things that could kill you quietly. Depression. Radiation. Love.

I didn't let myself overthink it or stand there for too long romanticizing my intent. I simply reached out and touched it. The jolt slammed through my body. My jaw snapped shut so hard my teeth rattled. I didn't scream, not at first; I couldn't inflate my lungs even if I had wanted to. My muscles locked up and for a split second my heart forgot how to beat. My body seized and I staggered backward as I slammed into the ground hard, eyes wide and blinking at the sky, every nerve ending twitched.

And then I laughed. I laughed because it hurt. I laughed because it didn't kill me. I laughed because I was still alone in the middle of nowhere, hoping something would take me out, and all I got was a new reason to pee weird for the next three days. I lay there for a while, dirt pressed into my cheek, heart thudding in my ears. The burn on my hand throbbed like it had its own pulse. The smell of my own singed skin filled my nostrils. A bird screamed overhead. My lungs ached when they finally remembered how to drag in air.

Then I heard the truck, but still, I didn't move. I figured if someone shot me for trespassing, at least I'd finally get some sleep. The engine slowed, then cut. I heard boots hit gravel. And then came a voice—low, male and cautious.

"You alright there, boy?"

I wasn't a boy. I was supposed to be a grown ass man, but I figured even though my age said I was in my thirties, my stolen childhood and good genes had me looking like I was twenty-four, max. I rolled onto my side. He stood over me like I was a stray dog that had wandered by. He didn't seem angry, or curious; he seemed oddly resigned to find me here.

"Define alright."

He squinted as I looked him over. He was likely in his mid-fifties, with a farmer's tan, a weather-lined face, and faded jeans. Maybe he was a rancher. Or maybe he was just a guy who'd seen too much weird shit in his life, and it had put that permanent scowl on his face.

"That's my fence," he said, confirming that he was in fact the owner of this property. "You, uh... you touch it?"

I held up my singed fingers. "I did. Yeah."

He exhaled through his nose. "You tryin' to die or somethin'?"

I didn't answer. We sat there together quietly while he called the police.

THE HOSPITAL WAS quiet in a suffocating kind of way. I didn't remember much of the drive there. All I could recall was getting pulled up off the dirt and someone inquiring if I could walk. A paramedic had checked my pulse and asked if I'd taken anything. I'd said, "Just voltage." No one had laughed.

They wheeled me in through a back entrance. The smell of antiseptic hit me first, sharp and sterile, like someone had been trying too hard to erase everything that happened here. The paperwork came next. A nurse behind a plastic window slid forms toward me like whatever form of mental illness I had was contagious. She didn't make eye contact with me. In fact, no one did.

I left the emergency contact line blank. They took my shoelaces, my phone, my bag, my cameras and my sense of control. Then they walked me into a room that was somehow both over-lit and dim at the same time. It boasted of beige walls, beige tiled floors, and windows that didn't open. Everything was padded without looking padded. It was all built to contain.

I was suddenly hyper aware of how alive my skin felt. How loud my heartbeat was. How empty my pockets were. Then I was asked if I wanted to hurt myself by a nurse with a flower print on her scrubs. I didn't say yes. I didn't say no either. Which apparently was the fast pass to a quick twenty-four-hour hold.

The nurse had a voice too soft for this kind of place. She gave me a pair of gray hospital socks and told me dinner would be at six. I didn't ask what was on the menu. I wasn't hungry.

The other patients drifted through the common area like ghosts—slow and half-asleep. One guy rocked back and forth in a chair by the TV, mouthing the words to a show with no sound. A woman stood in the hallway scratching at her wrist like she was trying to peel something invisible off. Another man, maybe my age, maybe younger, was pacing in circles near the window. He looked at me and smiled like he recognized me, but not from anywhere good.

"You new?" he asked.

"Guess so."

"They ever tell you the real reason they watch us sleep?"

I didn't respond.

"'Cause the moment you stop twitchin'," he whispered, "they know it worked." I kept an eye on him for the rest of my time there.

The intake evaluation happened three hours after I got there. With a social worker named Gina—mid-forties, with kind eyes and wearing a cardigan that didn't match her skirt. She looked exhausted but earnest. The kind of woman who probably kept protein bars in her purse for emergencies. The kind who still believed in her job, even after years of watching people break under the fluorescent lights.

She sat down across from me with a notepad and a hopeful smile.

"I'm just here to talk," she said.

That's what they all said.

"Can you walk me through what happened today?"

I shrugged. "I touched an electric fence."

"Why?"

"Curiosity."

"Was it painful?"

"Yeah. That's how I knew I'd done it right."

Her pen's movements faltered.

"Danny," she said, voice low, "did you want to hurt yourself?" How many people were going to ask me that and why did they suddenly care when they hadn't cared about me before I touched it?

"I didn't not want to."

"Do you want to die?"

I looked at her. Really looked. She had crow's feet around her eyes and soft wrinkles around her mouth, likely from smiling so often. She was probably someone's mom. Or someone's daughter. Or both. I wanted to tell her everything. I wanted to say I'd written a suicide letter, but I'm not dead yet. That I've stood under lightning and tried to feed myself to predators, and not once did it feel like enough. That the world kept spinning and I kept filming, and no one seemed to notice that the guy behind the camera didn't want to be here. I wanted to tell her that sometimes I did want to live—for maybe three seconds at a time—but it never lasted. I wanted to say, 'help me'. But then I remembered Zoloft. I thought about how it had flattened me. How it had made the pain go away by taking everything else with it. How I couldn't cry, or laugh, or even get mad. How I had just been left with the dull hum of not caring that felt worse than sadness. It had felt like being buried alive.

I remembered how my body still breathed, still ate, still existed—but my soul had checked out. Like I had been watching my life through a fogged-up window that I couldn't wipe clean. I remembered staring at my reflection and not seeing anyone I recognized. So instead, I smiled, big, and showed my teeth.

"I'm happy," I said. "I've never been better."

She didn't smile back, but the corner of her mouth twitched.

"Okay, Danny. We'll monitor you overnight. If everything stays stable, we'll discharge you in the morning."

"Looking forward to it."

I wasn't.

That night, I lay on the stiff mattress with my arms crossed over my chest and my eyes open. The ceiling had hairline cracks that ran like rivers, just like back at home. All the sad places seemed to come with ceiling cracks. The room was too warm; my socks itched my toes. But for the first time in a long time, no one expected anything from me, not even myself. No one was waiting for me to post content. No one was monetizing my likes or analyzing my tone. No one needed me to perform. It was terrifying. Because without all that... I no longer knew who the fuck I was.

The next morning when they let me go, I signed a paper that said I wouldn't harm myself or others and promised to follow up with a mental health professional in my area. I put down the name Dr. G. Nomad and an address in California that I made up on the spot. I didn't live in California, but they didn't know that.

They gave me back my bag and my phone and wished me well. No one stopped me when I walked out through the automatic doors and into the fading Iowa sunlight. I sat on the curb outside the building and watched a moth bash itself against the glass surrounding a single light bulb repeatedly like it had something to prove.

My phone buzzed. Fourteen missed texts. Six voicemails. Carter. I opened the most recent one.

CARTER

> Where the fuck are you man? I'm getting
> worried. Really worried, you crazy
> motherfucker.

I stared at his message for a long time. Then I opened the camera footage.

The clip was shaky, short, and honestly pretty boring. Just a guy walking through a field, touching a wire, and collapsing like a sack of meat. I think I might have peed myself. I would have leaned down to sniff the front of my jeans to confirm if I had or not, but I didn't want to get locked up again for crazy behavior, so I didn't.

But the video was real. It didn't need any edits or background music. The element of raw human stupidity and hope in its purest form was enough. I didn't even send it to Carter to edit. I just uploaded it in the parking lot of the psych ward.

I titled it: ME AND AN ELECTRIC FENCE

Caption: Ever wanted to know what electrocution tastes like? Iowa. It tastes like Iowa.

It got four point two million views in one day.

Someone commented:

EVEN THE COWS KNOW NOT TO DO THAT.

I didn't respond.

THE NEXT NIGHT I lay in a roadside motel bed with bad sheets and worse lighting, and I watched another moth. It too was bashing itself against the light bulb like it couldn't help wanting the thing that could ultimately destroy it. I thought about how quiet the psych ward had been. How the nurse called me "honey" and the walls made me feel even smaller than I already did. And I thought about that question again. Do you want to die? I knew this: I'd rather die on fire than live cold. That's why I walked into fields. That's why I touched fences. That's why I didn't tell the nurse the truth. Because I was afraid they'd save me the wrong way.

Die Trying 

@dietrying

20m Subscribers · 22 Videos

 SUBSCRIBE

March 2026

Iris decided the next life experience I had missed out on was the zoo. Which is how I found myself walking around the zoo with her, admiring all of the animals. I didn't even ponder how I could get myself into the lion pen. Which was a huge missed opportunity, but not one I would take in front of Iris. Not one I wanted to take today at all, if I was being honest with myself. I was having too much fun. Usually a place like this, that smelled of hay and day-old popcorn, that buzzed with a constant undertone of noise, would've been a place I'd hate to find myself but with Iris next to me, I found that I didn't. I hadn't known I was capable of smiling without forcing it, but there I was—grinning like an idiot while a baby goat with sideways eyes and milk breath tried to chew on my sleeve, pulling at the material with steady determination.

"I think he likes you," Iris said, holding up her phone. "Smile again."

"No."

"Too late." She'd taken a photo.

"You're violating my rights to privacy."

"You're building a core memory. Shut up and let me document it."

She wasn't joking. Not really. But she said it with that warm, teasing lilt—like everything else out of her mouth. It was as if her words were dipped in honey and wrapped in bubble wrap. Safe and ridiculous. It was the kind of tone you only use with people you cared about. I tried not to ponder why that made my heart feel funny. The goat next to me bleated. I scratched its head without thinking. Its ears twitched. It was stupid how much I liked it.

We walked around the petting zoo enclosure slowly. Peacocks screamed somewhere in the distance. Kids with juice mustaches and dirty hands ran past holding maps of the zoo upside down. Iris pointed at animals I hadn't cared about until just now. I made deadpan commentary to make her laugh. Her plan by taking me to the zoo had worked. Something in my chest had gone... soft. Iris handed me a little paper cup of pellets. "Try it."

"You try it."

She raised an eyebrow. "I already did. Twice. One bit me. It's your turn."

Reluctantly, I knelt. A trio of baby goats trotted over like they'd been waiting for me all day. One nuzzled my hand. Another butted my arm with its head. And just like that, I was six years old again—or maybe not quite six, because I never got to do this as a kid. I never went to petting zoos. I never had anyone hold up a phone to record me while I did something soft and safe and innocent. So yeah. I liked it. Too much. Something giddy grew behind my ribs, and I physically rubbed at it, trying to will it away.

"They like you," she said again, but softer this time. Like it meant something more than it had moments ago, like she could read my mind and see what was happening inside of me. I looked up. Her phone was still in her hand, but she wasn't filming anymore.

"What?" I asked, trying to make sense of the look on her face. She gave a tiny shake of her head, smiling to herself.

"Nothing."

"No. Say it."

She hesitated, then crouched beside me, tugging her jacket around her a little bit tighter. "You're not who you think you are."

"That sounds ominous."

"I just mean... you keep calling yourself broken and unsavable but look at you. You're out in the world. You're feeding goats. You're laughing."

"Because they're goats. And because that one's trying to eat your scarf."

She looked down. The goat in question bleated in protest as she laughed and gently pulled her scarf away.

"I'm serious, Danny."

I looked away. The sun was cutting through the clouds, casting a golden hue over the goats, almost making them look fake. Like tiny, illustrated animals chewing hay.

"I don't know how to be anyone else other than what I've always been," I said. I worried I was disappointing her. She had so much hope for me. And I had none at all.

"But I think you already are," she protested. I didn't say anything back. She stood and brushed hay off her jacket. I followed, dropping the empty pellet cup into the garbage can. As we walked toward the exit, I shoved my hands into my pockets and tried to ground myself. I focused on the cool breeze, the faint smell of manure, and the overpriced hot pretzels.

"You ever think about that?" she asked. I startled; I hadn't been listening.

"About all the goat poop that is on the bottom of my shoes?"

She nudged me. "About healing your inner child."

I stopped walking. "Don't say that."

"What?"

"Inner child."

She laughed. "Why not?"

"I told Carter if you ever said something like that, I'd have to quit."

Her smile finally faded slightly. "Would you really?"

"Hell yea. I'll stop answering your calls and never come back," I joked. Iris glanced at me, hurt clear on her face. The octave of her voice dipped just slightly.

"You wouldn't do that to me. I'd miss you."

There it was. That thing. That moment when the air changed and everything suddenly felt too loud, even though no one was currently speaking. Her words weren't dramatic or even flirty. But they were earnest and soft, and they hit something I didn't know was exposed inside of me. Something I hadn't known I still possessed. I looked at her. She was still walking, still pretending like she hadn't just shifted the gravity between us.

"Iris..."

"I know," she said quickly. "I shouldn't have said that. It was unprofessional—forget it."

"No. You said it."

"I say a lot of things."

I let it go and we kept walking. The tension between us stretched like a taut thread. A squirrel darted across the path in front of us, pulling me from my confused haze.

"I don't think I've ever had anyone say they'd miss me," I said, quietly, putting it out there.

"Then I'm glad I said it." Her words floated over to me, but she didn't look at me again.

We didn't talk much after that. The weight of today settled

between us in a way that I was comfortable ignoring but couldn't fully shake. We got warm drinks from a cart near the exit. Hers was tea, of course. She added too much honey. I pretended not to notice her watching me blow on mine before sipping.

"You're not gonna mention the goat video in next week's session, are you?" I asked, using humor to take my mind off how buttery sweet her words had felt on my brain and to make her talk to me again.

"No promises."

"I'll sue."

"Go ahead. I'll show the judge the video and win custody of your inner child."

"Jesus Christ, you're crazy."

She laughed—head back, real and bright. She was so beautiful it twisted something inside of me. And somehow knowing I had made her happy, even if just for a brief moment, hurt more than it should've because it made me worry what would happen to her when I was gone. When I was finally free of all my feelings, what kind of pain would I leave in my wake? I had never had any reason to consider that before. But now I couldn't shake the feeling like I had found one.

When we finally finished our drinks and said goodbye, Iris walked toward the subway entrance with one last look over her shoulder. I stood on the sidewalk longer than I needed to, just to watch her vanish into the belly of the city. I didn't want to go home. I didn't want to go anywhere. I wanted to bottle up this day so I could open it back up when I couldn't feel anything else and needed a reminder of something cute like a baby goat. That was the thing about core memories. You never realized you were making one until after the experience was done.

Chapter Thirty

Antenna Tower

Die Trying 

@dietrying

20m Subscribers · 22 Videos

 SUBSCRIBE

(Uploaded: July 25, 2025. 12:01 a.m.)

I didn't wake up wanting to die that day. Which was weird. Unsettling, even. Like waking up and finding your bed on the ceiling. Today I just felt the need to be high up. That's how I ended up sitting on top of a rusted antenna tower in the middle of nowhere, nine hundred feet in the air, with a turkey sandwich, and a crossword puzzle. Probably not exactly the kind of video my subscribers had in mind when they followed Die Trying, but I recorded it anyway.

The tower rose out of the field like a forgotten skeleton; each rung of its ladder corroded and flaking. There was a metallic smell in the air and as I gripped each rung, my hands came away sticky and covered in rust residue. The climb was easy. Too easy. The kind of ease that made it feel like I was cheating. There was no wind, no loose bolts, not even any adrenaline, unless I looked down. I tried not to do that. I climbed rung after rung after rung until the sky swallowed the land and the ground stopped looking like anything real. The air grew colder as I climbed. I filmed it, hoping they could hear more than just my heavy breathing in the background.

The platform at the top was barely big enough for me to sit cross-legged on. I anchored myself against the inner rails by bracing my boots against them. The metal was warm from the sun, and it smelled faintly of rain, even though it hadn't rained all day. A single red light blinked slowly beside me—probably warning planes not to crash into it. I liked the idea of something else being up here with me, even if it was just a light. I pulled out the sandwich first. Warm from my backpack. It didn't do much to make the dry bread, cheese and turkey with too much mayo taste better, but it didn't matter, I ate it anyway.

Then I took out the crossword. One of those little dollar booklets from a gas station.

"Five letters. Not dead, but not alive either."

I wrote in: "Empty."

Not the right answer. But it worked in my mind anyway.

For two hours, I didn't think about anything. Not the channel. Not Carter. Not my childhood. Not the list. I didn't even think about falling. I just sat there, breathing in the thin air, watching birds fly below me, which was a weird view to have. The sun moved in the sky and my skin grew pink. A helicopter passed in the distance, but it didn't come close. It was the most peace I'd felt all year. And then I ruined it. Because when you spend the majority of your whole life wanting to die and then you don't take advantage of the current situation, your brain starts yelling at you. *Why didn't you jump? Why didn't you dangle from the edge? Why didn't you at least pretend? This video will be the one that makes everyone unfollow you.* I started to feel stupid. Weak. Like I'd wasted the height. Wasted the silence. Wasted the moment. Like peace wasn't allowed unless I earned it through pain.

I tried to ignore it. I filled out the crossword until my pen ran out of ink. I ate the crust of my sandwich, but it tasted like sawdust. The sun began to dip lower, and the fields took on a copper hue. The red light next to me continued to blink; that and my self-deprecation were the two most consistent things up here.

The climb down was longer. Not physically—just emotionally. Every rung was a step back down into the noise. My hands slipped once as I began to sweat. My arm shook a little as I steadied myself. With every bit of my descent, my thoughts grew thicker and heavier; my shame returned and crowded my brain. By the time I hit the ground, the guilt and worry were clawing at my ribs. My legs ached, my palms were gritty, and my shirt was damp with sweat. I sat in the dirt for a while, letting the antenna tower stretch back up toward the sky without me. Letting the heat of the day fade from my skin. I wondered if today was proof that I was too weak to do this. Or too strong, or maybe both. I pulled out my phone and called Carter.

"Yo," he answered on the second ring. "Please tell me you didn't die somewhere with no signal."

"Nope. Still breathing."

"Well, shit. I owe Liam five bucks."

I let the silence stretch. He picked up on it fast.

"What's going on?"

"I'm getting bored of doing these."

A pause.

"Bored?"

"Yeah."

"You just climbed a fucking skyscraper in the middle of corn country."

"I brought a sandwich."

Another beat of silence. Then, "Dude."

"It's my most boring video."

Carter groaned. "You know how many people would kill to do what you just did?"

"I guess."

He exhaled. "Look. You've got what, five left?"

"Yeah."

"Then just make it happen. Knock 'em out. Wrap up the series. Go out with a bang. You're almost there."

I didn't say anything. But I knew what he meant. Not go out with a bang like *die*. Just... finish it. For the brand, for the arc, for the monetization. Each video brought in more than Carter's annual rent. Of course he wanted me to keep going. But what I didn't say out loud, what I couldn't say, was that I didn't just want to quit the channel. I kind of wanted to quit the list too. I didn't, though. I booked a flight that night. I packed light, just took the basics. And by morning, I was on my way to New Jersey. Destination: El Toro. The most dangerous roller coaster in the world. Because if I couldn't die quietly on top of a metal mountaintop, maybe I could do it while screaming my lungs out with strangers while pretending I was having a great time.

"THIS ONE FELT DIFFERENT. WATCHING YOU SIT UP THERE... KINDA GAVE ME CHILLS. SOMETIMES THE HARDEST THING TO DO IS TO JUST BE STILL."

"WATCHING YOU DO THAT CLIMB AND THEN JUST EAT A SANDWICH UP THERE... MAGICAL. I WANT MORE VIDEOS LIKE THIS ONE."

"I USED TO WORK ON TOWERS LIKE THAT. IT'S NO JOKE. THE WAY YOU FILMED THE SKY AND THE BIRDS WAS BEAUTIFUL. THANK YOU FOR SHOWING US THE QUIET SIDE OF DANGER."

"YOUR CROSSWORD ANSWER GOT ME. EMPTY. CUZ SAME."

"MY FAVORITE VIDEO YET. IT WASN'T CRAZY LIKE YOUR OTHER ONES, BUT I LIKED SEEING YOU BE PEACEFUL. PLEASE GIVE YOURSELF MORE OF THAT."

Chapter Thirty-One
Session Fourteen

Die Trying 

@dietrying

20m Subscribers · 22 Videos

🔔 **SUBSCRIBE** 👍

March 2026

I didn't think much of the texts at first. I had received a few midweek check-ins from Iris. A question about whether I'd tried the sushi place she'd told me about, a photo of a dog in a sweater that she saw on the subway, a "fun fact" about serotonin that I hadn't asked for. Yet I replied to all of them. Not too quickly, I didn't want her to think I had just been sitting here with nothing else to do but read her text messages as soon as they came in. That was exactly what I had been doing when they came in, but I didn't want her to know that. So, after waiting a bit and overthinking my responses, I did reply.

Then on Friday night, she sent me another text in response to something I had said earlier.

IRIS

Wait. You've never had a sleepover?

DANNY

How with everything you know about my childhood are you surprised that I haven't had a sleepover?

IRIS

Okay, well pack your bags. We're doing one.

DANNY

huh

IRIS

Next session is a sleepover. You and me. My place. I'll supply marshmallows and moral support.

I told myself I had no other choice but to agree. She sounded so excited. How could I let her down? I would let her give me all these missed life experiences, to make her happy, and then one day I'd leave and hope she wouldn't think of me again. I'd gulped at the thought of that and then told myself not to think about that either.

THE DAY of my next session, as I packed and repacked my bag, the panic began to set in slowly. I'd drafted three different excuses to text her but found myself deleting them. I imagined her face as she received my lame excuse as to why I couldn't attend her therapeutic sleepover and I couldn't do it. So, I finally shoved everything back into my bag and zipped it shut. I could survive one night with her even if it came with talking about my feelings and scented candles.

So instead of backing out on her, I texted Carter.

DANNY

SOS

DANNY

she is making me have a sleepover at her house tonight

DANNY

WHAT DO I DO?

It took him three minutes to respond. I chewed two of my fingernails off in that time.

CARTER

bag her

CARTER

but bring condoms

DANNY

are you 14 years old?

CARTER

a 14 year old would have fucked her by now

DANNY

ew. I can't go. What if that's what she's thinking?

CARTER

you're overthinking it. Just go

CARTER

bring the condoms just in case.

DANNY

I'm not gonna fuck her Carter.

CARTER

and here I thought you were brave...

EVENING HAD COME FASTER than I wanted it to, but I kept my word and took an Uber to her place. I stood outside Iris's apartment building with a backpack slung over my shoulder—a change of clothes, pajamas, deodorant and my toothbrush stuffed in it. I also held a bag full of Chinese food and had a bouquet of flowers tucked into the crook of my arm. I didn't know what you were supposed to bring to a sleepover as I had never been invited to one as a kid, and although I really didn't want to attend one as an adult, I still needed to do it right.

Iris opened the door wearing socks, leggings and a long, oversized hoodie that said, "it's not clocking to you" across the front. Her hair was up. Her face was makeup-free.

"Hi," she said, like this was all perfectly normal.

"You're underdressed for therapy." The words tumbled out of me. I hoped I didn't sound as awkward as I felt. She smiled and stepped back, opening the door more to make room for me to go in.

"Come in. I already set up the smores station."

Her apartment smelled like jasmine and toasted marshmallows. There were candles lit, but not in a weird romantic way, rather in a cozy, adult sleepover way. The lights were dim; her couch had a stack of blankets on it. She'd even built a pillow fort on one side and hung twinkling lights around it making it look like an adult fairy house. My chest tightened—not with dread, but with that weird ache I always got when I stepped into a scene of life that I clearly didn't belong in. I was so, so fucked.

We ate our dinner while sitting on the floor because all the couch cushions were being used for the fort. We had General Tso's, fried rice, egg rolls, wonton soup, and she also ate a veggie option that I didn't touch.

Iris told me stories about growing up attending a church youth group and sneaking out to see romance movies behind her dad's back. I told her about my first part-time job—stacking boxes at a thrift store run by a man named Gary who had named all his mannequins. She laughed so hard she snorted, then covered her face like her dribbling a bit of her iced tea down her chin wasn't adorable.

"Do you think he was like..." She blushed and didn't finish her sentence.

"Like what?"

She looked uncomfortable for the first time since I'd met her.

"You know... was inappropriate with the mannequins?"

"I don't think you can be. They're just one solid piece of plastic." I felt the tips of my ears go red. I was pathetic and I knew it. Carter would have already sweet-talked his way into her bed. He'd know what to say to make mannequins seem sexy. I, on the other hand, was like an awkward pre-pubescent teenager. She made a non-committal "hmm" sound, and we both sat there wondering if Gary had molested his mannequins after hours.

After we cleaned up from dinner, we watched the movie Wicked and made s'mores in the fire on her stove. She'd turned off the rest of lights and brought out flashlights for the scary story portion of the night. Hers was about a haunted doll in a glass case. Mine was about a foster home with walls that whispered. She didn't speak for a long time after I finished, in fact I thought I might have heard her sniffle. But I didn't say anything to ruin the moment. Eventually she said, "You always tell the truth when you're trying to scare me."

"Am I scary enough?" I asked, trying to make it sound like a joke. But I knew it didn't land that way.

"I'm not scared of you." She paused; her voice grew softer. "But sometimes I'm scared *for* you."

That hit harder than it should have. I looked over—her legs were tucked beneath her, a flashlight rested against her knee, her eyes caught the low amber glow from the one light she had turned back on in the kitchen, and she wasn't smiling.

"For what exactly?" I asked, quieter.

"For what's still living inside you that you haven't said out loud yet."

My throat tightened. She didn't press but she didn't look away either. And in that moment, I felt more vulnerable than I had standing on top of an elevator shaft or hanging out in a tornado.

"I don't want to be someone people are scared for," I muttered.

"I think you don't want to be someone people care about," she said gently. "Because then you'd have something to lose since you'd have the chance to care back."

I made a joke about being sure that sleepovers weren't meant to be this emotional, but deep down I knew she was right.

It was past midnight when I finally stood in her bathroom, toothbrush in hand, trying not to hyperventilate. Her counter was covered with neat rows of lotions, an electric water pic and creams that smelled like flowers. Everything around me felt too quiet even though I could hear the soft music she'd put on drifting down the hall. I could smell the lingering scent of coconut shampoo from the towel on the hook behind the door. I was in her space—the most real, unfiltered version of her—and it felt intimate in a way I hadn't prepared myself for. I splashed water on my face and stared at my reflection.

"You're just going to sleep," I whispered. "Don't fuck this up." My pep talk worked, and I finally opened the door and left the safety of her bathroom. When I stepped back into the living room, she was sitting cross-legged on the couch in a long-sleeved pajama top that looked like a hockey jersey and sweatpants. The shirt had the name Rozanov across the back. I wasn't a sports guy so I had no idea who he was. The glow from the kitchen light framed her like she was a painting set out on display in a gallery. Her feet were bare; her hair had fallen out of its bun.

She looked up and everything stopped. The silence between us crackled. Not loud. Not sudden. Not even obvious. But the moment was... charged. Like we were on the edge of something neither of us had a way to describe. I sat down at the other end of the couch. Close enough to feel it. Far enough not to act on it.

"Thanks for agreeing to do this," she said quietly.

"Thanks for inviting me."

She nodded. After a pause, she added, "You know... if we were ten years old, this would be the part where we made friendship bracelets and gossiped about our crushes."

"Who says I don't want to make bracelets?"

"I'll add it to your treatment plan."

I laughed. Then stopped. "Why are you doing this?"

She tilted her head. "Doing what?"

"This. The sleepover. The texting. The sushi. All of it. You know you've crossed a line." I knew I was being blunt, but I didn't really have time to beat around the bush. Her voice didn't falter when she said, "Yeah. I know."

"So why?"

She let out a long breath and then said, "Because I think you need it."

"You're my life coach, not my..."

She looked at me. Not simply a glance from over a pillow, but directly at me.

"Not your what?"

My throat tightened.

"Not my person," I said, quieter than I'd meant to be.

She didn't respond. Didn't move. Just sat with what I had said. Then she reached for the remote to turn off the music and said, softly, "I hope you sleep well tonight, Danny."

I did. I didn't have any nightmares. I didn't wake up with my fists clenched, thrashing amongst the blankets. I slept and experienced stillness in the night for the first time.

THE NEXT THING I KNEW, morning light filtered in through the windows. I blinked once. Twice. Then I sat up. Iris was already awake, and I found her curled up in the corner of the couch with a book in her lap. Her eyes flicked over to me from the top of the pages.

"Morning," she said.

I groaned. "Don't say it like that."

"Like what?"

"Like mornings are good."

She smiled. "Did you sleep well?"

"Unfortunately, very well, yes."

"Any nightmares?"

"Nope."

She raised an eyebrow. "That's kind of a big deal."

I rubbed my face; my skin was prickly from the hair that had grown in overnight. My voice came out gravelly. "I think my inner child liked the sleepover."

Her face lit up. "Did he?"

"Don't make it weird."

She set the book down and stood. Then she came over, knelt in front of me, and before I could process what was happening, her arms were around me as she hugged me. It was simple human-to-human contact. It didn't feel weird or like something it shouldn't. It was just arms around my torso and a cheek pressed lightly to my shoulder. I sat there, frozen until I let myself lean into it—just a little. Before I knew it, I was hugging her back. She was warm and soft against me. She smelled so good. And the contact made me feel safe and seen. I tried to memorize the shape of her. Why was my throat swelling up like that? I dropped my arms. She backed away. But for a second, I forgot why I had ever wanted to die.

My phone buzzed as I gathered my stuff and headed to the front door to leave.

CARTER

so did you bag her?

DANNY

you know I didn't.

DANNY

But it was a really good night. I think it wasn't just for me. I think she actually enjoyed it too.

CARTER

you don't say...

Chapter Thirty-Two
El Toro

(Uploaded: August 26, 2025. 6:42 p.m.)

Six Flags smelled like everything good and terrible about America—fried dough, hot pavement, sugar, sunscreen, and soda. After ten minutes of breathing in the air it felt like my lungs were coated in amusement park residue. Kids were screaming on the water slides and a guy in a giant foam character costume waved at everyone like maybe this was actually the greatest place on earth. Everyone around me looked sticky, tired and, very much alive.

I'd barely made it through the gates at the entrance of the park before someone recognized me.

"Oh my God, you're the guy from Die Trying, right?" A girl in her twenties with blue hair and braces pointed at me with a fried Oreo in her hand. I gave a shrug and finally admitted to being this elusive and anonymous guy she had been watching.

"Maybe."

Her eyes lit up. "Can we ride something with you? Are you doing anything insane today?"

Suddenly, my plan to try to die alone on the most dangerous

wooden coaster in the country started to unravel. I had hoped I could wait till the end of the day, when everyone had abandoned the roller coasters right before the park closed, and would ride El Toro by myself. I hoped that something would go wrong, and I'd get flung off the ride, but if I were to bring innocent people on with me, I could no longer hope for that. They wanted to live. They were here to have the time of their lives. In a quick game plan change, I gave up on that idea and told my fan and her friends to meet me at the ride later.

I didn't head straight for the roller coasters. It wasn't time yet. I wanted to feel a part of the crowd first. To experience the chaos firsthand. Unfortunately, it wasn't too much longer before another person spotted me and waved at me like I meant something. Like I was brave instead of broken. After that I wandered. I ate amusement park food like it was my last meal. I had a corn dog, a churro, a funnel cake, and a giant lemonade in a plastic cup shaped like a cartoon character I didn't recognize. I was like the hungry caterpillar if the caterpillar was depressed and had a death wish.

As I wandered around, more people stared. A few whispered. One guy offered to buy me a beer if I let him film me doing a backflip. I declined. I told him I was reckless, not athletic. He clapped me on the back and guffawed as if what I had just said was the most hilarious thing he had ever heard.

By noon, four more people had come up to me. Two recognized me from YouTube and one from TikTok. Apparently I had a fan account on there with a huge following. The guy told me his girlfriend loved my channel and asked if I'd say hi to her on Facetime. I said sure, and did as he asked. I didn't understand why it made them happy to meet me, but believe it or not, I found myself actually liking making people happy.

I had come here to flirt with death, not fans, yet that was how my day ended up shaping up to be.

When I was fully stuffed with disgusting food, I finally headed to the ride. El Toro loomed in the distance—made up of wooden beams and ancient rattling violence. It looked like something that should've been condemned or turned into a historical landmark by now, but instead it was still running with people strapped to it.

Over the years the coaster had already injured a few people. Back injuries. Whiplash. One dude had lost a tooth and filmed himself holding it up like a war trophy. The ride wasn't just fast; its movements were brutal. The first drop was nearly vertical, and the whole thing shook till you felt like praying even if you didn't believe in anything to pray to.

I'd scoped it out from a distance earlier in the day. Part of me had hoped something would be visibly wrong. A cracked beam. A loose bolt. An "Out of Order" sign that I could take as a sign from the universe. But it had run perfectly all day. Over and over. Taking screaming people, thrill-seekers, and tourists for the ride of their life. And now it was my turn.

I got in line with my camera and that's when they showed up. The girl was followed by a group of five—three girls, two guys—all probably in their early twenties like their blue-haired companion. They were so excited to meet me; a few were practically vibrating with it.

"Dude," one of them said, eyes wide. "You're him. You're him."

I nodded. "I am someone."

They laughed and called me humble.

We boarded the front car. I sat in the middle. One of the guys and one of the girls flanked me on either side. The harness came down with a metallic *thunk*. My chest tightened. One of the guys in front of us asked if I was filming. I said yes.

"Fucking amazing bro." He leaned over to high-five me. His hand was sticky. I tried not to make it obvious when I wiped it off on my t-shirt. The girl next to me grabbed my other hand right before we ascended the first hill. "This is gonna be fucking sick," she said. I thought about asking her to let go. But I didn't.

The climb was slow and noisy—it had that classic roller coaster click-click-click like a countdown to an explosion. My stomach crawled into my throat as I watched the sky get closer. I tried to focus on the clouds. Pretty soon I'd be plummeting; my body strapped to wood and gravity. The girl gripped my hand tighter, hers was sweaty. At the top, the world fell away. The drop was like being punched in the soul because it wasn't just a fall, it was an annihilation. My spine felt like it was being torn from my body, and I screamed before I could think about it. Loud and unfiltered. I couldn't hold it back even if I tried. The ride had a way of yanking it out of you.

The turns whipped us sideways. The track vibrated like it was alive and was trying to buck us off. My body rattled against the seat; my head jerked with every jolt. Someone laughed. I was screaming too hard to know if it was from terror or joy or both. And then, much to my dismay, halfway through the second drop, the nausea came on quickly, like a betrayal. I had done so much worse than this ride and had never seen the full contents of my stomach before. I tried to swallow it down, but the coaster had its own plans and at the next spin, I threw up. It wasn't dramatic, nothing projectile-like, but it was just enough to smell horrible and be messy. The girl beside me screamed again, but still she didn't let go of my hand. I spent the rest of the ride actively trying not to get vomit on anyone around me as I shoved the shame of being human as deep as it could possibly go.

When the ride ended, my legs felt like they didn't work, and as I limped back onto the platform, the group around me cheered.

"That was insane!" one guy shouted. "You good, bro?"

I gave a thumbs up with vomit still on my shirt. They whooped and said they had only been brave enough to go on the ride because of me. I hadn't known what to make of that.

I found a bench to sit on and wiped my mouth and my shirt with napkins from a pretzel stand, trying to decide whether I wanted to disappear or relive the whole thing. I smelled like something awful, but the group insisted on taking a few selfies with me before they left. They told me again that it was the best ride of their life. One girl said she'd never forget it. Honestly neither would I.

I UPLOADED the footage that night, puke scene included.

STUNT #17: EL TORO—THE COASTER THAT BROKE ME

The thumbnail was of me mid-scream, face pale, and a smear of something suspicious on my hoodie. The video got twenty-nine million views in two days.

The comments poured in.

> "AW HE LOOKS SO CUTE WHEN HE'S MAKING FRIENDS."

> "THE WAY HE SCREAMEDDDD LMAO I LOVE HIM."

> "BRO EVEN LOOKS HOT WHEN HE'S PUKING. SOMEONE TELL ME HOW?"

> "THIS WAS KIND OF... HEARTWARMING."

> "YOU FINALLY SMILED. AND IT WASN'T FAKE."

I scrolled for an hour and read every single comment. Even the dumb ones. By the time I closed my laptop, I didn't know how to feel. Because they were right, I had smiled and it had been real. For a few minutes—strapped into that ancient death trap, surrounded by strangers who knew who I was, I didn't think about dying. I hadn't wanted anything at all except to live through the next loop.

Chapter Thirty-Three

Session Fifteen

Die Trying ✓

@dietrying

20m Subscribers • 22 Videos

🔔 SUBSCRIBE 👍

March 2026

"All teens hung out at the mall," Iris told me. "It's a core part of growing up, so we're going."

I would have protested, but I knew it was futile, so I just begrudgingly got dressed and waited outside for her to pick me up, which she did, just after two.

She wore a long, silky brown skirt and a soft brown sweater. Her hair was pulled back in a braid, with sunglasses perched on top of her head like she'd just walked out of a coming-of-age movie. After she parked, I walked ahead of her and held the door by the mall entrance open. Loud music met my ears. I was already regretting letting her boss me around and making me come here.

"This is your worst idea yet," I said as we began walking past the different stores.

"That's what you said about sushi," she replied.

"Yeah, and then I'm pretty sure I choked on raw tuna and almost died."

"Dark humor seems to be your defense mechanism. Why don't you tell me more about that."

That shut me up. She smirked. I gave her the middle finger behind my back.

"I saw that," she told me.

"Good." I sounded like a petulant child, but I couldn't stop the laugh that followed from bubbling up in my chest.

We walked past the food court. It smelled like orange chicken, credit card debt, and too much cologne. I was halfway through pointing out the broken massage chair when Iris grabbed my wrist and said, "We're here."

I followed her gaze. Build-A-Bear Workshop.

"Oh."

"We're each making one," she said, already walking toward the store.

"You're aware that I'm an adult, right?" I jogged to catch up with her.

"By age maybe."

She giggled and dodged when I tried to swat at her arm.

Once we entered the store, I found that it was like happiness had thrown up in here. Other than the teen employee, who looked like she hadn't slept since Christmas, everything was so *cute*. Iris handed me a bear skin without hesitation. "This one looks like you."

I stared at it. It had lopsided ears and what looked like to be a weird belly button. I thought his eyes seemed haunted and I said so.

"I think he's adorable," Iris redirected.

"I feel seen," I grumbled, making her roll her eyes and laugh at me again.

"Now what?" I asked.

She smiled. "Now we bring it to life."

Iris made me go first. I picked up a red heart from the bowl. They told me to make a wish before I stuffed it inside my bear. I wished that once I was gone, Iris would find time to work on her own list of goals. I looked up to find her watching me, knowingly. I hated it so I stuck my tongue out at her. I was pretty sure she gave me the middle finger behind her back too.

"Naughty," I told her. Her cheeks flushed. Then we watched as the machine puffed my bear full of synthetic joy. The worker stitched him up with quick, sure strokes, talking like a Disney princess the entire time.

"What's his name?" she asked me.

I looked down at the bear.

"Regret."

Iris choked back a laugh.

"And yours?" I asked as the worker finished hers—a golden-brown bear with bright button eyes and a sparkly hoodie.

She considered briefly. "Joy," she finally told me.

"How original."

"She's healing your inner child. Regret needs friends."

We stood at the register with our bears in boxes.

"You know people are staring at us, right?" I muttered.

"Good. Maybe it'll inspire them to unpack their trauma with teddy bears too."

We got ice cream next. I went simple—mint chocolate chip in a waffle cone. She got some weird raspberry sorbet in a cup because she's a monster who doesn't like chocolate and I told her so. She made me taste her concoction off her spoon. I felt myself stiffen up in my pants as she fed me, and I had to make an excuse about not wanting to eat while standing so I could sit down and will it away.

We sat by a fountain in the center of the mall. Kids tossed coins in. A couple kissed on the bench across from us. The air smelled like sugar and chlorine. Iris set Joy between us. I placed Regret face-down.

"You don't like him?" she teased.

"I like him too much," I said. He was my very first teddy

bear, but I wasn't about to tell her that, although I figured she already knew. She didn't laugh or judge me. She just licked her spoon and leaned against the back of the leather bench.

"This is nice," she said quietly. I glanced at her. Her face was soft in the golden overhead light. She looked peaceful.

"You do this often when you were growing up?" I asked.

She shook her head. "I wasn't allowed to go to the mall alone. Too many temptations."

"Boys?"

"That and books at Barnes and Nobles. Tube tops. Bras from Victoria's Secret. Anything that made me feel free or pretty."

That hit harder than I expected. Her words made her feel real and less perfect in my mind, which made me like her even more. She looked at me then.

"I'm so happy you're here. You showed up for yourself today."

"Don't make it weird."

She smiled. "Too late."

I stood, "Come, it's my turn to take you shopping."

She blinked, surprised. "Danny—"

"No. This is important. I can't fix most things, but I can fix this. Come on."

She laughed, stumbling after me. "Where are we going?"

"To commit an act of holy rebellion," I said, dragging her straight into the lingerie store. The place was pink and way too warm. Lace and silk and satin were hung everywhere. I immediately regretted my confidence.

"You don't have to—" she started.

"I want to," I said, already blushing. "I've never bought a bra before, but I feel like I'm gonna be amazing at it."

She smiled, eyes shining. "You sure?"

"I don't have much," I said, quieter now. "But I do have

money. And I want you to have things you weren't allowed to have before, just like you want that for me."

Her smile faltered just slightly. In a good way. We walked through the store, browsing. I pretended not to notice how close she was to me as we stood looking at the wall of bras. She kept holding up different options. I made stupid comments like, "That looks like it would fit you well," or "that color matches your eyes." She rolled said eyes but didn't stop smiling.

Then Iris picked up a matching bra and underwear set, pale lavender with little embroidered flowers.

"This one's kind of soft and romantic," she said.

"Sold," I choked out.

I was suddenly imagining her in it. She looked at me. She knew. My face burned. She made me hold it while she looked through the sale basket. She was right, it was soft and silky. I'd never touched a woman's underwear before. Did she know that too?

I happily swiped my card at the register.

"Thank you, Danny," she told me with an almost shy smile. I felt her thank you swell up in my chest. Then we walked to the bookstore. She made a beeline for the romance section and immediately picked up a dirty book.

"Really?" I asked. Her grin was mischievous. "You said books and bras."

"I thought we were doing, like, Little Women, not... Hot Vicar of Lust Village or whatever this is."

She held it up. "Healing comes in many forms."

I stared at the book about two hockey players who fall in love. Then at the pink bag holding her new underwear. Then over at her. And I realized I was strung the fuck out on her. Not just in a "wow, she's beautiful" way, but in a *I might never recover from this* way. In a *Holy shit I think you may have actually changed me* way.

"Buy all the sex books," I stumbled over my words. We both blushed.

"I'll read them to you," she promised.

"I know how to read, just Iris," I grumbled.

"Sure you do."

Later, we went on the carousel. It was her idea. Of course it was. It creaked and groaned like this may be its last ride before it croaked, and the horse's paint was chipped in many places. But it was mostly empty, and the music was soft and nostalgic. She picked a white horse with roses painted on the saddle. I picked the black one behind hers—mostly so I could watch her. She turned in the middle of the ride to say something but stopped when she caught my gaze on her. The look she gave me was soft, amused, and curious. It made something inside of me tilt. The horses rose and fell, and I couldn't stop staring.

She laughed at something the operator said. Threw her head back. Her braid swung like a pendulum. My grip on the pole tightened. I'd only wanted a few things in my life and being around her had become one of them, and I felt like I was drowning in that realization. I didn't know if it was good or bad yet. I didn't know if I ever wanted to know.

We stepped off the carousel slowly. Our footsteps echoed through the mostly empty second floor of the mall.

"Do you think Regret had fun?" she asked, cradling her bear.

"He's traumatized."

"Match made in heaven," she quipped as we walked toward the doors to leave.

We reached the parking lot just before sunset. Iris unlocked the car but didn't open the door yet. I turned toward her; Regret still boxed under my arm.

"I'm not good at... this," I said.

"This?"

"Whatever this is."

She didn't ask me to explain myself. Instead, she reached into her bag and pulled out a tiny T-shirt. It was meant for my bear. Pale blue with white letters: YOU ARE ENOUGH.

"Joy has one too," she said, showing me. I swallowed hard. I looked down at the bear in my hands, a lopsided, patched-up, weird little thing.

"He's kind of like me," I said. "Kind of a mess."

She looked at me, eyes steady. Then, without skipping a beat, she smiled and said, "Guess I'm stuck with both of you then."

And something inside me crumbled in the best possible way. I didn't say it out loud. Of course I didn't. But I knew, at that moment, that I wanted to live long enough to give her more of this. More laughter. More ice cream. More bears with trauma names and carousel rides under dying mall lights. I wasn't ready to say I wanted to stay alive for much longer than that, but I was starting to hope I'd still be here at least by next week.

Chapter Thirty-Four
Tail of the Dragon

(Uploaded: September 11, 2025. 9:19 p.m.)

I hadn't even known the bastard was still alive. Not until he showed up on the news—all cleaned up and godly, wearing a deacon's robe like his soul didn't reek of rot. The segment was about church renovations or community outreach or some other bullshit, and there he was, shaking hands with a pastor and smiling like he hadn't ever locked a twelve-year-old boy in a basement and told him no one would ever love him. Foster father of the year. Deacon Harold. They even said the town—somewhere—in nowhere New Jersey—like the universe was handing me a GPS coordinate. Like it wanted me to recall where he was. So much time had passed that I had thought I had forgotten the address but maybe I had forced myself to forget it. Now that I remembered, I would never forget it again.

I didn't sleep that night. Or the one after. The nightmares came back with a vengeance. I'd wake up drenched, fists clenched, and throat raw from yelling. In one dream, I was back in that hallway again. In another, he was kneeling in front of a congregation, and I was the one bleeding up on the cross. By day three of no sleep, I couldn't tell if it was him I wanted to kill or myself. Instead of figuring it out, I packed a bag and drove south.

The drive there was just miles of highway, truckers, gas stations, and static on the radio. Without any music to distract me, I opened the window and listened to the thrum of my tires and the occasional whistle of the wind. By the time I drove into Tennessee, my head was buzzing. I'd pulled off to use the bathroom and splash some water on my face. The bathroom smelled like bleach and piss. My reflection in the cracked and dirty mirror looked slightly feral. I figured that made sense as I was about to take on the Tail of the Dragon. Only someone slightly deranged would do that at dangerous speeds on purpose.

The Tail of the Dragon was eleven miles long with three hundred and eighteen curves. It was a spine-snapping stretch of road through the borderlands of Tennessee and North Carolina, making it one of the most dangerous roads in the United States. People went for the thrill of driving from one end to the other. I went to see if the road would finally take me. I mounted two cameras on the dash at sunrise. One facing out and one facing in. Then I turned the key, hit record, and drove.

The first mile wasn't bad. The road was empty. Morning mist was still curling in, low and heavy like it didn't want to leave. It was quiet—too quiet—which was how I knew my brain was winding up to shatter me. By curve nine, my grip on the wheel was white knuckled. By curve fourteen, I was sweating like I was running a marathon. By curve twenty-eight, the panic attacks and memories hit like gunfire. Me at fourteen, cornered in the laundry room, him saying, "You want this, I know you do, Danny boy." Age twelve, screaming into a mattress so the neighbors wouldn't hear. Age fifteen, dissociating while staring at the wallpaper in the hallway until the flowers melted in my vision like bruises.

I hit the gas harder. The tires screamed. I nearly clipped the rail. But I didn't care. If I died here, it'd be cleaner this way than anything else I'd tried. The road kept coming, curve after curve, the sharp switchbacks threw me against the seatbelt. My chest heaved like I couldn't take in enough air, sweat rolled down the back of my neck and soaked into the collar of my shirt. I caught glimpses of drop-offs between the trees, the plummet off the edge made my stomach twist. For a second I imagined letting go, just taking my hands off the wheel and letting the mountain decide. But I didn't.

Somewhere around curve one hundred, the back tires skidded wide. I corrected too hard. The car lurched. The edge of the mountain blurred into view. My heart slammed against my ribs so hard I saw black for a second. And then—somehow—I was back on the road. I didn't slow down. If anything, I sped up. I wanted it. The crash. The silence. The end.

The middle stretch blurred. My brain went half-numb, half-on-fire. Every curve began to blend. Every turn brought the same thing, scenery flashing by, the engine growling at me, and my breath growing ragged in my throat. I began to talk to myself so I could hear my own voice; to prove I was in this car. Sometimes I cursed my choices, other times I reminded myself why I was doing this. They sounded the same to me.

The final curve nearly took me. A hairpin turn, almost blind because I couldn't see around the bend until I was there. I almost didn't make it. I actually saw myself flying off the edge, saw the crash, the blood, the fire. And then somehow, I was through. Alive.

After that last bend I pulled over, killed the engine and sat there shaking so hard I felt it in my bones. My pulse thundered in my ears. My throat felt raw although I had barely made a sound other than talking to myself. The camera light blinked steadily. Still recording. I was still here.

Goddamn it.

THAT NIGHT I uploaded the video. Twelve minutes of raw speed, violent curves, and a near-fatal crash.

STUNT #18: TAIL OF THE DRAGON

The thumbnail was a freeze-frame of the skid, tires nearly off the road, trees a blur in the background.

Within an hour, it was trending.

"YOU GOOD BRO?"

"I CAN'T STOP WATCHING THIS BUT IT'S ALSO MAKING ME SICK."

"LOOK AT HIS HANDS ON THE WHEEL AT THE 4:27 MARK. WTH."

"I WATCHED THIS FIVE TIMES. HE'S DISSOCIATING."
"DEAD EYES."

"SOMEONE GET HIM HELP."

CARTER

what the actual fuck, Danny. I'm beginning to worry. Should I worry my guy? Answer your goddamn phone.

I didn't.

Chapter Thirty-Five
The Park

Die Trying ✓

@dietrying

20m Subscribers · 22 Videos

April 2026

It was warm out. One of those early April days that flirted with summer, all breeze and sunlight and that faint scent of things waking up again. It wasn't a session day, but Iris had texted me to meet her at the park after she finished work. I did, and for once, I wasn't annoyed by her plans to immerse me in *real life*. The park buzzed with activity. Kids squealed in bursts of laughter. Dogs barked at passing squirrels. The sun hit my face in that perfect kind of way—warm, but not heavy, a reward for making it through winter. Iris made a beeline to the swings like it was the most natural thing in the world to do with me, like we hadn't spent months now bonding over my trauma.

"Come on," she called over her shoulder. I hesitated for a second, then followed. The swing set creaked under my weight; the metal chains were surprisingly warm against my fingers. We swayed in silence at first, kicking lazily at the wood chips by our feet. Then she created momentum by swinging back and forth, her legs outstretched, hair catching the light in a way that made me want to stare and look away at the same time. She looked free. I didn't know what that felt like. We swung in silence for another minute. My fingers curled around the chains; my legs moved on their own accord. She didn't push me, but I knew what she wanted. She wanted to know what secrets I was still keeping from her.

"I found him," I finally told her. I hadn't been able to stop thinking about it for the last seven months. She didn't stop swinging; she just tilted her head slightly as she watched me.

"The Deacon?"

I nodded, impressed by how quickly she knew who I was talking about. There were multiple options for who *him* could have been, but she knew what I was saying almost immediately. I couldn't say his name, doing so forced me to recognize that he still existed in the same world as me. "Yeah, back in September. I saw him on the news at some event. Now I know where he is, and I know that he is alive."

"What did that feel like?"

I didn't answer right away. A breeze moved through the trees; I watched the leaves dance under its caress.

"Like I still have unfinished business to attend to," I finally said. "Like the world has handed me a loaded gun."

She slowed her swing. "What are you thinking?"

I stared ahead. "That I want to kill him."

She didn't gasp, didn't flinch. She was just her usual brand of quiet. Not oppressively so. Not judging. Just giving me space to speak and think and be.

"Okay," she said softly. "Let's walk through it."

I turned to her. "What?"

"If you were going to confront him... how would that go? What would that look like?"

"I'd kill him."

"What if you approached it without violence?"

"I don't want that version."

"But if you had to use words... even before you did something physical, what would you say?"

I looked away, jaw tight. "I have nothing to say."

She finally turned fully toward me. "Are you sure about that?"

I kicked at the dirt, watching it scatter. "If I say something, it becomes real. If I say nothing, I stay in control and control is all I've got left."

Iris didn't argue with that, she just continued to swing slightly beside me, like the silence between us was a thread she didn't want to snap lest everything fall apart. Because this... this may finally be something she couldn't sew back together.

Just when the air grew thicker with the tension of what I was about to say, a voice interrupted us.

"Iris?"

We turned. A woman approached with a toddler on her hip. She looked like someone from a mommy blog—clean, dressed in pastel tones that matched her daughter's outfit, even her diaper bag looked organized. Iris's face lit up.

"Melanie, hey!"

The woman's gaze flicked between me and Iris and then she said, "Oh my god, Iris. He's adorable."

My whole body tensed, and my ears went hot. The woman was referring to me. I wanted to tell her that she was wrong but the part of me that always wanted to ruin good things finally stayed quiet. I let it hang there, and the lie of omission tasted sweet and ugly in my mouth. In direct contrast to my discomfort, Iris beamed.

"Isn't he?" She didn't correct her friend; she just let the assumption hang there in the sunshine. It made me want to disappear and also—somehow—be exactly who Melanie thought I was. As Iris chatted with her friend, I watched the little girl toddle toward the baby swings, laughing as she tried to pull herself up. I wasn't jealous. I wasn't. But there was something that felt sharply similar to jealousy that rolled around in my chest. If my path had looked different, could my life have ever been like this? Me, a dad, with a kid with someone who smiled like Iris? Could I have been someone's... parent? I looked down at my hands, unsure of what they were meant for. What were they good at? Potential violence? Setting up cameras? Typing to research the most dangerous roads in the country? Certainly not love, or gently holding a baby, or caressing my *wife's* skin. My own skin flushed hot, and I pushed the daydream away.

Once Iris said goodbye and turned back to me, I asked, "What the hell was that?" My tone sounded gruffer and sharper than I had intended. I didn't know why I felt so angry all of a sudden. No matter what I said or how I said it, it didn't pull the smile off of Iris's face. She remained her happy, collected self as she said, "*That* was Melanie. She assumed you were my boyfriend and it was easier not to correct her because I would never tell her you are actually my..." her voice trailed off because what were we? It certainly didn't feel like I was *just* her client anymore. My ears burned.

"Did she really think that?"

She tilted her head. "Why wouldn't she?"

I hated how much I didn't hate that. Iris wasn't just kind or funny or beautiful in her nerdy, too-honest way. She was good. The kind of good that lasted. The kind of person that didn't cheat or lie or touch kids or tell you to stop crying or threaten to have you medicated because your grief and pain made them uncomfortable. She made s'mores and wore fluffy socks and got excited about baby goats. She didn't flinch when I said I wanted to kill someone. She just asked me to walk her through it. And I —I had trauma coiled inside of me like barbed wire. Nightmares that made me sweat through sheets. A YouTube channel that documented every time I tried to die. A reputation as the guy who chased death because he didn't believe in healing. People like me didn't get people like her. But for a moment, a tiny flicker of space between heartbeats, I wondered what it would be like. If she were mine. If I was... lovable. And it made me wonder if someone like her could ever want someone like me, all of me, not just the jokes and the quiet smiles and the moments where I seemed *better*, but the whole package, the rage, the panic, the silence, the rot. And then she glanced at me, soft-eyed, still smiling, and said, "That was fun. Thank you." And just like that, I knew I'd die to protect her. Even if it meant protecting her from myself.

After a few more minutes on the swings, we found a dry and warm patch of grass and collapsed onto it. My heart hadn't stopped racing since my intrusive thoughts had bombarded me earlier.

"You're quieter than usual," she noticed.

I shrugged. "Just... thinking."

She picked at the grass, slow and thoughtful. "The worst things you've survived... they don't make you unlovable, Danny."

I didn't respond but a part of me—a very, very small part—wished she was right.

Chapter Thirty-Six
The Train

(Uploaded: October 31, 2025. 11:11 p.m.)

I found myself in the middle of nowhere waiting for my ride. There was nothing here other than train tracks and a few oddly bent telephone poles. The landscape was barren, boring, bland. Nothing like the city back home. Then again, most places weren't. I could hear the faint hum of the train approaching long before I saw it. The closer it got, the more it rattled behind my ribs, readying me to do the next thing on my list.

They say trains don't stop for their riders; instead they barrel through—without mercy, pausing momentarily to let you embark and then they're off again, desperate to get to their next destination. If you step on the tracks, it's over. The weight, the steel, the motion—it'll completely erase you. But that wasn't what I wanted. Not this time. I didn't want to get erased. I wanted to ride it. I wanted to grab onto something that wasn't made to hold me. Let it carry me away. Let the friction rip something open. Let the noise drown everything else out. The freight track I found sliced through a no-name patch of Montana. Nothing picturesque. Just bare brush, a cracked horizon, and air that smelled like dry rust and old leaves. The train came sooner than I had expected it to. It roared past me with a shriek of steel, like a monster with somewhere to be. All metal, smoke and noise. I ran for it. Stupidly. Recklessly. Every nerve in my body fired at once. My boots skidded on gravel as I launched myself at the side of a boxcar. I caught the rungs of the ladder, almost yanking my arm from its socket, and hauled myself up. One knee smashed into steel causing a jolt of pain to light up my leg, but I didn't let go.

The metal was cold and rough. The wind screamed past me. My body slammed against the car as I climbed up the rungs of the ladder, chest heaving, ears ringing. By the time I got to the top, I was breathless, bleeding, and gripping the steel beneath my hands knowing that it could save me or end me. I crawled flat and pressed myself against it. Chest to metal. Arms spread. The world blurred around me. The sky appeared too wide, the land was too empty, and I lay there thinking, *this should be it. Let this be the one. Let the wind throw me. Let a sharp turn do me in. Let something snap.* But it didn't. The train just kept going. And so did I. I could feel the rattle of every mile beneath me. I imagined the motion to be like being rocked inside the womb but it wasn't soothing, instead it invigorated me.

Somewhere along the stretch, I lifted my head just enough to look at the sky. It was a drab gray; the stars weren't peeking through yet. I thought about how funny it was that I liked the sky back home better than this one when it was the exact same sky. But the New York sky felt like it was alive, like it had a pulse, and something to say... where this one was just flat and empty. Maybe that was the point. The sky was the same every-where... but what you did under it was what made a place feel like home, even if home was a small apartment with nothing living in it but me.

I closed my eyes again, waiting for something to happen. But something else came instead. Silence. Not outside of me but within me. For the first time in weeks, everything went quiet. No static of anxiety, no screaming nightmares, no echo of what I'd done or what had been done to me. All that my senses knew was the metal and wind. And the knowledge that I was still here. Hours passed or minutes, I didn't know. I didn't jump, I didn't roll off, I didn't try harder to make something happen. I just... held on and allowed the peace to envelop me with every swaying motion. Eventually, the train slowed near a junction. The brakes screeched, the noise gyrated in my ears. I climbed down on shaky legs and got off the train like a man waking from a trance. I limped into the grass and sat down, watching everyone else disembark, ignoring their stares. Why? That was the only question I had left. Why was I still here? If I knew what my purpose was, if I knew what I was supposed to be doing, maybe then I could manage my fucked-up brain, maybe then I could handle this world. But not like this. I couldn't do it anymore like this. This way was clearly not working out for me.

By the time I'd made it back to my car, my phone had five missed calls and four texts from Carter.

CARTER

Dude, where are you?

CARTER

Just checking in. You alive? Hopefully yes. Preferably yes.

CARTER

Say something. Anything.

CARTER

Happy Halloween.

I stared at the screen for a long time. We had evolved into this odd little relationship where I had begun to feel bad when I didn't answer him. But sometimes answering a text message took literally all of the energy inside of me. So instead of texting something back that felt meaningless, that drained me of the little bit of shit I had left to give, I unlocked my phone, opened the camera, lifted it, and filmed the empty tracks behind me. The flat sky above them. The vast, uncaring silence around me.

Then I texted him the video with a message that said, "I'm still here." I didn't wish him a happy Halloween. I couldn't. The Deacon used to say Halloween was the devil's holiday, that good, godly people didn't celebrate it. No candy, no costumes, no jack-o'-lanterns. Just sermons about sin and eternal salvation. And yet the same man who preached purity would come into my room at night and put his hands where they didn't belong. I could never figure out how dressing up as Batman was evil but hurting me was fine. I recalled being so angry and betrayed when I learned that Jesus had died for the Deacon's sins because it let him do whatever he wanted to me, and he'd still get off scot-free. I remember watching the other kids through the window, plastic pumpkins clutched in their hands, faces lit up by porch lights and sugar highs. I had wanted to be out there with them so badly it had made my chest ache, but all I could do was press my forehead to the glass and hope that better days would one day find me.

"IMAGINE HE WRITES A BOOK AND TELLS US WHY HE'S DOING THIS SHIT. I'D PRE ORDER IT SO FAST."

"EVERY TIME HE POSTS A NEW VIDEO I SIGH WITH RELIEF."

"RIDING A TRAIN WHILE IT'S MOVING LIKE A NORMAL FRIDAY. MKAY."

"NONE OF US KNOW WHAT WE'RE DOING HERE, BABE. SOME OF US JUST HIDE THE CONFUSION BETTER."

Chapter Thirty-Seven

Session Sixteen

Die Trying ✓

@dietrying

20m Subscribers · 22 Videos

April 2026

The bar was warm in the way old neighborhood joints always are—walls scuffed with history, a jukebox that still worked was tucked near the back, and couples crowded the dance floor, swaying lazily to songs that hadn't been popular in two decades. The lights were low enough to blur imperfections, but unfortunately not dark enough to hide you from your own reflection in the mirror behind the bar. It was very obvious that I didn't belong here, but Iris insisted that I needed a night out at a bar for my next life experience.

Everyone here seemed to know each other. At least the bartenders greeted every patron like they did. The people on the dance floor moved like nobody was watching—and maybe nobody was at least not in the way I was watching Iris. She looked so good tonight. Not just in a *she's a really talented life-coach way.* She looked good in a way that had my childhood softening at the edges and giving me false bravery and hope that maybe I could be normal. For her. Her hair was loose, falling around her shoulders in soft waves that caught the yellow light.

Her laugh came even easier than it usually did, like she wasn't carrying anyone else's pain tonight. Not even mine.

She ordered something pink and frothy. I ordered a whiskey. Then another. I lost count after the third.

"You okay?" she asked after I knocked the last one back a little too quickly.

"Yeah," I lied, waving off the wince as the liquid slid down my throat in a sharp burn. I hid a cough behind my hand. "Just trying to keep up with your cotton-candy cocktail."

"It's called a Paloma," she said, amused. "It's grapefruit."

"Still sounds like something a grandmother would drink."

She laughed and leaned in, her elbow brushed mine where it rested on the bar. "Maybe me and the grandmas just like sweet things."

I looked at her then. Really looked. God, she was beautiful. Not fake, filtered, or curated. But real. So real. And warm. I hated how much I wanted to press my forehead to hers and whisper something reckless. I hated how much I didn't hate being here with her. Another song came on—one I only half recognized—but Iris lit up like it was her favorite.

"Oh my god, I haven't heard this in years," she said. "Come dance with me."

"No."

"Oh, come on. You survived alligator-infested waters. You can survive two minutes of Stevie Wonder."

"I'll survive it from here."

"You're scared," she teased, tilting her head. "Of dancing."

"I'm not scared. I just have a strict no-dignity-lost policy."

"Too late," she grinned, grabbing my hand. "You're already here with me. I'm afraid all dignity has been left at the door tonight."

She pulled me to the floor, and I didn't resist. I couldn't, not when she was smiling at me like that. Or maybe it was the whiskey. Maybe it was the song. Maybe it was the way her fingers had laced through mine. We didn't really dance, not in any coordinated way. We swayed. We moved. We existed in a little bubble of light and sound, making memories. Her hair brushed my cheek at one point, and it felt like a lightning strike against my skin. I wanted to wrap myself in it. I wanted to disappear in it.

"You're beautiful. You know that?" I said, slurring the words a little. My body jolted with shock as I said it, but I didn't regret it. It needed to be said. She needed to know.

She blinked. "You've been drinking."

"Doesn't make it less true."

Her cheeks flushed. "Thank you."

I laughed, but it wasn't joyful. It was cracked. "I don't say that kind of thing. Ever. But don't make a big deal out of it. Don't write about it in your notebook."

"I won't." She blinked at me, finally looking like I'd rattled her with my words.

"I mean it, Iris. You're really—" I gestured toward her vaguely. "You glow or something. Not like, in a spiritual way. Just... like a person who's never been broken."

That made her spine stiffen. I leaned closer. "I don't get people like you. You're not scared all the time. You smile for real. You wear soft sweaters and make pancakes, and you actually mean it when you say you want to help people."

She opened her mouth, but I wasn't done.

"I'm scared all the time," I whispered. "I don't even know of what anymore. Everything. Nothing. The second I start to feel happy; I panic. Like I don't deserve it. Like someone's gonna take it away from me."

She held her hand up in the air between us. Not touching me. Just there, hovering nearby, ready to grab onto me.

"I hate that he still lives in my head," I said, voice trembling now. "The Deacon. He's not here, but he is. Every day. I see him. I smell him. I hear his voice. And sometimes I think... maybe if I had just done something, anything, to shut him up. To stop him..."

"You don't have to talk about that if you don't want to," she interrupted me softly. But I did. "He ruined me, Iris. I don't know who I was before him. And I sure as hell don't know how to be anything other than what I am now. But you are so beautiful, and I couldn't let myself be too afraid to tell you that. And I hate how much I want to tell you that all the time."

Her expression softened into something unreadable. "You can tell me."

"No, I can't," I said, stepping back. "Because then it's real. And if it's real, I'm going to fuck it up."

She reached for my hand again, and I let her. Just for a second. Just long enough to pretend.

"You don't have to be perfect to be worth loving," she said softly. I blinked, and the words hit me like a punch to the sternum. She might as well have kissed me. I think it would've hurt less. Would have been less of a shock.

"You were right, you know. I'm not scared of dying," I said suddenly, the alcohol had my thoughts bouncing around in my head, jumping from thing to thing faster than I could keep up. "I'm scared of living and it not getting any better."

Her face didn't change. She didn't recoil. She most certainly didn't say I told you so. She just stood there, swaying slightly, eyes locked on mine like she could see every version of me that I was trying to bury.

"I know," she finally said. "But you're here now. And you're dancing, that's better than it was yesterday... isn't it?" Then she slid a little closer. Not dramatically. Just enough that I felt the shape of her hip brush mine.

"I like drunk Danny," she said softly. "He's honest."

"I'm not drunk," I lied.

She laughed and looped her arm through mine. "Okay, well then maybe I just like the real Danny."

The music changed—something slower now—and she didn't let go, she just swayed there beside me, her body warm against mine, her head tilted slightly like she was considering something dangerous.

"You ever dance like this before?" she asked.

"Never."

She put her hands around my waist, closer than we were before, so much so that I could smell her shampoo, could feel the warmth of her breath when she said, "Relax. I promise I won't bite..." And then she winked.

I swallowed hard, wishing I could get another drink. I had never seen her be so bold. I needed something to distract myself from how badly I wanted to touch her. She smiled like she knew, like she could feel it in the air between us, but she didn't push. She just stayed close as we danced slowly. Lazily. Like we had all the time in the world. For a second, I let myself forget the noise in my head. The nightmares. The Deacon. The letter. All of it. It was just her and the music and the little way her fingers played with the collar of my shirt like she couldn't help herself but touch me.

Then some guy showed up next to us. He was tall and scruffy, classic Brooklyn, wearing rings and a backwards cap, and he looked right at her—not even glancing in my direction although I was standing right here.

"Hey," he said with a crooked smirk. "You wanna dance?"

She didn't move. "I'm with someone."

The guy finally looked at me like I wasn't worth noticing.

"You with him?" he asked, like the words tasted weird. Something inside me snapped. Not in a rage kind of way. Just... cracked in a I've had quite the fuck enough kind of way.

"Yeah," Iris said, still looking at the guy. "With him."

He held up his hands as if to say, "my bad," and wandered off, but I couldn't stop hearing the way he'd said it. *With him?* Like I didn't make sense. Confirming my fears that someone like her couldn't possibly choose to be with someone like me. Iris turned back to me, soft and steady as always. "You okay?"

I shrugged. "Yeah." But I wasn't. Not even close. Because the truth was... I wanted to be chosen. And I didn't know how to live with that because I'd never wanted something like that before, and the shame that stemmed from the desire choked me. That was the beginning of the end of the night.

I returned to the bar without a word and knocked back another drink. Fast. Too fast. It burned, but I welcomed it. Needed it. Needed something to punch a hole in the tightness building in my chest. By the time Iris realized that everything was unraveling and we went outside, I was seriously drunk. Not falling-down drunk. Not fight-a-guy-in-an-alley drunk. Just loose. Unraveled. Honest in a way that made my throat clench with all the things that I had left unsaid that were now clamoring to get out.

"I really do hate how scared I am all the time," I said as we walked. "Of life. Of people. Of needing them."

Iris sucked in a breath as she listened and walked beside me, her jacket pulled tight, like the cool night air couldn't touch her if she didn't let it.

"I used to think I was brave for not being afraid to die," I said. "But I think... maybe that was the opposite of brave. I think real bravery is letting people in. And that terrifies me."

Her hand brushed mine, and I caught it. Held it. Just for a few blocks. Just until we got to her building. She opened the door and let me in without saying anything. Tonight, her apartment smelled like berries and ginger tea. I stumbled over the edge of her rug as she led me to the living room, and I collapsed on her couch like gravity had given up pretending it could hold me up for one more second.

"I'm sorry," I muttered, face in my hands. All the stupid things I had said came rushing back to me. I felt dizzy. "I didn't mean to drink that much." I'd ruined it. She'd been acting flirty, like she was just a girl, and not my life coach, and I'd gone ahead and drank too much, thought too deeply, and let everything dysregulate me to the point where I'd lost a chance that I'd never get back again. I wanted to shake myself and scream. I wanted to ask myself why I sabotaged everything the second it started to feel good, started to feel normal.

"It's okay." Her words shook me from my shame spiral.

"I shouldn't be here." Was I still slurring?

"You're exactly where you need to be," she assured me. And just like that, I broke. My shoulders shook. My eyes burned. I didn't sob, not really, not like I had on the couch in her office. But the tears came. Hot, tired, half-silent, flowing down my cheeks, and dripping off my chin. Iris sat down and gently pulled me toward her lap, brushing my hair back like I was a kid who'd scraped both knees and couldn't figure out why it hurt so badly.

"I didn't want to die tonight," I admitted to her. She kissed my temple, and it was the gentlest pressure I'd ever felt.

"Then don't." She cleared her throat and added, "Please."

Oh, I got tangled up in that please. I was suspended in the air from hearing her breathy voice say that word. Practically beg it.

She ran her fingers through my hair, brushing it back. "You're okay. I've got you."

I wanted to believe her. God, I wanted to. My chest convulsed again, and I buried my face in her lap like a child. She didn't move away. She just stayed there. Fingers remained in my hair. She whispered things I couldn't hear but somehow understood anyway. And then I felt it again—her lips against my temple. Gentle. Unassuming. The kind of kiss you give someone you love in silence. I didn't say anything. I couldn't. I just felt more tears slip free and slide down the bridge of my nose.

Eventually they slowed, and I felt my breathing sync with hers. Her hand never stopped moving against my scalp. Her legs were warm beneath my cheek. And somewhere between grief and exhaustion, I whispered, "Don't leave."

"I won't," she said. "I'm right here."

I fell asleep like that. Face pressed against the safest place I'd ever known. Wrapped in something that felt dangerously like love.

WHEN I OPENED MY EYES, it was morning. Light was filtering through the gauzy curtains in her living room, pale and gold and too gentle for how wrecked I felt inside. My head throbbed. My throat was dry. But worse than that was the unmistakable memory of breaking open in front of her. I stayed perfectly still, hoping maybe if I didn't move, the weight of my mortification wouldn't crush me.

She'd let me cry in her lap. She'd kissed my temple. She'd stayed. The couch was warm beneath me. My head rested on a pillow now instead of her thighs, and a soft blanket was pulled up to my chest. I didn't remember her moving out from underneath me. I didn't remember much of anything after the sobbing stopped, except the way her fingers had threaded through my hair like she'd been anchoring me to this world. I heard faint sounds in the kitchen. The kettle whistling. A cabinet door closing. Then muffled footsteps. I should sit up. I should leave. I should say something. But all I could do was stare at the ceiling and feel the ghost of her lips on my skin like a brand I hadn't asked for but still didn't want to lose. The couch dipped near my knees a few minutes later, and I turned my head slowly. She was sitting beside me, holding out a mug.

"Ginger tea," she said, like it was the most normal thing in the world to find me here, hungover, on her couch, after a good crying sesh the night before.

I stared at it. Then I took it.

"Thanks," I said, my voice was hoarse.

"You were really out. I didn't want to wake you."

"You should have. I was probably snoring."

"You weren't."

I sipped the tea. It burned my tongue slightly, but the warmth steadied me.

"I said a lot of things," I muttered. She didn't rush to answer. Just tucked one leg beneath her and let the silence stretch.

"You did," she said eventually. "But none of it bothered me."

I looked at her.

"I wasn't trying to be a bother," I said. "I was just—"

"Healing," she finished for me. "Yeah. I know."

I winced. If she weren't my life coach—if this were a woman I was actually trying to impress, seduce—I'd have zero chance after yesterday. No woman could possibly be attracted to a guy with a death wish who cried the minute he felt anything soft. Like wow, Danny, you've really got it going on. The runny nose definitely would've sealed the deal. Good job.

"Sorry," I intoned, lips against the rim of the mug.

She softened. "Danny. You don't need to apologize for being real."

My throat tightened again.

"You could've sent me home," I said quietly.

"I could've," she agreed. "But I didn't want to."

I watched her fingers on her own mug. They were steady.

Calm. Like she wasn't at all shaken by the fact that the mess of me had cried himself to sleep on her couch.

"I must've looked pathetic," I whispered.

"No," she said. "You looked like someone who needed to be held. That's not pathetic. That's human."

I wanted to say thank you, but the words got stuck in my chest like shards of glass. Instead, I reached for her hand and let my fingers brush against hers. She didn't pull away.

"I don't like when people see me like this," I said. "It's weird."

"I know."

We sat together for a long moment—quiet, steeped in warmth and unsaid things. Eventually, she squeezed my hand gently and stood. "There's toast if you want it."

"I think my inner child is hungover," I croaked. She laughed from the kitchen.

"That's progress."

I sat there on her couch, still wrapped in her blanket, sipping ginger tea in the quiet morning light—and thought about the fact that if any of my attempts had been successful, I would have never experienced last night or this morning and that would have been sad. That realization sent my nervous system into overdrive, and I had to gulp my next sip of tea so as not to choke, but I didn't freak out. I didn't get angry. I didn't spiral into self-loathing; I just let myself be okay with noticing the feeling of gratitude that I had failed at every single attempt because it had brought me right here. It was an odd kind of irony because on one hand, I wished my life could have been different and on the other hand, everything that had happened had led me here, and part of me couldn't be mad about that.

Chapter Thirty-Eight

The Morgue

(Uploaded: November 12, 2025. 3:01 a.m.)

I had lost interest in the rest of the ways I had planned to try to die. I left my list abandoned in the note on my phone. I hadn't planned on doing another attempt video this week. It was pathetic, really, how I couldn't even muster up the energy to try to finally just end it. But working through my list was starting to feel so repetitive. Drowning, electrocution, storms, freezing— same story, different scenery. The near-death high had gone stale. My body kept surviving, and I'd stopped feeling intrigued by it.

It was on a whim that I decided to visit death tonight instead of chasing it.

To get a little preview of what I was up against. What I was really pursuing.

To see what it felt like to exist where the noise ended.

At around 2 a.m., I drove to the closest hospital and parked in the back lot where people were wheeled out, not in. After walking for a bit, I found a side entrance with just one fluorescent light brightening up the doorway that buzzed like dying flies. The air was damp. The concrete walls seemed to contain a kind of quiet that only existed in places where screams used to be.

I was surprised to find that the door wasn't locked. I pulled it open and slipped inside. Hospitals, no matter what department you were in, smelled like false hope, antiseptic, recycled air, and cafeteria coffee. Everyone pretended the scents could mask the stench of death, but I called bullshit. This entire building was heavy with denial. Machines breathed for people who couldn't. Monitors beeped like they were counting down to something better than this. The living lingered here for too long, and the dead stayed just long enough to be entered into a registry.

The morgue was two flights down—past the vending machines, past the chapel with its fake candles still glowing for no one. The elevator didn't respond even after I pressed the button too many times, so after waiting impatiently, not wanting to get caught, I took the stairs, my hand ran down the metal railing before I realized that I probably shouldn't be leaving any of my DNA behind.

The stairs led to a hallway which finally brought me to the swinging door with a red sign on it that read AUTHORIZED PERSONNEL ONLY.

I figured I was qualified enough on the topic of death to be authorized for this kind of room, so I ignored the sign and pushed the door open just enough to let me in.

The air felt like it shifted as soon as I entered—it grew denser and heavy with grief. I found it ironic to see how ugly this room was. The rest of the hospital looked like they had a few rich donors, and their billing department knew how to up code, but down here it was like they had a meeting and determined, why bother. Who gave a shit what the dead thought of the ambiance. The tiles had to be original to the building and were the color of old teeth. The fluorescent hum from the light above me began to make my brain hurt. I tried to ignore it as I set my camera up on a gurney and hit record. My breath fogged in front of me, curling and vanishing.

I should've left right then. Called it quits. Thought better of what I was about to do. But I didn't. This might not be the scariest thing I had done, but I was pretty sure it was the most unhinged.

There were twelve drawers along the wall, each labeled with a small metal tag and a red light above it. Half were glowing, indicating that they were occupied.

I walked down the line of them; my sneakers squeaked against the floor. Every drawer looked the same—same size, same lock, same silence—but each one also felt different. Like they were whispering to me, waiting for me to join them at the end of my journey.

The light on drawer seven wasn't lit up. I presumed that meant it was empty. I stood there staring at it, wondering who'd been in there last. Were they old or young? Had they come in alone or had an entire group of family members sobbed as they had been wheeled out of the room? Or had they been quietly cremated, turned into dust before the world even noticed they were gone?

The handle on the drawer was cold and when I tugged, it got unstuck and then shrieked as I pulled it open, the sound cutting through the stillness like it was letting out years of pain. Inside was just a steel tray. I imagined I saw a faint stain, the shadow of someone who'd recently been erased.

I don't know what made me do it, maybe curiosity or maybe it was a punishment for everything that had brought me to this moment, or maybe it was both—but something pushed me to climb in.

I lay down. The slab of metal seemed to cradle me. The fit was tighter than I had expected; the sides pressed against my shoulders. The air felt wet and thin, I felt compelled to take a gasping breath before I pulled the tray shut from the inside until the light disappeared.

Suddenly, everything was dark. Real dark. The kind that eats the light and the sound and your bravery.

For a moment, panic kicked in. Would I run out of air? Did the drawers automatically lock? Was I going to die with the dead? My inhales became short gasps, and my pulse hammered in my chest so loudly that I was sure all the dead people around me could hear it. My brain protested my idiotic actions as usual, but as always, I ignored it and stayed put. I wanted to see what came after the fear.

It smelled like bleach in here and something faintly human. The thought made me nauseous. I pressed my palms to the walls and felt the compressor humming, the morgue's mechanical heartbeat. The only thing alive in here besides me.

I imagined that the drawer was locked from the outside. I imagined them finding me, wondering why the hell their corpse was still dressed in a hoodie and jeans. I wondered what my followers would think when no next upload came. Would the silence feel something like this?

The thought of getting stuck in here and the cold forcing me into a sleep I'd never wake up from didn't scare me but leaving my followers with more questions and no answers, imagining Carter calling my phone until the service ran out and the voicemail changed to someone else's name, that didn't sit right with me.

I lay there until time stopped meaning anything. Until my fingers went numb and my chest burned from the lack of oxygen. I whispered into the dark, maybe to whomever would fill this space after me, maybe to the dead who were already here, maybe to myself. "Is this it? Is this all we get?"

The answer came from the hum of machinery. Not yes. Not

no. Just the endless indifference of existence continuing without us the next morning.

I thought about all the people who'd laid here before me—all their previous heartbeats, every laugh, every stupid dream—all compressed into a tag and a number. I pictured what my own tag would look like:

Unidentified Male, thirties. Found Alone. Cause: Recklessly chased death.

The drawer began to sweat around me; condensation dripped like dew on a spring morning. The air thickened with my breath. This is what it had come down to. My two alternatives: Continue living and try to find a way to exist in the pain. To sleep with the nightmares. To sustain myself even amongst the self-loathing. Or end up here, naked and alone on this sheet of metal before being deposited unceremoniously into the earth. I had always known that those were my options. But it had never felt quite so real until right now.

When I finally shoved at the tray, I found myself relieved that it opened, the too-bright light hit my face like it was surprised to see me again. I took a gulping breath of air, filling my desperate lungs with it. Then I slid out, legs stiff, hoodie damp with the promise of death and my own sweat. I caught my reflection in the shine of the opposite drawer—I was pale and wide-eyed, looking almost like the ghost I had hoped to become.

I shut the drawer and whispered, "See ya," though I wasn't sure who I was talking to—the cameras that were watching me, death itself, or the echo of who I used to be and was leaving behind.

I grabbed the camera, wiped the lens, and pressed the power button. The red light flickered once and then blinked off. The hum of the machines filled the room again.

As I left, I saw a clipboard hanging by the door, the last tag read: Held for Transfer.

That was the thing about death—even after everything was supposed to be done with and over, still more came after it.

When I left the hospital, dawn was bleeding through the sky—thin pink shone amongst the clouds. A janitor pushed a mop past the exit without looking at me. Apparently, he didn't give a shit that a live person was leaving the morgue exit, a place where people who looked like me were supposed to be wheeled out of by the living who wore scrubs, not walking out on their own accord. But he was focused on starting another day of scrubbing death off the floors, so he didn't give me any trouble. Or maybe I had actually died and was already a ghost, so he couldn't see me. That thought almost troubled me enough to run up to him and say something to confirm that I was still here, but the risk of spending another night in the psych ward stopped me.

I sat in my rental car for a while, engine off, listening to the world wake up. The chirp of the birds. The sirens in the distance. Life was emerging for another day, stubborn as ever. And I thought—maybe I was wrong about peace. Maybe it wasn't found in the silence. Maybe it was actually earned in the noise.

CARTER

what in the actual fuck did I just edit

DANNY

an artistic exploration of mortality

CARTER

bro I can't even pretend that I get you anymore

DANNY

weirdly good lighting tho

CARTER

you took a siesta in the morgue and you want to talk to me about lighting?

DANNY

I mean it's the first thing I noticed.

CARTER

I swear you do this shit just to fuck with me.

DANNY

sure man.

CARTER

...you scare me sometimes

DANNY

join the club

"MAN WENT FROM ADRENALINE JUNKIE TO PHILOSOPHER OF DEATH AND I DON'T KNOW HOW I FEEL ABOUT IT."

"WHY DOES THE QUIET IN THIS ONE SOUND LOUDER THAN ANY OF HIS OTHER VIDEOS?"

"I FELT THE COLD THROUGH THE SCREEN."

"'SEE YA.' HIT HARDER THAN ANY STUNT HE'S EVER DONE."

"WHAT THE FUCK."

"SOMEONE PLEASE CHECK ON HIM."

"MOST PEACEFUL VIDEO HE'S POSTED—AND THAT'S WHAT TERRIFIES ME."

Chapter Thirty-Nine

Session Seventeen

Die Trying 

@dietrying

20m Subscribers · 22 Videos

 SUBSCRIBE

April 2026

I ris called me the morning of my next session. She said not to worry, we were not doing therapy, obviously, it was "an experiment in playful mindfulness with a side of creative processing." Which was her long-winded, painfully Iris way of saying: we're going to a pottery painting studio.

"Are there snacks?" I asked as we walked in.

"There's a vending machine if that counts."

The place was small, cozy, and warm with the faint smell of clay and acrylic. A couple of kids were painting ceramic dinosaurs near the front, one of them proudly declared his would have laser eyes. I respected that. I was always amazed at watching kids be kids. Kids who felt safe enough to be creative or even be a little sassy to their parents. A kid who was able to be rude, knowing they wouldn't get hit later, was a beautiful thing to see.

We were directed to the back table where the store attendant gave us options of figurines and a collection of paint bottles with varying shades of colors.

"You're not gonna make me cry again, are you?" I said as I

sat down. I liked to call myself out, put the awkward thing out in the open so that no one else could do it. My logic had always been if I made fun of myself, it wouldn't sting when someone else did it. It was largely flawed, and although I knew that, I kept doing it. She rolled her eyes and grinned.

"Only if your inner child finds the experience emotionally moving."

"My inner child is still hungover."

That earned me a snort. God, I loved making her snort. We each picked a piece to paint. I chose a unique little ceramic fox. She went with a plain mug and started painting tiny vines along the handle. Of course she was the type to paint vines. I didn't realize how quiet I'd gotten until she leaned over, peering at my fox.

"Danny."

I froze. "What?"

"You're really good at that. Like... really good. Why didn't you tell me you could paint?"

I glanced down at the fox. The details had come together without me thinking about it—shading, lines, tiny expressions. "I didn't know I could," I said honestly. "I've never tried this before."

She looked at me like I'd just told her I could speak fluent elvish or perform heart surgery. "You're full of surprises."

"Careful," I said. "You're starting to sound impressed. That's dangerous territory."

"I am impressed. And a little suspicious."

"Suspicious of what?"

She tilted her head. "Of how many things you might actually be good at, but never let yourself believe, or explore."

That stopped me cold. I looked down at the fox again and didn't respond. But I painted with a little more confidence after that and actually enjoyed it. He came out cute and I found myself looking forward to putting him on a ledge in my apartment. Maybe next to the succulents. All the happy feelings overwhelmed me; they were so foreign that they almost made me feel nauseous. Like when you had too much of a good thing —gorging on birthday cake or finishing the last slice of pizza when you actually had no more room for another bite.

We grabbed lunch after. Paninis and iced tea from some overpriced café with green chairs and painfully aesthetic flower vases on every table. Iris talked for most of the meal. I watched her hands—I loved how she chatted with them without even noticing that she was doing it. I also loved how she never once looked bored with me, even when I said almost nothing.

I was feeling better. Lighter. More like a human and less like an exposed nerve. The crying on her couch last week had cracked something open in me, and it was soothing to me that somehow, she hadn't run. And now I was starting to feel... okay... maybe... Not good. Not healed. But okay enough to laugh at her dumb jokes and let her touch my wrist when she asked if I liked my food and didn't flinch. Okay enough to wonder what it meant when she looked at me like *that*.

In the back of my mind, I knew I was paying her. Paying her to care. To listen. To spend time with me. That was the deal. But it didn't feel like *just* that anymore. It felt real. Too real. Like maybe she wanted to be here. Like maybe she wasn't keeping track of the minutes anymore. And that messed with my head. Because no matter how much better I was doing, I was still the kind of man who sobbed like a child on a woman's couch. That wasn't exactly...attractive. It wasn't manly. It wasn't cool. But she hadn't run away, she didn't look at me any differently, I reminded myself for the nine millionth time. She'd just held me. And that fucked with me—because if I really let myself think about it—it made me want more.

When we finished lunch, we took an Uber to the pool. It

was an indoor saltwater pool at a place that Iris swore by. She said she took hot yoga classes there. Because of course she did. "It's cleaner," she said, "and the floaty sensation is good for trauma processing."

"You made that up."

"No, it's science."

We changed in separate locker rooms. I almost bailed when I saw my reflection. I was naturally muscular, but pale. I had remnants of scars on my shoulder and hip. My body was a reminder of everything I had gone through. But then I recalled how her fingers had threaded through my hair last week and the way she'd kissed my temple. I hadn't lied when I said I'd never let anyone see me like that—crying and stupid and vulnerable— and she hadn't looked away. So, I straightened my shoulders in brave resolve, and walked out in my swim trunks and waited for her.

When she stepped out of the women's locker room, I skipped my next inhale and ended up choking on my own saliva. She was wearing a simple, black, one-piece bathing suit. But her bare shoulders paired with that easy, lopsided grin, and that little thing she did with her ponytail so it swung behind her when she walked, had me staring at her like she was a Victoria's Secret model on the runway. She caught me staring and faltered for a second, then waved at me. Suddenly I was sixteen again, tongue-tied, horny, and terrified of getting it wrong.

"You're staring," she teased, saying the quiet part out loud.

"This is just how my eyes work."

She rolled her own eyes and shoved me on my shoulder. "Let's swim."

We did. Sort of. She floated like a sea otter, graceful and at ease. I mostly doggy-paddled, panicked, and hoped I looked cooler than I felt. At one point, she swam behind me and pushed me gently toward the wall. "Let go. You don't always have to control everything."

So, I let go of my rules and need for control, and then I finally began to enjoy myself. After swimming multiple laps across the pool, we swam over to the shallow end, near a bench submerged just beneath the water. She sat on it. I hovered nearby awkwardly treading water, trying to ignore the way the material of her bathing suit molded so perfectly to her body.

She patted the space beside her. "Come on. I'm harmless."

"I'm worried about the biting you spoke of last week." The words tumbled out of me. She blushed and it sent a flicker through me. I loved making her blush. I didn't do it nearly often enough. She patted the bench next to her again and I sat. Close enough to feel the heat of her thigh. The water made everything feel surreal—weightless and suspended. Like I had nothing to worry about. Everything would be fine. I closed my eyes as her arm brushed against mine, and I swear it felt like a brand on my skin.

"You think you could get used to doing this kind of thing?" she asked. My eyes popped open.

"What, swimming with life coaches?"

She grinned. "Having fun. Letting people see you."

"Most people don't want to."

"I do."

I pondered what she meant by that, and we ended up sitting in the silence for a beat too long, until I cleared my throat.

"So... after the twenty sessions are up... is that it?"

She blinked. "What do you mean?"

"I mean..." I shrugged. "Am I just a paying client to you? Or would you—hang out with me after? If I wanted to."

Her expression softened, but she didn't answer right away. It was enough to make me regret asking.

"I'm not asking for anything," I added quickly. "I just—

sometimes... I wonder if you'd still care about me if you weren't monetarily obligated to."

"Danny." She looked at me fully. Water clung to her lashes. "You think this is still just a job?"

"I don't know what it is."

She reached out and lightly touched my wrist under the water. Her fingers were growing cold, but they felt like fire against my skin. "If you disappeared tomorrow, I'd notice. It would matter. To me."

I couldn't look at her. My throat burned too much.

"You're not just a client," she said. "You're..." She stopped herself, then laughed quietly. "You're someone I think about even when I'm not supposed to."

And just like that, my heart did something stupid. It grew attached. It opened up and let the feelings in, till I felt physically queasy from them. I swam away under the pretense of wanting to get one more lap in to work off the panini I had eaten, but I knew she was onto me. And I was okay with that.

We got out of the pool once our fingers had turned to prunes and the saline water started making my eyes red. I offered her my towel like an idiot. She laughed and reminded me that she had one of her own.

In the locker room, I took my time in the shower. I pressed my palms against the cool tile and stared at my reflection in the small mirror that was probably meant for shaving, or something. The same face stared back at me. The same everything. But something felt different. Like I was slowly becoming someone else. Someone I didn't hate.

I dried off, got dressed, and came out to find that Iris was waiting in the front lobby with damp hair and a bag of gummy bears. She offered me a handful of just the red ones.

"You remembered," I said.

"You said they're the only good ones."

I popped one in my mouth with a grin.

We didn't talk much in the Uber on the way back. The radio was low. Her arm was gently pressed to mine, and I didn't move away. Right before we pulled up in front of my apartment, she said, "You're different lately."

"How so?"

"Lighter. But also... more you."

I snorted. "I don't even know what that means."

"You will."

The driver parked but I didn't open the door. I almost said something about last week, about crying in her lap and her not leaving. About this week, and the water and her fingers on my wrist. But I didn't know how to say any of it without sounding like a clingy lunatic, so I settled for, "Thanks. For today."

She smiled like she knew all the things I wasn't saying. "Anytime."

I got out, closed the door gently, and walked away without looking back. But when I reached my door and turned around, the car was still there. Waiting. Just for a few seconds longer.

Chapter Forty

Chicken

Die Trying 

@dietrying

20m Subscribers • 22 Videos

SUBSCRIBE

(Recorded: December 12th, 2025.
Uploaded: January 21, 2026. 12:04 p.m.)

I hadn't even planned for this to be my last stunt. My twentieth and final attempt. It just happened. Like a serendipitous horror movie. I had been driving through New Jersey with nowhere to be, nowhere in particular to go. The sun was low and flaming behind me, casting a golden glow over the road, almost making it look molten. I'd stopped at a gas station and was getting back into the rental car after filling up the tank when suddenly there he was. Sitting in a gray Toyota Camry. Boring, bland. Just like him. At first, I thought my brain had conjured him because there was no way the man who had abused me for seven years was eating a bag of chips in his car by the pump next to me at a remote gas station. Except I couldn't have made him up, so it was most definitely him. You didn't forget the devil. You couldn't. The Deacon. The man who stole my childhood from me and called it love.

And now, here he was. Completely unaware that I was next to him. I didn't move right away. I couldn't. I just stared. If looks could kill, he would have been on fire. I watched as he licked crumbs off his fingers and then wiped the excess oil onto the corner of the chip bag. I watched his head bob to some soft rock song I knew he was playing on the radio, although l couldn't hear it. But I could imagine it. I knew him well. I watched him exist like he hadn't carved open my life and then pissed on the wound.

My heart was beating so fast, I could feel it in the tips of my fingers. I waited until he pulled out, watched to see which way he went, and then I sped up, going the opposite way. I was shaking by the time I got off the next exit and cut through a side street, getting back on the highway, this time heading North— my heart was still pounding the entire time.

It only took a few minutes before I spotted him again. On the other side of the road. Probably all relaxed after his little snack. Driving like he had nothing to fear. But he did; I would make sure of it.

I barely thought about it before I did it. I turned the wheel and crossed the yellow line, heading straight for him. I was so glad I hadn't died any of the other nineteen times I had tried because doing it this way was the best way I could imagine it happening. At first, he didn't seem to register that a car was coming right at him. He probably thought I was a drunk driver who would drift back to the other side before he got to this part of the road. But I kept gunning for him, and I could almost see the moment realization struck him. I could imagine the flicker of fear behind the windshield. Could almost see the jerk of his hands on the wheel. His mouth going slack, in a gasp, in a prayer.

"Well, it was too fucking late for that," I taunted, even though I knew he couldn't hear me. "Where's your God now, bitch?"

I pushed harder on the gas. For every night he hurt me. For every time he tried to convince me it wasn't what I thought it was. For every time he punished me for trying to protect myself. I flattened my foot against the gas pedal, smashing it to the floor.

Seventy. Eighty. Ninety.

The car trembled beneath me; the tires sliced through the air like they were begging to leave the ground. The road blurred at the edges, and everything tunneled until it was just me, him, and fate deciding which one of us had more to lose. He veered a little. Overcorrected. Then straightened. He still thought I'd back down. He didn't know who I was, but I imagined he'd be shocked if he found out that the boy who cowered behind the headboard and stared at the ceiling, praying for mercy, was now the monster gunning him down with my car.

I wasn't that boy anymore. *Say it*, I begged silently. *Say my name like you used to. Say Danny boy. I fucking dare you.* We were seconds apart now. My hands were steady. My jaw locked. I could feel the scream inside my engine trying to match the one in my head. I braced for impact just as he flinched.

The Camry swerved hard onto the shoulder. The tires shrieked against gravel, fishtailing in a panic. A cloud of dust swallowed his car as I rocketed past, windows rattling, and my pulse detonated in my chest like a grenade.

I didn't crash. I didn't kill him. But I could have. I hadn't flinched. I hadn't tried to save myself this time. And the high that knowledge gave me had me trembling. I kept driving another quarter mile before I lost the grip I had on myself. I pulled over to the side of the road and flung the door open so I could stumble onto the cracked asphalt as the December wind tore through my shirt like it wanted at my skin.

I needed to throw up. But I didn't. I just stood there, hunched over, gasping like I'd been underwater too long, gagging from what had just almost happened. My vision blurred. My knees buckled. This wasn't adrenaline. This was panic. A tsunami of it. And yet, through all of it, I wondered—why hadn't I been allowed to just finish it?

Why hadn't the universe let me ram my car straight through his door and end it all right there? I would have killed two birds with one stone, literally. Not to protect anyone else. Not for justice. Just to silence the fucking noise in my head. Because ever since seeing that interview of him on my TV, every time I closed my eyes, I saw him. Every time I slept, I felt him. Every time I tried to breathe, my lungs reminded me of the day I lost everything that had made me human. And now that I'd found him—now that I knew where he lived, where he prayed, where he smiled for cameras and kissed babies, I couldn't un-know it. I kept picturing it. How easy it would be, to show up with a knife, a gun, or even my bare fucking hands. I couldn't die alone anymore. Not when he still walked free. If someone had offered me a button that could only kill one of us—I wasn't choosing me. And yeah, maybe that was progress. Maybe that was growth. Or maybe it was just a different flavor of fucked up.

Later that night, back home, I emailed the video from today over to Carter. It was short, five minutes max. It didn't show much other than me speeding, my heavy breathing and then him swerving. The most impactful part of the video was the silence after.

I planned on titling it: "A Monster On The Garden state."
Location Tag: New Jersey
Posted To: Die Trying
I imagined the comments would roll in something like:

"WHO WAS IN THE OTHER CAR? THIS ONE FELT
PERSONAL."

"THIS ONE SCARED ME. IT WASN'T BEAUTIFUL
LIKE THE OTHERS. IT FELT LIKE PAIN."

"STILL HOT THO. HOW ARE YOU ALWAYS HOT
EVEN WHEN YOU LOOK DEAD INSIDE."

"THAT MAN IN THE OTHER CAR SHOULD BE
THANKING GOD YOU DIDN'T KILL HIM."

"I'M PRAYING FOR YOU. WHATEVER THIS ONE WAS
ABOUT... I HOPE YOU FIND PEACE."

CARTER

Who the fuck was in that car? And why haven't
you been answering my phone calls lately.
Fuck you Danny. Stop ignoring me.

Chapter Forty-One

Session Eighteen

April 2026

I ris told me it was my turn to choose what we would do for our next session. She said she wanted to be pushed outside her comfort zone and see what it was like to live on the edge like I did.

"Whatever you choose," she said, "make it something that scares me a little. I think I need that."

Dangerous words to say to someone like me. I told her to meet me in the woods. I brought the harnesses. We were going zip-lining. The zip line wasn't part of any official park or recreational center. It was deep in the woods, known mostly by word of mouth through forums and a couple of unlisted YouTube videos. The kind of place you'd only find if you were looking for something borderline stupid to do. And I always was.

The platform was maybe thirty, thirty-five feet, nothing insane by my standards, but enough to make your knees shake as you questioned your life choices. The line stretched across a steep hill down into a mossy ravine, disappearing into the trees below. One wrong move and they wouldn't break your fall.

You'd shatter. But I wouldn't let that happen. Not when I had someone to protect. Even if that someone was also me.

Iris stared up at the platform, her mouth slightly gaping open. Her throat bobbed as she swallowed, a strand of her hair lifted off her in the breeze. I had to look away as the sunlight hit the curve of her neck. Suddenly, it wasn't the anticipation of flying above the tree line that had my pulse jumping.

"You okay?" I asked, nudging her with my elbow. "You look like you might finally be at a loss for words."

"This is way higher than I thought it would be."

"You asked for this."

"I didn't ask to die, Danny."

"No," I smirked, "that is my thing, remember?"

She groaned and smacked my arm, but her hand lingered there longer than it needed to, as if she were checking that I was still real. For a brief second her fingers traced along the edge of my muscle, and I wondered if she found comfort in touching me. I didn't want to admit that I hoped she did. But I did. I really did. I did so much that the want tingled up my arm, and I turned away yet again and cleared my throat to distract myself.

It took me a while to convince her to climb up. She insisted I be right behind her so the entire climb she had her ass practically in my face. I'd never done something this crazy with a semi before but there was a first time for everything, and my first time was right now. It was interesting how my brain had decided she was safe to lust after. I'd never really done that before either, and my body was very excited for the opportunity.

At the top, the wood creaked under our boots. I pulled out the gear and dropped to one knee, flipping open the buckles and loops with practiced ease. Iris stood still, watching me like I was some kind of mythical creature in his natural habitat.

"Sit," I said, tapping the bench built into the platform.

She obeyed. Her breathing was faster now. Her shoulders

were stiff. Her eyes darted everywhere but my face. I crouched in front of her, pulled the harness around her thighs and up her hips, and began strapping her in—tightening, tugging, testing. My fingers brushed her sides more than once, and each time I felt her tense and then pretend that she hadn't. Her thighs were warm through the fabric. Her breath hitched again when I looped the strap through her legs and cinched it snug against her inner thigh. The air between us thickened. I could smell the soap she used and the coffee she had drank this morning from where I hovered between her legs. I almost forgot how to speak as my thumbs ran down the material of her leggings, just once. I'd never wanted to do something like that before, yet now I found myself aching to touch her.

"You good?" I asked when I finally found my voice, checking the carabiner. She nodded too quickly.

"Yeah. Just... trying not to pass out."

"You're safe."

"You would say that even if I wasn't."

"For me absolutely," I grinned. "But in this case, you actually are. I would never let anything hurt you, just Iris."

She stood once she was fully clipped in. Her legs were shaky. Her hands fumbled with the gloves.

"God, this is so stupid," she muttered. "Why did I say yes to this?"

"You asked me to push you out of your comfort zone."

"Yeah, well, consider me shoved."

"Iris."

She looked up. I leaned in a little.

"Do you trust me?"

She swallowed. "Yes." The word fell from her lips so softly I almost didn't hear it. Something about the way she said it hit me right behind the ribs. No one had ever handed me their trust before. I had never given anyone reason to. I wanted to hold it like a baby egg in the palm of my hands. I felt too afraid to move and break the moment, but I stepped away from her and nodded once. "Then don't look down. Just step forward."

She walked a few steps. Then froze.

"Danny... please."

Oh, my body liked how she said that. She was clipped in, gloves on, helmet slightly crooked. Her body leaned forward like she wanted to jump but couldn't quite convince her feet to agree. I stood behind her, fingers lightly gripping the base of her harness—not to push, just to anchor.

"You okay?" I asked, softer this time.

"No," she said, her voice high and tight. "No, I am very much not okay. This was stupid. I am a life coach, Danny, not a —" She threw one arm out, gesturing at the trees. "—not a flying squirrel."

I bit the inside of my cheek to keep from laughing. "You want to go back down?"

"I—" She glanced down the hill, then back at me. Her eyes flashed. "Don't you dare let me go back down."

I grinned. "Then what do you want?"

"I don't know!" she snapped. "Stop asking me questions! You're the thrill-seeking, death-defying weirdo—just tell me what to do!" She was red in the face now. Breathing fast. Her words came out in one big tumble of panic and pride. And for some reason, it was... adorable. No, scratch that—it was hot. I liked seeing her flustered. I liked knowing that for once she was the one spinning out while I was calm, steady, and grounded. I liked that she needed *me* to be the one in control.

"Hey," I said, stepping beside her. "Breathe."

"I am breathing."

"You're hyperventilating."

"Shut up."

I laughed. "Okay, now you're just being mean."

She exhaled shakily and turned away, mumbling something I didn't catch.

"What was that?"

"I said," she muttered, "I'm sorry. I just got overwhelmed."

"I know."

"I wasn't expecting to feel this—vulnerable."

"Iris." I leaned against the railing beside her, our shoulders nearly touching. "That's the entire point of a comfort zone. If you weren't terrified, it wouldn't be brave."

"You sound like me."

"Gross. Please take that back."

She cracked a smile—barely—and then turned to me.

"Okay," she said. "You win. Coach me through it."

I raised a brow. "You want me to life coach the life coach?"

"I'm giving you full permission to boss me around. For the next ten minutes, I'm yours."

Wrong thing to say, sweetheart. I was now sporting a full hard on in my pants. I tried to readjust myself as inconspicuously as possible. I needed to keep this situation to myself.

"Okay, how about I go first. If I die, get off the platform. If I make it, jump and follow me. I'll be your guinea pig, darling."

Her eyes rested briefly on my lips before nodding. She didn't even admonish me for talking about dying. That's how I knew just how anxious she really was. I clipped in beside her. Close enough to feel the tension in her shoulders and the tremble in her fingers.

"You good?" I asked.

Her eyes darted to mine. "Yes."

"Good." I tightened the final strap on her harness and gave the line a test tug. "Then follow my lead. I'll go first. You wait until I text you the all clear, got it?"

She nodded; her bottom lip caught between her teeth. I stepped onto the edge. The trees stretched wide and wild beneath us. The drop was steeper than it looked from the bottom, and the wind rushed up like it was hungry. For me, it felt like home. I jumped. The wind swallowed me whole. Branches blurred. My body zinged with that familiar electric buzz of weightlessness and risk and freedom. It was perfect. It was amazing how enjoyable these crazy things could be when you weren't trying to find ways not to make it out. When all I had was the thrill, it was actually even better.

When I made it to the bottom and unclipped, I texted her to follow me. Nothing. A second passed. Then two. And then— Iris must have jumped, I was too far away to see it when it happened, but I heard it. She screamed the entire way down. It wasn't a terrified scream. Okay, it started out that way. But halfway through it twisted into something giddy and breathless and wild. When she finally came into view her eyes were wide, her hair was tangled beneath her helmet, and when she landed, she stumbled straight into me. I felt her body against mine, her chest heaving, her sweaty strands of hair stuck to my neck. I liked the feel of her tucked up against me. Way more than I had any right to.

"Told you I got you," I said to her, laughing, fighting the feeling to run a finger down her sweaty cheek and touch her soft lips. She looked up at me, breathless, cheeks flushed, eyes bright, hair a mess around her. She was chaos and sunlight and victory, and I wanted to bottle up the moment and keep it just to prove it was real. For a moment I thought she might kiss me. For a moment I wanted her to. But she shook me free as she laughed.

"Oh my God," she panted, vibrating with her excitement. "That was the scariest thing I've ever done in my life."

Instinctively I caught her by the waist, bringing her back to me, her hands found their way to my chest. "You didn't pass out. I'm impressed."

"You were right," she said. "It was amazing and horrible. But I did it."

"You flew."

"I screamed like a banshee the whole way."

"I won't tell anyone."

She stepped back just enough to look up at me. Her flushed face glowed from the rush. For a second, we just stared at each other—this weird little moment of mutual awe and adrenaline and maybe something *more* passed between us.

"I needed that," she said, voice soft now. "To feel like I could survive something terrifying."

"You did more than survive," I said. "You conquered it."

She smiled. "Thank you." And then she lifted her hand and pressed her fingertips to mine. The contact was feather-light. Deliberate. I didn't move; I didn't want to break whatever fragile thing was forming between us. Even once her hand dropped, I felt her touch everywhere.

LATER, back in the car, she glanced over at me.

"You really enjoyed that," she said.

"What? Watching you panic? Definitely."

"No, I mean helping. Coaching me."

I shrugged, but yeah—I did. It felt good to be the strong one. To steady her hands, to clip her in, to remind her to breathe, to be needed; to know I could be the brave one for someone else and not just the reckless guy chasing death for likes.

The entire day, I hadn't felt broken. I'd felt... capable. Wanted. In the quiet hum of the ride back, I caught her watching me, smiling to herself. It felt like maybe the wires between us were finally starting to cross. Whatever it was buzzed between us, alive and heavy, a secret neither of us would say out loud. When her eyes caught mine in her reflection in the window, it felt like she was seeing something she hadn't planned on finding and for the first time ever I really wasn't afraid if she had.

DANNY

bro

CARTER

what??

CARTER

Did you accidentally tell her you love her?

CARTER

Did you touch her boob?

DANNY

we zip lined. she touched my hand after. not by accident. she wanted to

CARTER

Bro... not the hand! Are you sure she's not pregnant by now?

DANNY

don't start with me

CARTER

Too late

CARTER

if she touched your hand after zip lining you're basically married

CARTER

I don't make the rules

DANNY

shut up

CARTER

You shut up. Don't ruin this. Do not get weird and disappear on her for three weeks

DANNY

I uploaded a video of it. Go look. I'm gonna crawl into a hole now

CARTER

You're monetizing her finger flirting you. Fuck me. BRB

"WAIT WHO IS THAT? WHO IS THIS MYSTERY GIRL? I WANT TO SEE HER FACE!"

"NOT THE, "I TOLD YOU I GOT YOU.' I'M IN LOVE WITH THEM BOTH."

"THE WAY HE LOOKS AT HER. IF MY FUTURE HUSBAND DOESN'T LOOK AT ME LIKE THAT I DON'T WANT IT."

"TELL US EXACTLY WHAT PRAYER YOU SAID TO GET THIS."

"MAY A LOVE LIKE THIS FIND ME."

"NO BC I WILL FISTFIGHT HER. GET YOUR HANDS OFF MY HUSBAND."

"I'M SO CONFUSED HOW WE WENT FROM ALMOST COMMITTING MURDER IN A CAR TO EYE FUCKING IN A FOREST BUT I MUST ADMIT I'M SO HERE FOR IT."

"WE HAVEN'T GOTTEN A VIDEO IN SO LONG I WAS SO SCARED, OH EM GEE I'M GONNA PASS OUT I'M SO HAPPY TO SEE THIS MOFO!"

IRIS

ummm. The comments on your latest video (confused eye emoji)

IRIS

Are these people ok?

IRIS

Your fans think I'm your girlfriend now.

DANNY

You did scream my name while I was strapping you in.

DANNY

Very misleading.

IRIS

You could've cut that out. lol

DANNY

And miss out on the "Don't steal my man" comments? I think not.

IRIS

Someone said, "He's off the market. My condolences to the rest of us."

IRIS

I almost feel guilty.

DANNY

Why?

IRIS

Because I'm not actually your girlfriend.

DANNY

Right.

DANNY

You know better than any of them how I'm exactly what people don't want to date. One big walking red flag.

IRIS

You keep saying that.

IRIS

But I'm still here.

DANNY

Good night, just Iris

IRIS

Good night, Danny

Chapter Forty-Two

Session Nineteen

May 2026

I was feeling better. Lighter. More like a human and less like a gaping wound with mental health issues. The zip line had shown me that things could be a boost of dopamine for me without being life threatening. And the girl screaming beside me had been a huge bonus. The fact that she'd clung to me and cursed at me and laughed like I was someone safe, someone fun, had made me feel almost normal. Even afterward, when the internet spiraled out over the mystery girl in my video and people started calling her my girlfriend, she didn't bolt. She just sent me a screenshot of the comments and said, "So... do I get to steal your hoodies now?"

In the back of my mind, I knew I was paying her to spend time with me. That this was technically still a session. But it felt real. She felt real. Like she wanted to be here. Not because she had to. Not because it was her job. And that confused the hell out of me. Because I knew it wasn't very stable to cry your eyes out on a woman's couch one week and then get turned on while watching her zip line the next. But somehow... here I was. Healing, even though I didn't want to. Wanting her, even though I shouldn't.

When I showed up to our next session, I brought her a coffee. I didn't know what kind she liked. I just remembered she'd once said she liked it iced, sweet, and "embarrassingly girly," and for some reason, I wanted to be the one who remembered that. Who showed up with her favorite things. She blinked at me when I handed it over.

"For me?" she asked.

"Nah," I said. "For the other life coach in my life."

She smiled so wide it hit me in the chest. We were running out of sessions. I could feel it like a clock ticking down the time under my skin. Other than broaching the subject lightly the other week, I hadn't really asked her yet—if she'd see me after this. If I'd still be allowed to want to be around her once the job was over. But it was starting to feel like a real question. Like maybe, somehow, she'd want it too.

She'd spread art supplies across the small table in her office. Not like a teacher laying out a project, but like a friend who already knew what would make me sit down and stay awhile. Charcoal pencils. Watercolors. Blank paper. No instructions.

"I know it's ironic, but this is the part of life that I hate," I said, dragging a chair over. "The end."

I didn't mean the session. Or the art. I meant the countdown to the end of this. Us. The way it felt like something was slipping away from me before I had the guts to really grab it. Iris sat across from me, curling one leg under herself like she always did. She didn't push. Didn't make it clinical. She just said softly, "Have you thought about what you want things to look like after session twenty?"

I stared at the page in front of me. Drew a line. Then another. I didn't know what I was drawing yet. Maybe nothing.

"I guess I thought I'd be gone by now, so I never thought

about it." My hand stilled. I waited for the dread to claw up my throat like it used to. But it didn't.

"But I won't be," I said finally. "Gone, I mean."

Her voice was gentle but direct. "Do you still think about it?"

It was the question we'd danced around for weeks. Dressed it up in metaphor. Skipped over it with humor. But now, sitting here with a charcoal pencil and her eyes on mine, I didn't feel the urge to lie.

"I don't know," I said. "Not in the way I used to."

Iris nodded slowly, her expression unreadable in the best way. "That's progress. Even if it doesn't feel like it yet."

We sat in the quiet for a while. I added more lines to my paper. They were starting to look like something. Mountains, maybe. Or scars. I wasn't sure which.

"What if I'm not ready?" I asked. "What if I say I'm not better yet and need to continue our sessions just so I don't lose this—lose you?"

She didn't react with surprise. Or pity. Just understanding, with the hint of something else hovering beneath the surface.

"You're allowed to not be ready for change," she said, almost purposefully not addressing what I was really trying to say. "Plus, the goal of healing isn't to be better. It's about learning to stay with yourself, even on the days when it hurts to exist."

I swallowed hard. "Is it bad if I still need you?"

Her voice was a little quieter when she replied. "Needing someone isn't bad, Danny. It's normal human nature... to need."

I tapped the pencil against the page, thinking. Not drawing anymore. Just... bracing myself.

"What if I wanted more?" I pushed further, trying to sound casual while I helped her understand. "Hypothetically."

Iris didn't look up right away. She kept brushing color onto her page with a little sponge, soft swirls of blues and greens.

"More from what?" she finally breathed out.

"From life. From... people." My throat tightened. "From you."

That made her pause. Her hand holding the sponge stilled.

"I mean—hypothetically," I added quickly. "If someone had, like, been basically feral for a few years and suddenly started wanting to be... less feral. Would that person wanting someone else to... stay. Would that be crazy?"

She looked at me now. Not with professional curiosity. Not with caution. But with something softer. Warmer. Like she already knew what I meant and had been waiting for me to say it.

"No," she said. "That wouldn't be crazy at all."

I blew out a relieved breath; a shaky laugh followed it. "Good. Because the hypothetical guy I'm talking about would be so screwed if it was."

Her lips quirked. "And would this hypothetical guy happen to draw like he's been doing it in secret for years?"

I rolled my eyes. "Don't change the subject."

"I'm not. I'm just impressed."

"You're deflecting."

She smiled. "Maybe a little."

We fell into comfortable silence, and soon my page wasn't just a mess of color anymore. It was a field—wild and sweeping. Grass that bled into a lavender sky. A fence in the distance. Not a live wire or anything threatening. Just... a place that said you can stop here for a while. A place someone might call home if they were brave enough to admit they wanted one. I didn't realize I'd drawn it until I stopped and put my pencil down. Iris leaned over, and I could feel her body heat again. Her shoulder almost touched mine. Her eyes traced every line like they were pieces of me.

"Danny," she breathed. "That's... beautiful."

I laughed under my breath, half-embarrassed, half-shocked. "I was just messing around."

"You weren't. You made something gentle."

"I'm not gentle."

"You could be," she said softly. "If someone let you."

I looked at her then. Was painfully aware of her closeness.

"Do you like it?" I asked.

"I love it."

She touched the corner of the page, like she didn't want to smudge anything, but I wanted her to. I wanted her to smudge me. I shivered, not even really understanding what that meant, I busied myself with cleaning up the art supplies and then we moved to the couch. Not for any specific reason, really, we just naturally migrated there. As if we'd done this a thousand times already.

She curled one leg beneath her. I stayed upright at first. But then the silence filled in around us again, and I let myself sink back beside her. My arm brushed hers. She didn't move away. I watched her for a second before speaking. I memorized her profile and the soft way she breathed. I remembered the way she looked at my drawing like it had meant something I'd never managed to say aloud.

"Do you think I'm too crazy for you?" I finally felt bold enough to spit it out. I'd stood in the middle of a tornado for God's sake; I could do this. Her eyes turned toward me, wide and searching.

"Danny," she corrected, "you're not crazy."

I gave her a crooked smile. "That's not a no."

"You're complicated. You've been through hell." Her voice dropped with her admission. "But no. You're not too anything for me."

I felt something shift in my chest. Something heavy and terrifying, and stupidly hopeful.

"I still don't know what happens after this," I said.

"Maybe you don't have to know yet."

She was close. Our shoulders were almost touching again.

"I'm afraid," I admitted quietly.

Her eyes flicked up to mine.

"Of what?"

I forced a breath through my nose. "Of not... seeing you every week. Of going back to whatever I was before this."

I expected her to reassure me with some non therapisty-sounding logic. But she didn't. She just nodded slowly, her gaze soft and impossibly kind.

"I think I'm afraid of that too," she admitted.

That stopped my heart for a second. "What do you mean?" I asked too fast.

She smiled like I'd caught her saying something she hadn't meant to say out loud. But she didn't backtrack.

"I mean," she said, "I've seen a lot of clients. I've worked with a lot of people. But you... you matter to me more than anyone ever has."

Her voice dipped lower. "More than you probably should."

I couldn't breathe.

"I thought maybe I'd imagined it," I said.

"You didn't."

The ache that bloomed in my chest wasn't sad. It was something else. Something rarer. It was what hope felt like when you hadn't felt it in so long you forgot how heavy it could be. It was then that I finally let my shoulder lean into hers, just barely. Just a feather touch of her warmth, but it was enough to ignite every nerve ending in my body.

"I think I have to do it," I said. "Before I can really move on. I need to confront him. I keep thinking I can move forward without doing it, but... I can't. He's still in my head. And if I don't face him—if I don't say what needs to be said—I don't think I'll ever be free."

She looked at me with that unblinking steadiness she always had, like she could hold the weight of anything for me.

"I'll take you," she said.

"What?"

"Next session. If you're sure. I'll go with you."

"Why?"

"Because you don't have to do everything alone anymore."

That cracked something wide open in me. We sat in comfortable silence again, but this time, my hand brushed hers on the cushion between us and she didn't pull hers away.

DANNY

She said she'll come do something important with me next week

CARTER

That sounds ominous

DANNY

Yeah. Just a thing I need to take care of before I finish up therapy.

CARTER

Pretty sure you're not in therapy, my guy

DANNY

You know what I mean

DANNY

PS she said I matter to her and her hand was like…ON mine. Like FULL PALM TO PALM CONTACT

CARTER

Omg. Not the fucking hands again.

CARTER

you are aware that is not even first base. right?
Like you're not even in the stadium yet.

DANNY

stfu

CARTER

I knew it. You're in love.

DANNY

I am NOT in love.

DANNY

I am mentally unwell with a soft spot for a
woman who wears cardigans and knows how
to validate my trauma.

CARTER

that's literally the same thing, buddy.

DANNY

Also like what if she touches me again and
wants more than just hands and I freak out.

CARTER

What if she breathes and you spontaneously
combust

DANNY

It's entirely possible.

DANNY

She smelled like vanilla today.

CARTER

Bro.

CARTER

Ask her out.

DANNY

I can't ask her out yet.

DANNY

I'm still technically her emotionally wrecked PAYING CLIENT

CARTER

Okay, but after that…you're gonna marry her, right?

DANNY

I will deny this entire conversation in a court of law

CARTER

Sure.

CARTER

Just remember to invite me to the wedding, Mr. & Mrs. Trauma Bond

THAT NIGHT I had another nightmare. My chest was buzzing. Not with panic, not dread—not exactly this time. Just something electric and unsettled. Something I didn't know how to name anymore. I begrudgingly got out of bed, knowing I wouldn't be getting any more sleep tonight. I rubbed a hand over my face, then got up to grab my laptop.

The screen lit up, harsh and quiet in the dark. I blinked; my eyes needed a minute to adjust. I opened a new document. Just a blank page. I stared at the blinking cursor. My fingers didn't move. Not at first. Then I started typing. Slow to start. Then faster. When I was done, I didn't stop to reread. Didn't pause to second guess. I just shocked myself by falling back to sleep, the cursor blinked on the first sentence.

If you're reading this...

Chapter Forty-Three
The End
Session Twenty

May 2026

I woke up too early. Not because of nightmares this time, but because I knew what day it was. The weight of it pressed into my chest before I even opened my eyes. My first thought was simple and stupid, I don't want to do this. My second was even worse, I have to. If I was to ask Iris out. To take a chance on me. To let her show me what life, real living, could feel like, I had to take this monster out of the closet once and for all.

The light in my apartment was gray and muted, the kind of filtered morning that made the world feel quieter than usual, like even the sky was holding its breath. I swung my legs over the edge of the couch and sat there for a long time, trying to convince my body to get up. My leg was already shaking. Not tapping, not bouncing, it was shaking. A full, nervous, tremoring rattle from knee to ankle like I was made of live wires. I pressed my hand down on my thigh to stop it. It didn't work.

Eventually, I made it to the kitchen. I warmed up water in a mug in the microwave. Scooped some instant coffee grounds into it and stirred. Mindlessly. Everything felt heavier than it should've. I spilled some on the counter and didn't wipe it up. This was it. The day I'd been avoiding and fantasizing about in equal measure. The day I found the man who took everything from me and decided whether or not to let him live. Or if I were to be a little more realistic and a tad less dramatic, I would confront him and make sure I got a recording of his confession to give to the police.

I sat on the couch with my lukewarm coffee, but I didn't drink it. I just held it between my hands like I hoped it might anchor me. I stared at the blank laptop screen, at the empty wall, at the light bleeding in through the paper blinds. Every tick of the time on my phone felt like a punch to the ribs.

What if he wasn't home? What if he was? What if I froze? What if I didn't? I ran through every version of the day in my head, every possible outcome, every kind of reaction. I pictured killing him. I pictured throwing up on his welcome mat. I pictured knocking and no one answering, and having to carry all my rage back home with nowhere to put it. I thought about Iris. About her driving me there. About her sitting beside me, not asking anything of me, just being there for me. I didn't deserve her. But I wanted her anyway.

The knock came at 9:04. I jumped like I'd been shot. When I opened the door, there she was—in a jean skirt, soft booties, a thin slate-blue top that matched the exact color of calm. Her hair was loose. Her face was makeup-free. She looked like comfort. Like warmth. Like the kind of person you could trust to walk with you into hell.

"Hi," she said, almost like she wasn't sure if she should smile so she didn't. Her usual smile missing from her face unnerved me some more.

"Hey."

Her eyes dropped to the coffee mug in my hand. "You drink that yet?"

"No," I said. "I just held it until it got cold."

She didn't laugh, but finally she smiled. "Are you ready?"

"Nope." I grabbed my zip-up and locked the door behind me. "Let's go."

The rental car smelled like lavender and gum. There was a half-empty bottle of water in the cup holder and a tote bag in the backseat that said, "feelings are real." I buckled my seat belt and immediately unbuckled it again.

"I can't do this," I muttered.

"Yes, you can."

I stared at the dashboard. My hands were already sweating. My foot tapped against the floor mat like it had a mind of its own. Iris didn't say anything else—but when I gave her the go-ahead, she started driving.

The highway blurred past us in streaks of gray and green. The further we got from the city, the quieter everything felt. Trees lined both sides of the road. The sky overhead was color-less, thick with clouds that hadn't decided if they were going to cry or not. I didn't talk; I just fidgeted. I put the window down, then put it up. I adjusted the vent and scratched my neck. The entire time my leg kept bouncing like it had a damn motor in it.

At one point, Iris reached over and placed her hand gently on my knee.

"Breathe," she said, her voice a balm to my scratchy soul. "You don't have to do anything. But you do have to keep breathing."

I nodded but I couldn't look at her. If I looked at her, I'd cry, and I'd already done enough of that to last a lifetime.

Halfway there, I broke.

"Turn around."

"What?"

"Please. Just—turn around. This is a mistake. I'm not ready. I'm not strong enough. I'm not—"

"Danny."

Her voice was soft but firm.

"I will not make you go inside. You don't even have to get out of the car if you don't want to. I'm just here to drive. I'm just here to sit with you. Nothing else."

I ran my hands through my hair. My throat was tight. "What if I go in and I lose it?"

"Then we deal with it."

"What if I go in and I don't feel anything? What if he wins again?"

Her hand squeezed mine gently this time. "He doesn't win today. No matter what happens, you showed up for yourself. That's more than he ever did for you."

I nodded and bit my lip until I tasted blood. I had to do this. I had to move on. I needed to.

We pulled off the highway and the streets narrowed. Brick buildings turned into suburbs. The homes here were tidy. The lawns trimmed. One had a 'God is good' bumper sticker on a minivan parked in the driveway. It was the kind of place where people waved to each other while hiding vodka in their tumblers. Where no one asked questions unless the grass got too long. Where monsters wore aftershave and smiled for the HOA newsletter. The kind of place that taught boys like me to stay quiet.

Iris glanced at me. "We're here."

I nodded, jaw clenched. My hands started shaking again. I stuffed them into the pockets of my hoodie; my hand closed around the recording device I had stuffed in there. Iris pulled up to the curb, the tires crunched softly against the gravel at the edge of the driveway. She didn't say anything at first. She just sat there, hands tight on the wheel, staring ahead at the house with its beige siding and white-trimmed windows. The shutters were new. There was a fresh coat of paint on the front door. A ceramic welcome sign hung from the mailbox like the peaceful slogan meant something. But I knew better.

Underneath the vinyl siding and hydrangeas, the house hadn't changed. Not really. It still had the same cold bones. The same memories clung to the air like mildew on drywall. I sat frozen in the passenger seat, yet my leg still bounced violently, making my heel thud against the floor mat.

My eyes were fixed on the front step. The same step I used to sit on while waiting to be let back inside after being punished for things that weren't my fault. The same one I'd stared at through the window multiple times, wishing I could run. Wishing I had someone in my life that would care that I was gone. It looked smaller now. That was the fucked-up part. I thought it would tower. I thought I'd feel crushed beneath it. But it was just a house. Just a door. Just a front step.

"I'll wait right here," she said. "There's no rush. You don't have to go in until you're ready. You don't have to go in at all."

I didn't answer. My hand moved toward the door handle, hesitating for a moment like even that decision had weight. I unbuckled my seat belt slowly. Sat still for a while as it fell back into place. A tremble built in my hands and the way my ribs clenched around my lungs felt less like protection and more like a cage. Then I did something I hadn't planned on doing.

I didn't open the door. Instead, I turned and leaned across the center console. Iris's breath caught quietly, but she didn't move away. She just looked at me, eyes searching mine, waiting. Her hands stayed on her lap, open. Calm. But there was something brimming there. A magnetic force began to churn around me, bringing me closer to her. Something unspoken and patient and aching bloomed.

I didn't touch her. Not yet. I just looked, memorizing her face.

"I need to do this," I whispered. "But before I do…"

I trailed off. Any words felt too big, too small. Both all at once.

"Is this okay?" I asked instead. Voice low, rough. Like the question cost me something to say. Her eyes flicked to my mouth, then back to my eyes.

And she nodded. "Yes."

I closed the space between us in a quick movement and I kissed her. Not fast. Not frenzied. There was no hunger to it, no overwhelming heat. It was surprisingly soft. Solid. Like a heart-beat reminding you that you existed in the middle of a storm. Her lips met mine with a kind of gentleness that made my chest hurt. Not because it wasn't real—but because it was. So real. My feelings for her weren't shadowed by lust or a kiss of passion, rather they shone through, genuine, in the moment. Gentle, soothing kisses, and soft sighs.

Her hand rose slowly, fingers brushed the side of my jaw, her thumb rested just beneath my cheekbone. It was the kind of touch that said *I see you*. The kind that said *you're not just a project. Not just a broken thing I'm trying to fix.* The kind of touch you give to someone you hope will come back.

My eyes squeezed shut. I tried not to fall into it. Tried not to obsess over the shape of her hand on my face or the taste of mint gum on her tongue. But I did. Of course I did.

The kiss broke softly, and I rested my forehead against hers, breathing unevenly. I didn't want to move. Didn't want to break whatever magic was holding me together. But the real world was waiting. Just twenty feet away.

I reached into my jacket pocket and pulled out the envelope. I laid it carefully on the console between us.

"What's this?" she asked, her voice barely above a whisper. Her lips were puffy from our kiss, her cheeks were flushed, and I felt pride that I had put that look on her face. "Read it after I leave the car," I said.

She didn't ask me again. She just looked at me with that same softness. I saw grief behind her eyes that I'd never seen on anyone's face before for me. Knowing that she felt sad for me, that she had come here for me, that she had given her first kiss to me... It was what gave me the final push of strength that I needed.

I opened the door.

The cool spring air hit my face, slapping me out of my terrified stupor. Waking me up from the lust that had crept into the peripheral of my brain. I stepped out slowly, feet feeling like lead on the pavement, the car door clicked shut behind me.

I walked toward the house. The wind blew the wreath on the door just enough to make it creak. The sound made me flinch. But I didn't stop. I climbed the steps I hadn't touched in more than a decade and a half, and stood in front of the door I'd once pressed my ear against, hoping to hear someone—anyone—coming to save me.

And I knocked. The door was beige now. Not red like it used to be. The siding was cleaner, the lawn freshly cut, the bushes manicured because all he gave a damn about was how things looked from the outside.

But it was the same house. The same porch. The same crack in the step that used to slice my shin when I didn't move fast enough. My hand trembled as I lifted it to knock again. Just once more. Quick. Cowardly.

I half hoped he wasn't home. That maybe I'd imagined him. That maybe I was still a kid, and this reality was all a nightmare, and maybe none of this had ever happened at all.

But then I heard the sound. Footsteps. Then a pause. Then the door handle jiggled. Then it opened. And there he was.

His hair was grayer. He was thicker in the face, with jowls now where there used to be sharp lines. His eyes, still small and piggish, narrowed in confusion. He blinked once, then again. And then he smiled.

"Danny boy," he said, voice syrupy, like we were old friends catching up.

My breath halted. The sound of it—that name—hit something raw in me like salt in a wound that had never healed. I stared at him, stunned.

"You came back," he said, like I had just gone out to get milk at the age of seventeen and had finally returned all these years later. "Look at you. All grown up."

I didn't respond. The word no was in my throat, but it got stuck. He pushed the screen door open wider, like I was an invited guest. "What's it been? Twelve years?"

Fourteen.

"I wasn't sure you'd ever come around again."

I took a step back, not forward. My palms grew slick.

"I didn't come to reminisce," I managed, voice sharp. "I came to say what you never let me say back then."

His smile flickered. But it didn't go away fully.

"Alright," he said, stepping outside to join me, arms crossed. "Go on then. Say what you came to say."

I hesitated. Because I hadn't planned the words. I hadn't written a speech. I hadn't thought I'd actually get this far.

"You ruined my life," I said finally. "You took everything from me. My safety. My childhood. My fucking sanity."

He tutted softly, as if I'd disappointed him.

"Now, now," he said. "That's not fair."

My hands curled into fists.

"Fair?" I spat. "You want to talk about fair? You drugged me. Touched me. Gaslit me into thinking it was love. You said I was your favorite."

"You were," he said, matter-of-factly. "You were a good boy. Obedient. Soft."

My stomach turned.

"You don't get to talk to me like that," I hissed. "Not anymore."

He took a step closer, voice lowering.

"You came here for closure?" he asked. "Or maybe for more of something else?"

I shook my head, disgusted. "I came here to reclaim my life."

He chuckled.

"You always were dramatic, Danny boy."

That name again. Like a switch, I snapped.

"Don't call me that," I growled.

But he did. He said it again. Slower this time. "Danny boy." Like it was his to say. Like he still owned it. Owned me.

The world shrunk. I heard a high-pitched ringing in my ears. My vision pulsed around the edges; a red fog crawled in like smoke through broken glass. He leaned closer, smiling like he had won.

"Be honest," he whispered. "You wouldn't be here if a part of you didn't want it again."

Something in me obliterated. I didn't remember making the decision. My body just moved, and I lunged at him. My fist connected with his jaw, my knuckles cracked against bone. His head jerked sideways with a sound like wet paper tearing, and he stumbled backward through the door frame. The porch creaked beneath me as I followed him inside, shoving him hard enough that he crashed into the entryway table and knocked over a decorative bowl that held a bunch of keys. He scrambled to push himself up, but I was on him before he could move. I punched him again. And again. Blood sprayed—from his lip, his cheek, my wrist. I didn't care. I didn't fucking care.

"Was I asking for it when I was ten?" I roared, shaking him by the collar. "Or did you know how much I hated it? Was that what turned you on?"

Something wet smeared from his face to my hand. Was he crying? Or maybe it was sweat. I hoped it was blood.

"You ruined me!" I yelled louder this time. "You made me hate myself. I've spent every year since wanting to die because of you."

He tried to speak, but I slammed him into the wall.

"Shut up! Shut the fuck up!"

His eyes were wide. Terrified. But it wasn't enough. It would never be enough to undo what he had done.

"You raped a child," I hissed, dragging him by his shirt and slamming him into the other side of the hallway. Picture frames fell. Glass shattered. The skin around his eye was already turning purple. I didn't stop. I couldn't stop.

"You stripped away everything good in me. Everything human. And then you made me think I was crazy when I asked you to stop!"

He sputtered and coughed, blood dotted his lips.

"You're sick," I said. "You're a monster hiding behind prayer and lawn fertilizer and fake-ass church sermons."

He tried to crawl away. I grabbed his ankle and yanked him back. The back of his head thudded against the floor. He groaned. Whimpered. But I didn't feel sorry. Because I remembered the sound of his belt sliding through the loops on his pants. I remembered the way he used to hum. I remembered him whispering, "You like this, don't you, Danny boy?" And I saw red all over again. I hit him. Again and again. My hand went numb, I thought it might be broken, but it didn't matter. I heard a scream. My name in the distance. And I grew panicked. Was that Iris?

And then came the sirens. They split through the fog that had taken over my brain and reality slammed back in. I looked down and saw what I had done. He was a mess of blood and bruises on the floor, moaning softly, eyes rolling in his head. I staggered back, my heart pounding. What had I done? My right hand wasn't working. It was bent wrong. Bone jutted out slightly from beneath my skin. I shoved it in my jacket pocket. Hid the damage against the recorder that was still on. Just like I used to hide everything else in this goddamn house.

I stepped outside, blinking in the sudden flood of red and blue lights. Cops were everywhere. Guns drawn. Screaming.

"Hands above your head!"

I couldn't react fast enough. Not because I was resisting. Because I was gone. I was completely dissociated out of my body. I was not thirty-one. I was twelve. I had just been cornered in the garage with his breath in my ear and my throat too tight to scream. My hands stayed in my pockets. Iris yelled my name. Screamed something as she began to run toward me.

"Danny, put your hands up!" she cried. "Please!"

I turned. My hand bulged in my pocket, pushing out the thin material.

"He has a gun!"

And then—BANG. Oh fuck. The bang wasn't like the ones in the movies. There was no dramatic echo, no slow-motion fall. Just a pop—short, sharp, and cruel. And then the weight left my body like it had been yanked out of me by something invisible, and I dropped to my knees. Then the pavement rushed up and kissed my face. I somehow managed to turn onto my back. I blinked, and the world blurred. Everything sounded like it was underwater. The sirens, the yelling, someone saying my name, I knew they were all there, but I couldn't connect the sounds to anything real. There was a tightness in my chest. Then heat. Then—oh. The pain came. It tore through me, savage and wild, not sharp like a stab, but hot, like something was boiling inside me, melting muscle from bone. My breath caught. My lungs refused to work. I coughed—and blood spilled out of my mouth, thick and metallic, warm against my lips. I couldn't feel my legs, couldn't move anything. But my mind was aware. Hyperaware. Of the cold concrete. Of the sky spinning above me. Of a high-pitched screaming that didn't stop until it was suddenly close. Iris. She was here.

"Danny—no, no, no, no—Danny—look at me!" Her hands were on my face, my chest, trying to stop the blood, trying to hold me together in one piece. I tried to smile, but my lips wouldn't cooperate. I tasted the blood. I could feel it dribbling over my lips and down my chin.

"You're okay. You're gonna be okay." Her voice cracked. "Stay with me. Please."

Her hand lifted and I saw all the blood. There was so much of it. Too much. It soaked through her sleeve. Streaked her cheek. Turned her whole body frantic. I looked at her. Really looked. She was crying, and somehow she was still so beautiful. She was sobbing, and somehow she was still so strong. She was here. For me.

"Iris," I whispered, coughing, voice barely there. "You did it."

Her face crumpled. "Did what? Danny, no—please—what did I do?"

I blinked again. The sky was brighter now. Or maybe it was just my vision going white at the edges.

"I really don't want to die."

Her mouth opened in a sob. "Then stay. Please stay."

I tried to nod. Tried to tell her I would. That I was sorry. That I loved her. That I wished we had more time. That she'd given me everything and then some. But the words got lost somewhere in my throat, swallowed up by blood and silence. Then everything went dark.

And I died.

I finally fucking died.

Chapter Forty-Four

Iris

Die Trying 

@dietrying

20m Subscribers · 22 Videos

SUBSCRIBE 

I watched him walk toward that house like he was heading into a battlefield, and in a way, he was. His shoulders looked even broader than usual, squared with something that might have been courage or maybe just sheer exhaustion. Maybe both. The wind caught his hair, tugged at the hem of his hoodie, but he hadn't flinched. Hadn't hesitated. Not until he reached the front steps. Then he did what he always did, paused just long enough to break my heart. And then I watched him knock.

I held my breath until my vision swam a little, then let out a shaky exhale that fogged up the windshield. One hand was touching my lips where his had just been. The other still gripped the envelope he'd left on the console. My name was written across it in his messy, all-caps handwriting like he hadn't known how else to make it mean something. My fingers hovered over the letters. Part of me didn't want to open it. Like it would be cheating. Like it would be admitting that I was afraid of what was inside. Afraid of admitting how I felt. Afraid of thinking of a time where I hadn't been in orbit around a world where he existed. But I was. I was so afraid. Not just of what would happen inside that house, but of what I imagined would happen after. After he screamed, after he cried, after he exhumed everything that had been poisoning him for decades, what would be left? Would he still need me? Would he still want me? Would he be worse? Would it destroy all of his healing, and would I really, truly lose him?

Because somewhere along the way I had stopped pretending that it was just a job. Somewhere between session four and session ten—maybe even earlier—I had started memorizing the way his voice cracked when he talked about hope like it was a language he'd forgotten. Or had never known. I had started noticing the way his hands shook when he smiled, how he always tried to hide it. How he looked at the world like he didn't want to be in it—and then, somehow, like he did.

God help me, I had fallen for him. Not in the way you're supposed to fall for someone. It wasn't slow or subtle. It was inconvenient. Inappropriate. Complicated. But it was real.

I took a deep breath, and opened the envelope.

> If you're reading this, it means I went inside.
>
> It means I found the nerve. The courage. Or maybe just the final breaking point. I'm not sure which yet.
>
> But I needed you to know something before I walked through that door—something I might never get the words out to say, not in the right order, not out loud. And if somehow I don't come back, it can't stay unsaid.
>
> You saved me.
>
> I know you're going to argue with that. You'll say I did the work. You'll say I showed up. But you were the reason I showed up. You were the reason I didn't walk into traffic, or touch a power line, or jump from a rooftop. I didn't stop because I stopped wanting to die. I stopped because I started wanting... something else. Something soft. Something steady. Something that was you.
>
> You're the first person who saw me—really saw me—

and didn't look away. You stayed when I was sharp, when I was heavy, when I was too much. You stayed when I couldn't meet your eyes. You stayed when I cried on your couch like some broken kid. And I think that's when it happened. That's when it started. The thing I don't know how to say. But I think you already know.

I'm still not afraid of death.

But I am now more afraid of missing out on life with you. I'm afraid of missing out on you.

If somehow fate intervenes and I don't come back, I want you to know that being loved by you, (I know you never said it and maybe I'm being presumptuous but fuck if I didn't feel it) in even the smallest ways, was the thing that made me want more. It was real to me. I hope it was real to you too. I hope, somewhere in your heart, you know what you mean to me. That if I had a choice, if I could rewrite all the pages of my life, they'd lead me straight to you. Faster. Sooner. More whole. But I can't change it, so I'll take it exactly how it was. Because I have no other choice but to love you with all my broken, fucked up pieces.

And just in case I don't get to say it with my own mouth, I need you to know that I put your name on my bank account. Because there's no one else I would give my life to. Not just my things... my life.

You're it for me, Iris. You're the only ending that ever made staying make sense for.

Wait for me, sweetheart.

— me

I PARKED across the street from the cemetery; my hands rested on the steering wheel even after the engine went silent. The sun in the sky was suddenly covered by a gray cloud giving off a soft, moody kind of light that made everything feel like it was waiting for something to happen. The trees rustled gently above, casting long shadows across the rows of stones that stretched out like stories untold.

For a moment, I didn't move. I just looked at the gates. Then I saw Carter. He stood near the entrance in a black shirt and black pants. His hands were shoved into his pockets, hair sticking up like he hadn't bothered to fix it, and when he saw me, he smiled—just a little. Not the bright kind. The quiet kind. The kind you save for people who've been through hell with you. I got out of the car and walked toward him.

"Hey," he said, voice low, almost reverent.

"Hi."

We stood there, side by side, both looking at the cemetery gates like they might bite.

"They make these places look so peaceful," he said, kicking at a pebble near his boot. I exhaled and smiled faintly.

"It's a big day."

He nodded, sobering. "Yeah. It is."

We started walking together. The gravel path crunched underfoot, the smell of cut grass mingled with the faint earthy scent of damp stone. All around us were headstones with last names and dates, and etched prayers. I tried not to imagine what people would think if they saw us, two quiet figures moving through a place meant for endings. Carter was silent until he asked, "Do you think he knew? How much people gave a shit?"

My throat tightened. "He knew."

"Good," he murmured. We passed an angel statue, weather-worn and soft with moss. Carter stopped and reached out, brushing a finger along the edge of its wing. He looked over at me.

"I know you're sick of me saying this. But thank you for what you did for him."

I shook my head. "I didn't do anything. I just sat with him long enough for him to remember who he was. Who he could be."

"Don't be humble. It's disgusting." He nudged my shoulder. I laughed, eyes suddenly watery.

"Shut up."

We walked for a bit, saying nothing, letting the quiet say the rest. Then we veered off the path near a cluster of sycamores, where a worn foot trail dipped left through the trees.

"The irony is not lost on me that this shortcut is through a cemetery," Carter said, snorting. I followed him, pushing a tree branch out of the way, nodding in agreement. Ironic indeed. My heart started to pound with anticipation. The kind that crackled behind your ribs and gave you butterflies. The trees opened to a clearing where a dock jutted out over a lake—calm and blue-gray like glass, framed by hills that looked like they'd seen every season and then some. The cemetery lay just beyond the rise behind us, but here... it was a different world. Seven people stood waiting for us on the dock. Three women. Four men. One in a beanie with healing cuts wrapped in bandages on his wrists. One with a guitar strapped to his back. One with pink hair and combat boots. A woman in a denim jacket and red lipstick. Another with a notebook, her fingers stained with ink. They looked up as Carter and I approached.

"Welcome back to the Undead Club," Carter announced with a grin, spreading his arms like a game show host. Laughter broke out across the dock. Not polite laughter but real, belly-deep; we earned this kind of laughter. One of the men stepped forward, he was in his mid-twenties, with a head full of wild curls, he had the brightest blue eyes under dark heavy brows.

"It's been three weeks since my last attempt," he told us, holding up his wrists. Once I got close enough, I wrapped my arms around him.

"Three weeks and counting to infinity," I whispered into his shoulder.

"Fuck yeah," he said in agreement, stepping back with a smile that looked like it hadn't touched his face in a long time. The others clapped for him, celebrating his milestone as though it were their own, and for some of them it was. You could feel it in the air —that this wasn't just a dock. It wasn't just a lake. It was a sacred space carved out for a unique kind of healing. A place where broken people found each other, where grief didn't hide in shadows, and joy wasn't rationed and controlled. It had started with these seven but was rapidly growing beyond my wildest dreams.

A few months ago, it was just me, Carter, a post on social media, and a long list of desperate application emails in our inbox. And now here we were, building something that shouldn't have to exist—but did. A refuge. A rebellion. A way forward. For those left behind by society with nowhere else to go. The ones with the biggest feelings, the most brutal back stories, and a strong yearning for something more than just what life had handed them.

Carter slung a DSLR off his shoulder and started adjusting the settings.

"Documenting the next episode of the rebirth?" I teased.

He shrugged. "The world didn't care when they were trying to die. Maybe it'll pay attention now that we're all trying to live."

And then—a sound tore through the air, interrupting him. The roar of a motorboat engine. Everyone on the dock turned toward the water, hands shielding their eyes from the glint of the sun shining off the lake. Behind the boat, a figure was waterboarding like a damn maniac, arms stretched wide, teeth bared in a laugh so wild and alive you could see it clear as day despite the space between us. Water spray flew in every direction as he zigzagged behind the boat, carving joy into the water like it owed him something. And it did.

"Am I next?" one of the girls shouted. "I want a turn at dopamine instead of death!"

We all broke into laughter. I loved hearing them use the little phrases that I'd come up with because it made the truly meaningful things that they were learning a little easier to handle. A little rhyme eased them into saying the things they needed to say. A little humor helped them face their demons. A little dopamine made life worth living.

"He's insane!"

"Look at him go!"

"He's gonna eat shit and we're all gonna cheer!"

"That's not a death wish, that's a fucking life wish!"

The boat circled once before pulling up to the dock, slowing to a smooth stop like it had rehearsed the moment. Danny let go of the tow rope and coasted in, hopping off the board with a fluid motion that said I belong here now. His muscles rippled as he stretched, revealing a long, healing scar just under his ribs—evidence of how close we'd come to losing him. Before I could say a word, he was already climbing up onto the dock, eyes locked on mine. And then he ran over, and despite my protests that he was all wet, he picked me up. Just scooped me into his arms like the world wasn't watching, like we weren't surrounded by half a dozen people and a camera, and a scarred history stretching out behind us. He spun me in a full circle, my laughter caught in my throat, and my arms went around his neck. His skin was sun-warmed and wet. His eyes... alive. Gloriously, achingly alive.

"Iris," he said as he put me down, voice breathless and reverent, like my name was his favorite word.

"Yes?" I asked, heart hammering.

"You're here."

"Always am."

He kissed me. It was the kind of kiss that rewrote endings. That said, we're still here, still trying, still choosing each other. There was nothing hesitant about it; just a thousand unspoken moments crashed into one single, infinite second. Someone groaned in protest.

"Oh my God, get a room," Carter called from behind the camera.

Danny pulled back with a smirk. "You're just jealous."

Carter threw up the middle finger as he dove back behind the camera again and the group around us laughed, the kind of laughter that reminded me that although we were all still healing, we had each found space for real, unfettered happiness.

Carter lowered the camera once more and called out, "By the way—Die Trying's latest video just hit fourteen million views. And we've got fifty new people registered for the next support group meeting. We're going to need a second boat."

Danny whistled. "Hell yeah. I've got so many things to add to our dopamine list. They're gonna love it."

I grinned, brushing a strand of wet hair off his forehead. "I'll answer the emails."

He leaned his forehead against mine. "I know you will. And hey, just a reminder, you're the reason I'm loving my life."

"I know," I whispered back. He told me so every day. "And you're the reason they're enjoying theirs." I pointed to the group on the dock who were playing rock, paper, scissors to choose who got the next go at dopamine instead of death, a chaotic ride around the lake on the wake board. Danny looked around the dock—at the mismatched group of fighters and survivors. Then he looked at Carter, who was beaming like an idiot behind his camera. Then at the lake that shimmered like it had been made for this exact moment.

"I'm just..." He paused, overwhelmed. "I'm just really fucking happy."

Everyone's voices blended around us, into a sort of hum. Soft laughter, water slapping against wood, the occasional whoop as someone dared to dream out loud. Carter's camera clicked again as Danny toweled off beside me. The angry scar across his chest reminded us both of everything that had brought us here.

I watched as Danny looked around at the beautiful, broken humans who had all, in one way or another, crawled their way back from the edge. Some were still climbing. Some had just begun. But all of them were here. Breathing, laughing, and choosing to stay. We watched as the boat swung out onto the lake. Someone shouted something about needing a hit of serotonin. Another voice yelled back, "Dopamine, bitch!" and the dock erupted into laughter once more.

Danny grinned, shaking his head. "They're insane."

"They're yours."

"They're *ours*," he said. And it knocked something loose in my chest. The air smelled like sunscreen and the lake, and someone had turned on a portable speaker, so music spilled across the water. Laughter rang out from the dock, followed by the splash of a cannonball. Carter yelled at one of the boys to "go easy on the GoPro battery" while the newest member of this group asked if anyone had brought snacks. Danny grinned and reached for my hand. His fingers laced through mine, now dry and warm. He looked back out at the water, eyes glinting in the sun. And then he said the last thing I expected to hear today.

"Remember how I used to think the bravest thing I ever did was try to die?"

He looked at me and my heart leapt into my throat. How could I forget? I was thrown back to that day, recalling the police thinking he had a gun, watching his body shudder in an unnatural way and then thud to the ground; running over to find way too much blood pumping out of him, and then his body growing cold. The weeks that followed would forever be ingrained in my memory. The police; that a neighbor had called, had very quickly discovered that they had shot an unarmed man; between that, the recording in his pocket, and the Deacon telling them that Danny had not attacked him but rather had been using self-defense, not a single charge had been brought against him. He had been airlifted to the hospital where they had kept him in surgery for hours repairing the damage the bullet had done to him. When he finally woke up and found me and Carter by his bedside, he cried. Long sobs that shook me to my core. Then with his puffy eyes and his heart rate jumping all over the monitor screen, he told me that he loved me. It had been my turn to cry and also laugh because Carter grumbled something in the background about being chopped liver. Danny had admitted how much he cared about Carter too, which had pacified him. For the two weeks of his recovery in the hospital I had barely left his side, and when I did, it was to bring him sushi, cozy blankets, and a mug that said Not Dead Yet on it in big black letters. Apparently, Carter had finally made merch. Danny thought it was amazing and asked out loud, "What if we give this out as a prize when other people survive?" And that was how our idea of organizing a support group had come to fruition. A place where people learned to heal and ask hard questions in our not-therapy sessions but also flood their brains with dopamine in a safe way from Danny's ever-growing list of activities. A place where they found community and connection. Where we explored things like healing through art and nature. Where we encouraged people to cry if they wanted to or break mugs in our rage room if they needed. Each journey was individual and unique, but so beautiful to witness and walk alongside.

Danny squeezed my hand as I leaned in closer, taking in his scent and nuzzling along his neck. He grinned and kept talking.

"But now I know the bravest thing I've ever done is this, baby. Letting someone love me... and loving them back."

I could've broken apart right then and there, just from those words. Not only because in his self-discovery journey, I, too, had found myself. I, too, had fallen in love and unlearned scripts that had been holding me back. I, too, had leaned into living bravely, boldly and without worrying what the rules were. As much as he claimed I taught him, he had taught me so much more. He had given me my first kiss, a fresh perspective on life, and the ability to let my heart race for the sheer joy of it even if it meant ziplining, which I still hated, but finally understood the appeal. This man—this man who had kissed death twenty-one times and survived—was choosing life not out of fear, not out of guilt, but out of wanting to stay. And not just simply to stay. But to live. To love. To feel. He pulled me even closer against him, his voice soft in my ear.

"This is what enough finally feels like."

And it was.

Epilogue

Die Trying 

@dietrying

20m Subscribers • 22 Videos

🔔 SUBSCRIBE 👍

December 2026

IRIS

I know I said I wanted to wait but I am done waiting.

IRIS

I know you're in a meeting with those fancy podcasters but when you see this, if you want to… hurry home.

IRIS

Carter left condoms here the last time he came over for a movie night. It's probably wasteful if we don't use them before they expire.

IRIS

Oh never mind. They don't expire for a while. We've got time. I will wait until you're ready too.

DANNY

I'm coming home.

DANNY

I'm ready. Don't you dare change your mind.

DANNY

Iris?

DANNY

Did you fall asleep?

IRIS

photo

DANNY

Oh shit. Stay just like that. I'm almost home.

I'd never imagined being someone top-rated podcasters would want to have on their show, but apparently, I was. My YouTube fame, the chaos of my videos, and the success we'd had with the Undead Club had gotten so much attention that Carter had started acting as my manager. He had finally convinced me that we could help so many more people if I would stop being such a fucking idiot and would go on a few podcasts, his words not mine. A few months ago, I had finally done one and realized that it wasn't so scary and the hosts were genuinely interested in me, and led the conversation so kindly that I actually enjoyed myself, so I agreed to do another. The hosts on that one cried when they heard my story, and the ratings shot through the roof. When the hosts of tonight's interview reached out, I thought Carter had been joking. Why would a man with a top-rated podcast who had interviewed the most famous people want to talk to little old me? I'd almost said no, but I was glad I hadn't. We had talked about so many important things, and my story would get to so many more ears that when I left the studio I had felt like I was on a high. Then I saw Iris's text and my heart had rolled over in my chest. Giddy, frantic, excited, happy... none of that could possibly describe the cacophony of feelings that had erupted inside of me.

Once I got back to our building, I skipped the elevator because it would take too long to get me to her and instead, I took the stairs two at a time. My scar twinged slightly like it always did from quick movements, but I ignored it. I would just have to keep getting used to it. I wasn't slowing down my life for a bullet wound scar. Nope, I had way too much to do than let that stop me. My breath burned in my throat. Not from the climb, but from the way her texts echoed in my mind. "I am done waiting." The words crawled up my sternum and burrowed their way into my heart. Everything about her turned me on. Sleeping next to her at night, her warmth, soft and pliable beside me. Watching her brush her hair, the comb gliding through the strands, making me wish it were my fingers. The way she blew on her mugs of tea, the heat steaming up her glasses, her lips pursed and full. Her laugh, her smell, her love for garage sales and thrift stores. Her mind, her safety, her body. All of it made me desire her. My own body tightened at the thought. In the past few months, I had finally allowed myself to go there. To want more than just run my fingers along the nape of her neck and laugh when she shivered, as she pushed at me. "Stop, that tickles, Danny," she'd say as her body defied her words, and she'd curl up closer to me. I'd begun to feel safe with allowing my eyes to linger on the curves of her waist and the soft skin on her thighs. I'd begun to expect the hitch of her breath while giving her a massage as my hands would hesitate along the edges of her underwear before moving away. We'd been flirting for so long now. Feeling safer and safer to let down the last of our walls, me protecting the most vulnerable pieces of me, her protecting a promise she had made so long ago she could barely remember why.

I quickly punched in the code and unlocked the door to our

apartment. Even thinking the words, *our apartment* was pretty cool because I never thought I'd live long enough to call something this pretty, mine. But here we were. I hadn't ever dreamed of any of this. Not the soft hum of the fancy ice maker on the counter. Not the scatter of blankets on her reading chair or the row of mismatched mugs that lined the kitchen shelf. Not the thirteen plants that I'd learned to mist, water, prune, and not kill. And definitely not the woman currently humming to herself in the next room, half-dressed and glowing like the angel she was who'd saved my life.

I smelled her body wash, telling me she had recently showered. The notes of vanilla and jasmine clung to the air, almost caressing my face. The lights in the kitchen were low, bleeding soft gold all over the walls. For a moment, I just stood there, memorizing the sound of safety.

Somehow, I'd gotten lucky enough to be here. In *our* apartment that had all the best parts of her in it; it was warm, slightly cluttered, yet quiet and cozy in all the right ways. Perfect from my hoodie draped over the back of our couch, to her slippers parked beside my boots at the door. Sometimes I'd catch myself staring at the ordinary things like a spoon in the sink or a shopping list, and I'd tear up. Because the ordinary meant I'd stayed. I was here. And staying meant learning how to want things that weren't dangerous. That I wanted more than an ending.

Tonight, what I wanted was her.

I was peeling off my coat and toeing off my shoes when she came into the doorway of our bedroom looking a little nervous. I'd seen her annoyed, excited, sad, happy, patient... overly kind. But this? I'd never quite seen this version of her yet. She glowed with her decision to be so bold with me, to step off into this unknown territory with me. Her hair was braided, her skin flushed, and the tie of her robe hung loose like she had just untied it but was considering retying it. I worried she might be unsure if she was actually ready.

"You okay?" I asked.

She nodded but didn't speak. Her hands fidgeted with the edge of her robe until she met my eyes. "I'm ready."

"Are you sure?" I whispered as I followed her into the room, my heart a full-on orchestra inside my chest.

She walked over to me as I sat on the bed, and she straddled my lap with a grace that stunned me. "I've never been surer. Are you?"

I let out a slow breath; my hands shook slightly as I steadied them against her hips. "I am ready for you." I thought I heard her let out a soft gasp as she leaned in and pressed her lips to mine. The touch did not startle me. It didn't make me nauseous. It didn't bring up unwanted images or nightmares. All I felt was her sitting in my lap, my body thickening against the warm weight. All I heard was her breath and the sound of us together. All I could think about was how much I loved her. How I hoped I wouldn't mess this up for her by it ending too quickly. I let out a groan as she shifted in my lap.

We continued to kiss; it had started soft and slow, but it didn't stay that way. There was a hunger that crept in around the edges. Months of teasing glances and brush-of-the-hand moments had led us here. In the never-ending courtship and flirtation stage, I had discovered that hope and desire was a kind of pressure too, and tonight, it would finally break. Her lips were warm and sure; she tasted faintly of mint and rose. Every tilt of her mouth, every pass of her tongue unraveled me a little more. I'd gone so many years without ever wanting anything like this and now I couldn't get enough.

She tugged my shirt up and over my head. Her fingertips felt blazing hot as they skimmed my chest like she was memorizing every scar and every bone.

"You're beautiful," she murmured. "Even the parts that hurt you."

I almost laughed, almost cried. Instead, I pulled her in for another kiss that stole the breath from both of us. When we fell back onto the sheets, it was clumsy and heated—knees bumping, breathless laughter, her hair tangled around my fingers like a tether. I made her gasp. She made me swear. We fumbled with each other's clothes, laughed again, kissed through the nerves. Soon we were naked, and a condom had been rolled down my length; she had watched me figure it out, eyes wide, lips puffy from my kisses. I hadn't been able to look at her for fear of this being over before we even started. I trembled as her chest pressed against mine, her warm skin was so soft, so foreign to me. I shook with my want of her. I ached as her thighs wrapped around me and then time slowed.

"Is this okay?" I asked for what must have been the one hundredth time against her lips. *Please say it's okay, I can't stop now.*

I could feel her wet warmth pulsing against me, and I had to fight not to just thrust up and rub myself against her. She had me shaking at the edge of control. But I would pause until I received permission. I'd rather go insane with want than ever push her faster than she could handle. I would wait forever if that's what it took. Iris's gaze met my eyes, I could see her love for me swimming in them, yet they were glazed over with lust as well. It was so potent, so desperate I had to look away so as not to spin her over and pin her to the mattress. I wanted to taste her everywhere. I wanted to discover all the secrets of her body. I wanted to make her scream. I shocked myself with the thought and I bit the inside of my cheek to make my imagination halt. This was Iris, *my Iris*, I needed to go slow with her. I needed to go slow with me. She reached up, her fingers slid up my neck, grounding me. She turned my face back to hers and then she nodded with a look of almost desperation that melted me from the inside out. "Okay," I breathed. It felt like a prayer and a thank you wrapped in one. I pressed forward—carefully—slowly, and her breath caught. Mine did too. I hadn't known what to expect. But she was so hot. So tight. So wet. *Don't come. Don't come. Don't come.* I wiped away her tears with my thumb, I kissed away her gasps of pain, I waited, tremulously, until she urged me to keep moving.

And then... it was just us. Bodies tangled. Breath synced. Fingers trailed over soft skin and ribs and pelvic bones and then to a soft, wet heat that had me calling out, gasping, and falling into her. I memorized the sounds she made, the way her hands gripped my back, the whispered yesyesyes when I kissed her just right. Her name left my mouth like a prayer. Mine left hers like a promise. She pulled me down. I let go. We fell together into each other. Into groaning bed springs, taut muscles, panting breaths, seeking hips, another flash of pain from her, a moment of desperation from me, and then finally really moving in synchrony until I was convinced I saw the pearly gates of heaven because nothing had ever felt so glorious in all my life. The sounds she made wrecked me. They were so soft and real. Her hands gently led me to where she was aching, swollen and needing me. Teaching me to strum her, starting gentle but then applying more pressure until she gasped and shook and clamped around me so hard I saw stars behind my eyes. It didn't take too much longer after that. Just a few more strokes, a few more quick movements of my hips, a few more gasps from behind clenched teeth until I grunted out my love for her as I flooded the latex and felt myself fall off the edge of a cliff, tumbling into a place where I could never imagine my life without her. Into a place where my obsession for her grew in leaps and bounds. The things we could learn to do to one another. I felt excited to trace all of her with my tongue. To make her do that half gasp, half cry again. Against my fingers, against my mouth.

I would do it again, just as soon as I could feel my body once more. We lay in a heap of blankets and discarded clothes; the windows were open just enough to let in the winter air. She curled into me. I tugged the blanket over her body. I didn't want to, I wanted to stare, I never wanted to look away from her rosy flushed skin but she was cold, so I pulled the comforter over us as she lay down on me once more, her head rested on my chest, one hand over my heart like she was checking that it was still beating. It was. For her, it always would be. Even one day when we were both long gone. Her fingers traced the scar from the bullet. I kissed her temple. I breathed in her scent. I basked in this moment. She was *mine*. This life was mine.

"Still glad you stayed?" she whispered suddenly, shaking me from my thoughts.

I glanced around the room—the plants on the windowsill, her pile of books on the night table, back to her, then to the discarded condom wrapper on the floor. Then back to us.

"I'm more glad than I ever thought I could be," I told her. She giggled as I kissed the tip of her nose and brushed the wayward strands of hair off her face. She promised me she wanted more, told me how good it had been. I asked her if she was lying; I knew it had hurt. She insisted it had been amazing. She didn't know why we had waited, she wanted to do it again, and eat chocolate, and take a nap, but not in that order. She laughed as I kissed my way down her neck, but her laughter turned to groans as I took one nipple in my mouth and then kept moving lower, tracing the lines of her ribs with my tongue, nipping on the jut of her pelvic bone, and then reveling in the sound she made as her body bowed when my tongue delved deep against her warm wet skin. "If I had died before tasting this," I told her, "I would have been very angry with myself."

She laughed, then moaned again as she gripped my hair, pulling me as close as she could get me. I got her chocolate after I used three more condoms and fed it to her, piece by piece, as I listened to her talk. Then we slept.

I didn't dream of blood or pain or falling off cliffs. I didn't wake up choking on fear or guilt. I didn't wake up at all. I slept. Deeply. Fully. Safely. Wrapped in her warmth, her breath against my neck, the steady rhythm of her heart beside mine.

And finally—just being alive was enough.

The End

ACKNOWLEDGMENTS

I literally didn't write this letter for you, my readers, until right before I sent the manuscript in for formatting. Not because I didn't know what to say, but because this book asked something different of me than my others did. I didn't want this letter to feel like a neat bow or an inspirational takeaway. I wanted it to be brutally honest. Because this book required me to sit in the uncomfortable truths of life and stay there long enough to be able to tell it to you through Danny's experience.

This story came to me one day as I was driving and I pushed off a different project to write it because the world just feels so exhausting sometimes, and so much evil exists. So many people are walking around with their own version of Danny's story. I decided to write a book that showed what it looks like to keep going when you're not sure you believe in "better." I wrote Danny's story to remind all of us that survival doesn't always look brave, and healing doesn't always look pretty.

So, thank you for reading this book. Truly. Thank you for trusting me with something this raw. If any part of it felt familiar, or heavy, or quietly comforting, I hope you know you weren't alone while reading it—and you aren't alone now.

I also need to say this: I would not have finished this book without my BETA reader Hannah and the support of my newly formed street team. You sharing about my books, your encouragement, your belief—especially on the days I wanted to walk away—kept me going. You reminded me why this story mattered when I got sick of having to be a content creator, not just an author. Your support and encouragement showed up consistently, loudly, and with so much heart and I don't take that lightly.

This book exists for the people that stayed. Because *you* chose to stay.

Thank you for reading. And thank you for being here.

Love,

Rae

ABOUT THE AUTHOR

Rae Lloyd is a romance author with a deep passion for the written word. Having been an avid reader since a very young age, she was inspired by the thousands of books she consumed since childhood. With this being her fourth book release Rae's dream of having her writings published has truly come to fruition. She can be found writing in between living life with her three daughters and her husband, as well as hanging out with her many adorable pets, baking gluten-free desserts, or cultivating beauty in her wig salon. This is Rae's fourth book but she has many more stories brewing in her mind, stay tuned for more to come.

To stay in touch and receive all book updates, subscribe to get emails at https://www.raelloyd.com.

You can also find Rae on TikTok and Instagram username - @raelloydwrites.

You can join Rae's Facebook group called Rae's Readers.

ALSO BY RAE LLOYD

This Is What It Feels Like https://a.co/d/oFPm2g1

-> Where we first met Carter

Love's Crescendo https://a.co/d/1mPTPpq

We https://a.co/d/gJuwPTK

-> Where we saw Carter again

If you or someone you love is struggling, help is available. In the
USA you can call or text 988 to reach the Suicide & Crisis
Lifeline.
If you're outside the USA, please visit findahelpline.com to
locate support in your country.

www.ingramcontent.com/pod-product-compliance
Lightning Source LLC
Chambersburg PA
CBHW051300130726
47987CB00004B/1608